No
Reservations

TITLES BY STEPHANIE JULIAN

By Private Invitation
No Reservations

Reservations

STEPHANIE JULIAN

HEAT | NEW YORK

THE BERKLEY PUBLISHING GROUP
Published by the Penguin Group
Penguin Group (USA)
375 Hudson Street, New York, New York 10014, USA

USA I Canada I UK I Ireland I Australia I New Zealand I India I South Africa I China

Penguin Books Ltd., Registered Offices: 80 Strand, London WC2R 0RL, England
For more information about the Penguin Group, visit penguin.com.

This book is an original publication of The Berkley Publishing Group.

Library of Congress Cataloging-in-Publication Data

Julian, Stephanie.
No reservations / Stephanie Julian. —Heat trade paperback ed.
p. cm.
ISBN 978-0-425-26288-7
1. Hotelkeepers—Fiction. 2. Businesswomen—Fiction. I. Title.
PS3610.U5346N63 2013
813'.6—dc23
2013006078

PUBLISHING HISTORY
Heat trade paperback edition / September 2013

PRINTED IN THE UNITED STATES OF AMERICA

10 9 8 7 6 5 4 3 2 1

Cover photograph of Ring: Kang Kim / Gallerystock.
Cover design by Lesley Worrell.
Text design by Laura K. Corless.

No Reservations

One

❧

New Year's Eve

"I'm afraid you don't look like you're having a very good time. As one of the hosts, I have to say I'm slightly offended."

The deep, masculine voice cut through the haze that had developed over Kate Song's attention, drawing her gaze upward until she looked into the darkest blue eyes she'd ever seen.

If she were the romantic type, which she really wasn't, she'd say they were the dark blue of a calm sea set in an arrestingly handsome face.

Strong forehead. Straight nose. Gorgeous cheekbones. Dark hair cut a little too long to be considered conservative but not long enough to be rebellious.

Even if he'd been wearing anything other than the custom-made tuxedo—like say, the penguin costume that unfortunate fool in the corner had chosen to wear to this high-class New Year's Eve party—he'd still look exactly like what he was.

A rich playboy with endless pockets and probably an ego twice as big.

And he stared at her as if she were next on his to-do list.

Buy small European country before breakfast. Acquire Fortune 500 company after lunch. Host fancy shindig at night.

Why he'd added *Sweet talk sour-looking guest at fancy shindig* to that list, she didn't know. And couldn't afford to indulge.

"Then I'd have to reply that your powers of observation leave something to be desired."

Kate made sure she kept her tone disinterested and let her gaze slide back to the dance floor. Her best friend was out there, dancing with a gorgeous guy who'd practically swept her off her feet the second they'd arrived at this party.

Annabelle had needed this night out and Kate hadn't wanted her to go alone. Even Kate's fiancé, Arnie, had realized how much this would mean to Annabelle. He'd told Kate to go, have fun.

He certainly hadn't meant for her to flirt with a gorgeous stranger while she was there.

Low, amused laughter from above made her eyebrows arch as she slid another glance his way.

"Wow," he said, "I don't think I've ever been told off quite that politely before."

One corner of his masculine lips had quirked up and his eyes had narrowed.

And her heart gave a little flutter.

No way. None of that tonight.

None of that ever, apparently.

Crap. Just . . . crap.

Hell, she couldn't even get her snarky subconscious to lay off tonight.

She didn't have to force a chagrined smile as her gaze lingered this time. And found her attention captivated.

He truly was a beautiful man. And she didn't mean he was pretty.

No, he was distinctly, utterly masculine in a way that made her want to rub up against him and purr.

Danger ahead. Especially for an engaged woman.

Who was having doubts left, right, and center lately.

Sighing, she gestured to the seat next to her. "I'm sorry. Would you like to sit? I have to warn you, though. I'm probably not going to be very good company tonight."

"And why is that?"

Because I can't decide what I want to do with my life. Because I'm engaged to a man I'm not sure I love enough to marry.

"Because I foolishly thought these shoes would be a smart idea, and now my feet hurt."

He laughed, low and a little husky and so very enticing, as he slid into the chair on the opposite side of the round table.

"Well, I'm glad to know it's not the company."

It definitely was *not* the company. Despite her assurances to Annabelle that she would be fine by herself, she wanted the company. Hadn't wanted to be sitting here, alone, looking like a spinster chaperone.

Annabelle would freak if she thought she'd been neglecting Kate and would refuse to leave her alone for the rest of the night. Then Annabelle would miss out on the fun she seemed to be having with the blond, blue-eyed Adonis who'd arrowed in on her from their first moment at the party.

So Kate would suck it up while she sat here and talked to this seriously handsome playboy.

And what could it hurt? After all, it was just a conversation between two adults who didn't know each other amid a crowd of people who weren't paying any attention to them.

She stuck her hand across the table. "I'm Kate."

He took it for a firm shake, not holding on too long. Just long enough for the heat to seep from his skin into hers. She almost embarrassed herself by curling around his fingers and not letting go. "Tyler. Very nice to meet you. Now, about those shoes . . ."

With a smile, she stuck out one leg to show off the offending platform-soled, spike-heeled black patent leather pumps . . . and realized she was exposing more skin than she normally showed unless she was wearing a bathing suit or going to bed.

More than a dozen petal-shaped pieces of tulle created the skirt of her handmade fairy costume, and those pieces fell open to reveal her thigh all the way to the bottom of the barely decent, green satin underskirt.

She'd known when she'd been creating the matching costumes for Annabelle and herself that they were sexy, racy, and like nothing she'd ever worn in public.

And that had been part of the appeal. To display a little piece of her life that she normally kept hidden to people she didn't know and would never see again.

Kate took pride in the fact that the beautiful costumes held their own among the other custom-made pieces at this high-class party in one of the most exclusive hotels in Philadelphia. A party she never would have attended had it not been for Annabelle's recent breakup.

"They're beautiful." Tyler's voice deepened as his gaze lingered a little longer than necessary on her leg.

When he lifted his gaze, it wasn't a fast or furtive journey. But neither was it salacious.

She didn't feel uncomfortable.

She felt sexy. Enticing. Utterly female.

More so than she'd ever felt in her life.

Her heart racing, she pulled her leg back beneath the table.

"Yes, well, they're definitely not made for dancing for any length of time."

"Surely one dance wouldn't be too painful. Or you could take them off."

Was he asking her to dance? His gaze held hers and heat flashed through her body, flushing her cheeks with color. She regretted removing the half mask she'd worn with her costume. It might've hid the blush.

"I'm not sure that would be such a good idea."

But it would probably be amazing.

His gaze never wavered. "And why is that?"

Because I want you.

The thought didn't surprise her, but she couldn't be sure she meant it.

Did she really want this man? Or was it just that he seemed to want her?

Did it matter?

Seriously, what could one dance hurt?

Watching Tyler's steady gaze narrow, Kate felt her lungs constrict until she struggled to draw in a deeper breath.

A dance with another man wouldn't matter one bit.

A dance with this man . . .

Would upset her carefully crafted world.

Because, yes, she wanted him.

Her breasts felt heavier, her nipples tight. Her sex clenched and she felt herself get wetter with each passing second.

It took her fiancé Arnie several minutes of foreplay to work her into this state.

This man had induced it in seconds with only a single touch.

Why?

Hell if she knew. Several other men had asked her to dance. None of them had produced this reaction.

Why him?

Blinking, she transferred her gaze out onto the dance floor and, after a few seconds, caught a flash of Annabelle's bright hair.

"Because I'm engaged."

He didn't respond right away but his attention never wavered.

"And he's not here with you tonight."

Tyler didn't phrase it as a question, but she didn't hear any condemnation in his tone, either.

"No. My friend and I came alone."

"Are you enjoying the music, at least?"

She couldn't decide if she was upset that he didn't push her to dance with him, or relieved. "The band's very good. Just not my style."

"What do you like?"

He actually sounded interested. Another point in the guy's favor. They just kept racking up. "Classical, mostly. Some trance. Film scores. I like to create a mood while I work but I don't want lyrics interrupting my train of thought."

"I know exactly what you mean. Do you play an instrument?"

She let a smile curve her lips. "Violin. My father's Korean and my mother was Italian. They always claimed it was in my genes. And I enjoy it. It's just not my first love."

"And what is?"

"Fashion design."

"I can see you have a talent for it. You made both costumes, didn't you?"

"Yes, I did."

"They're beautiful." His gaze slid down then, but again, she didn't get the sense that he was ogling her. "The attention to detail is amazing."

Her heart tripped over itself. Yes, Annabelle had gushed about them, but hearing this man praise her design made her flush with pleasure.

His gaze caught hers again and held.

And Kate felt her world shift.

Two

❧

Present

Tyler Golden stopped just outside the Adamstown antiques store where his brother, Jared, planned to make a very public display of intention.

His grandmother, Beatrice, and Jed had already entered the building.

Through the front window, Tyler saw store owner, Annabelle Elder, the woman Jed could no longer live without.

She moved through the crowd, her bright red hair flashing under the lights. Annabelle had a wide smile to go along with her vibrant hair and vivid green eyes and a sweet nature that eased Jed's harder edges. When she laughed, everyone in her vicinity was drawn to her.

Everyone except Tyler.

His attention had latched on to the woman at Annabelle's side.

Kate Song, Annabelle's best friend. Her long, dark hair accentuated the paleness of her skin. Her huge, dark eyes and exotic features blended into a beauty that had tugged at Tyler's libido since the moment he'd seen her.

The first woman to do so since his fiancée.

It'd been almost two years since Mia had died and, of course, the first woman Tyler had been attracted to had turned out to be engaged.

Apparently, his luck hadn't changed much.

A cold breeze slid by him as the women moved into another room, out of sight. Tyler decided it was past time to join his family and pushed through the front door.

Once inside, he stopped for a quick look around.

The shop looked clean, open, elegant. Not a dusty and disorganized jumble like a stereotypical antiques store.

People stood in small groups everywhere . . . talking, laughing, having a good time. No one he recognized, but that was probably because he wasn't an art person like Jed.

Annabelle was celebrating the opening of her very own art gallery featuring the work of her late father, a world-famous artist whose murder, along with that of Annabelle's mother and the man she considered her second father, had created a worldwide scandal several years ago. Annabelle was finally taking back her birthright and her name as Peter O'Malley's daughter.

Tyler wished her all the best, and he'd make damn sure she and Jed had the time and the privacy they needed to make their relationship work. If it meant he had to call in some favors from a few well-placed friends, he wouldn't hesitate.

He could be ruthless when it came to his family.

Though he hadn't been able to do a damn thing to help Mia. And she hadn't—

No.

Pushing that thought out of his mind, he made his way through the crowd to his grandmother and brother, just as Annabelle spotted them from the front of the gallery, where she was welcoming the guests.

"I have one more person I'd like to thank," she said. "Without him, I don't think I'd be in this position. Ladies and gentlemen, Jared Golden was the catalyst for tonight's event. He provided me with the final piece to my father's Passion series. Thank you, Jared, and thank you all for coming tonight."

Annabelle turned to Kate, still at her side, and the women exchanged a few words, their gazes darting toward Jed before Kate's slid to him. And held.

His grandmother said something he didn't hear, but Jed and Beatrice moved forward and Tyler followed along, his gaze never leaving Kate's.

Annabelle stepped in front of them and Tyler forced himself to focus on her.

She wore a smile so bright, he couldn't help but return it.

"Mrs. Golden." Annabelle reached for his grandmother's hand. "I'm so glad you could come."

"I wouldn't have missed it for the world, Annabelle. Your shop is beautiful, and the gallery is amazing."

Their conversation continued but Tyler couldn't follow. His attention had shifted back to Kate.

She looked stunning, covered from neck to ankles in champagne-colored silk. Tyler would've never thought a dress that completely covered every inch of a woman's body could be anything other than concealing.

This one . . .

Hell, this dress conformed to every curve, no matter how slight, and accentuated her femininity to an exponential level.

He wanted to run his hands over the shiny material. Wondered if she was wearing anything under the dress, because he couldn't see any lines. And he was looking damn hard.

His temperature began to rise and he knew it wasn't because the gallery was full of people. It was Kate.

Suddenly, Kate stepped up beside Belle and held out her hand, palm up.

"But the set shouldn't be parted," Annabelle said.

Set? What set?

His grandmother gasped and he turned to see her expression break into an amazed smile. "Oh, Annabelle, you found the ring."

Ah. The missing piece of his grandmother's stolen jewelry. Annabelle had worn the pin, stolen from his grandmother decades ago and lost for years until Annabelle's late grandfather had bought it at a yard sale, to Haven's New Year's Eve party.

Jed, the idiot, had nearly lost Annabelle when she'd overheard him telling Tyler about the piece. She'd thrown it at him in anger the morning after the party, and it'd taken Jed days to find her.

"Actually, Kate did," Annabelle continued. "She picked it up at one of the stands at Renninger's Flea Market. If you hadn't shown up tonight, I would have contacted you tomorrow."

Beatrice's smile couldn't be contained. "Well, now, I'm absolutely stunned." She turned to Kate with a smile Tyler had learned to be wary of. "Kate, why don't you give that to Tyler? He'll hold on to it for me. Won't you, sweetheart?"

Since he never refused his grandmother anything, he nodded and dutifully held out his hand. "Of course, Nana."

Their gazes locked as Kate stepped closer. She placed the ring in the center of his palm, her fingertips brushing against his skin for a brief second before she pulled back.

He forced his hand to remain open when all he wanted was to grab her and pull her against him.

From the corner of his eye, he saw Jed and Annabelle exchange soft words and a kiss.

Good for Jed.

Tyler fought the urge to do the same to Kate.

His hand clenched around the ring and he nodded, not trusting himself to speak. Not sure his voice wouldn't betray his simmering desire for this woman.

Because somewhere in this crowd, he was pretty sure he'd find her fiancé.

He waited for her to move away, to drop his gaze and put him out of his misery.

Instead, she held it. And stepped closer.

Now he caught a whiff of the spicy scent she wore. Not perfume. It didn't have that underlying astringent smell most perfumes carried. This smelled more organic.

And much more enticing. It made him want to nuzzle his nose into her neck and lick a path from her collarbone to just behind her ear.

"How have you been, Tyler?"

The sound of her voice jolted through him like a mild electric shock. Luckily, he controlled any outward response that could've embarrassed the hell out of both of them.

Instead, he nodded. "I've been fine. And you?"

She hesitated, her head tilting to one side, as if weighing her response. Or maybe she was reacting to his cold tone. He hadn't meant to sound so damn distant, but he didn't want to put her in an awkward position either.

If she were free—

"I've been better, actually."

She smiled but he saw it didn't reach her eyes.

Irrational fear made his heart pound and sent a chill through his body even as he stepped closer. "Is everything okay?"

She nodded but began to worry her bottom lip with her teeth. "Everything's fine. I just . . . I mean, there's nothing physically wrong."

He frowned, wanting to pull her away from the crowd, from all the people and the noise. Get her alone.

Which wasn't going to happen.

"Did something happen? Do you need help?"

He'd do whatever she needed, get her whatever she wanted.

The corners of her mouth lifted and he was struck by the fact that he didn't think he'd ever really seen her smile, as if she didn't have a worry in the world.

Her smiles were always tinged with . . . something. Not fear, but something that held her back from total enjoyment.

"Actually . . . could we talk for a few minutes? Alone?"

He bit back the immediate urge to say "Absolutely" and hustle her out of the building. She'd think he was an idiot, not to mention it'd probably cause a scene.

He nodded. "Of course. Where—"

She took his hand, the one not holding the ring, and tugged him toward the front room and the door. But not before giving a furtive look over her shoulder.

As if searching for someone. He looked too, but no one appeared to be watching them.

She dropped his hand as they entered the less-crowded front room. She smiled and nodded at a few people but never stopped to talk, kept moving forward. They reached the front door in less than a minute and she pushed through, releasing a barely audible sigh of relief when she stood on the sidewalk.

The cool night air slapped against his senses but didn't make a dent in his internal temperature, which was working its way to a boil.

And wasn't helped by the fact that his gaze kept trailing down her back to watch her swaying ass.

You're a dog.

True. And still, he couldn't make himself not look. *Shit.*

He thought she'd stop now that they'd reached the sidewalk in front of the building. Instead, she continued on, not running but not taking a leisurely stroll either. Finally, when she reached the intersection at Main Street, she stopped at the corner and took a deep breath, which she released with an audible rush.

She didn't say anything right away, just stared straight ahead. He was pretty sure she wasn't looking at anything in particular.

He, on the other hand, allowed his attention to shift over his surroundings.

Brick townhouses and small wooden homes with picket fences. A beautiful church and a Victorian bed-and-breakfast. Several storefronts farther up the street.

All the properties appeared well-maintained. *Quaint* described it perfectly.

Considering that he and Jed had just bought a large property not too far from town that they planned to turn into an exclusive spa retreat in the next few months, he should be more interested.

Time enough for that later, he decided.

Right now, he focused all his energy on Kate. He wanted to enjoy these few stolen moments before he had to walk away from her. Again.

He gave her a full minute before he couldn't keep quiet any longer. "Kate, is everything okay?"

With a sigh, she turned to face him, arms crossed over her chest as if she were cold. Slipping his leather jacket off his shoulders, he wrapped it around hers. She didn't tell him not to, and he could've sworn he saw her shiver, even after she drew it together in front of her.

Her gaze lingered on his for a few seconds before she looked up into the sky.

Following her gaze, he realized he could see a hell of a lot more stars here than he could in center-city Philadelphia.

Nice.

But far less interesting than she was.

"I've spent all of my life here," she finally said. "It's so peaceful. Quiet."

Since he had no idea where she was going with this, he nodded, though she couldn't see because she was still staring up at the sky. "Seems like it would be."

She looked over her shoulder at him, dark eyes huge. "Are you going to be spending a lot of time up here getting the spa going? Or will Jared handle that?"

Did she want him to be here often? "We have good people in place at Haven, so I'll probably be able to spend some time here. Jed tends to go a little wild if I'm not around to rein him in occasionally."

There was that half smile again. "You two work well together. You get along well, too, don't you?"

"Yeah, we do. Better now that we're older."

He took a step closer, unable to stop, but clenched his hands into fists so he wouldn't reach for her and pull her against him.

Her smile spread. "I bet Jared was a hell-raiser as a teenager."

Tyler laughed and felt his lips curve in an answering smile. "You could say that."

Her head tilted to the side. "And you were always the stable one, weren't you?"

"Would you be surprised if I told you I wasn't?"

She shook her head and a ribbon of straight silky black hair fell over her shoulder. He wanted to wind it around his hand and tug her closer. "No, because I don't really know you, do I?"

"True." He took a deep breath. "Would you like to know me better, Kate?"

She paused, and a deep-seated longing curled through him, tightening his stomach into a knot.

"I broke off my engagement."

He blinked, momentarily stunned. Then the dark, fiery lust that'd been percolating deep in his gut began to rise. "I'm sorry."

But he wasn't. Hell, how could he be sorry when he wanted her so badly his teeth fucking ached with it?

She turned away and tilted her head back to look into the sky again. "I'm not. It was a long time coming and the right thing to do."

He heard a "but" in there and wanted to prod her until she spilled. Instead, he remained silent, waiting for the rest of the story. He knew there had to be more.

"Arnie's a nice guy. A real sweetheart."

Tyler's jaw clenched but he forced it to release before she turned and caught him looking like he wanted to hurt someone. Mia had literally flinched away from him in fear the few times he'd ever looked at her like this. He'd learned to submerge most of his darker emotions, knowing Mia had loved him enough to satisfy some of his cravings but had been unable to handle all of him. And he'd been okay with that because he'd loved her, and love meant compromise.

He didn't think Kate was afraid of much of anything.

"He'll be better off without me."

His gaze narrowed. "Why do you say that?"

"Because I didn't love him the way he deserves."

The caveman part of his brain wanted to pump his fist in the air. Luckily, the more civilized part talked him out of it. "Then he wasn't the right man for you, Kate."

She paused. "Do you believe in soul mates?"

Dangerous territory.

He closed the few feet between them so he was standing by her side. The top of her head barely came up to his shoulder and he fought the urge to pull her into his arms and lift her until her eyes were on a level with his . . . and their mouths were aligned.

Stuffing his hands in his pockets, touching the ring she'd given him earlier, he sighed. "I'm not sure anymore. I used to. I even thought I'd found mine. And then she died."

Those dark eyes met his again, her expression genuinely sorrowful. "I'm so sorry, Tyler. I know how awful it is to lose someone you love. Do you still miss her?"

Did he? "It's been almost two years. The pain's more like a dull ache that I know is still there but . . . it doesn't bother me all the time."

"But it *does* still bother you?"

"When I think about her now . . ."

He got angry, more often than not. And that made him feel like shit. So he didn't think about her.

"What?" she prompted.

He sighed. "I get mad. Which is stupid. Mia had a brain tumor that killed her a year after she was diagnosed. She couldn't control it. She could do nothing to change it."

And yet . . .

"So why do you get mad?"

Because if she'd gotten her symptoms checked earlier, she might've lived. If she'd fought harder—

"Because I couldn't do anything for her."

And it'd been his job to take care of her.

"So now you think you should be able to cure cancer?"

The dry sarcasm in her voice finally drew out his smile, even through thoughts of Mia.

"Maybe I should."

She huffed. "Yeah, and maybe one day I'll be able to weave wool into gold."

Which was as good a segue as any. "Jed told me he talked to you about a lingerie boutique for the spa. He also said you haven't given him an answer yet."

She stiffened, and he could've kicked himself. He didn't want to lose her. Didn't want her to walk away and leave him. Not now.

"That's because I'm not sure it's such a good idea."

"Why not?"

"Because I'm not sure I'm ready to put myself out there like that."

It was a reasonable doubt, he supposed. Especially for someone who'd never tried it before. "Have you shown your designs to Jed? He has a great eye."

It was something he and his brother shared, though Jared mainly dealt with art and Tyler with architecture. Lingerie wasn't much different than art, he figured.

She nodded. "He's seen some of my pieces."

Tyler smiled. "Let me guess . . . on Annabelle."

She arched perfect eyebrows at him. "Of course. No way was *I* modeling for him."

Damn right she wasn't. Tyler would've had to punch his brother.

"Then he's seen that you have talent. Trust me. Jed's as much a businessman as I am. He wouldn't have offered if he didn't think you could do it and make money. Not even to get in good with Annabelle."

Her gaze shifted away for a split second. "Maybe you'd like to see some of my work? Judge for yourself?"

His throat went completely dry and his heart started to gallop.

Was she offering to model for him? Would he be able to keep his hands off her if she did?

Kate pointed over her shoulder. "My apartment's just up the street. I could show you a few of my sketches and I have several samples."

Okay, not offering to model for him. *Damn.*

He forced a smile. "If you'd like to show me, I'd love to see them."

Her expression totally transformed. This was the smile he'd been waiting to see. No trace of sarcasm, just pure, sweet pleasure.

His pulse began to pound and his cock throbbed.

"Then follow me," she said.

He fell into step beside her and silence settled between them, the only sound the click of Kate's heels against the pavement and the almost inaudible hum of traffic on the highway to the east.

He could almost imagine they were the only two people awake at the moment. A few windows glowed from within but most were dark. Annabelle had probably invited the entire town to the gallery opening.

A few streetlights provided enough illumination for them to make their way along the sidewalk but didn't glare down at them.

The air smelled fresher here, cleaner. Philadelphia air always had an underlying scent of decay and diesel fumes.

It took only a minute to reach their destination—a three-story, brick town house with a small porch.

"My apartment's on the second floor," she said as she pushed open the white picket gate between her townhouse and the identical one next to it. "The entrance is on the side."

A security light flashed on and he released the breath he hadn't been aware he'd been holding.

As a city dweller, you learned to be wary of shadows. It'd be so easy for someone to hide in the dark spots along the side of the house, waiting for her to return. She hadn't even looked for danger before opening the gate.

As they walked up the wooden stairs along the side of the house, he allowed his gaze to drop again to the slight sway of her slim ass beneath the dress. His hands clenched, his fingers practically itching to touch her. He wanted to crowd up against her and bend her over right here. Ease up her dress, unzip his pants, and slide his cock between her thighs and inside.

He managed to clamp down on those thoughts before she reached the landing at the top and opened the door, ushering him inside and closing the door behind her.

She'd left a light on and the room that came into view made him smile.

It fit her.

Bright red walls with deep purple curtains on the two large windows at the front of the building. A gold love seat and a purple and gold patterned chaise formed a small seating area in front of a tiny, ornate fireplace on the left side of the room with a TV in the corner. Pictures covered the walls, all in different frames. Sketches, photos, watercolors, oils. He couldn't discern a theme but the jumble seemed to work well together.

"Would you like something to drink? I don't have much alcohol but I do have soda."

He turned to find her in the small kitchen area at the back of the house. Bright white cabinets and counters and a small round table with four chairs, all in black, looked pristine.

Everything had a place in her apartment and everything was in its place.

"Soda's fine."

As she turned to the refrigerator, he caught a glimpse of what looked like her workroom behind the living room. The jumble of color drew him closer. He knew he shouldn't be traipsing around her home, poking into places, but he couldn't seem to stop himself.

He reached for the light switch on the wall and the second he flipped it, he realized he had to have the woman in his bed or die trying.

Holy hell. He was going to have to give Jed a raise, which meant nothing considering they split the profits fifty-fifty. Still . . . *Jesus*.

"I've been a sketching demon the past couple of weeks. Obviously it's not all good. Some of it's crap, actually, but—"

"Kate. Nothing in here is crap."

Actually, the word he'd use would be *amazing*.

She'd tapped into every man's secret sexual fantasies. Tiny bits of lace and satin stitched together in ways designed to fuel a man's desires.

The short back wall had been lined with shelves, where mounds of fabric were separated according to color. In the front of the room, a sewing table and drafting table sat facing one another in front of the large double window.

Another table topped with a grid formed a triangle with the other two.

Most of the room, however, was given over to dress forms.

There were at least eight and all wore lingerie. Other pieces hung from a thin metal cable that stretched along the entire length of the white side wall.

Every piece enticed him to stroke it, rub it between his fingers. Or tear it off a willing woman's body.

All colors of the rainbow. Every conceivable fabric. Lace, satin, velvet, silk, cotton. Even a few pieces of leather. Panties, thongs, bras, corsets.

Did all the air in the room just evaporate?

His cock responded with a surge and he took some time to will his erection to recede. At least to the point that it wouldn't be so damn obvious.

When she brushed by him, his skin broke out in gooseflesh.

She headed toward one of the mannequins displaying a camisole created from sheer cream lace and triangles of peach satin that would barely cover a woman's nipples. "I'm not sure I like the peach and the cream on this piece. I think it may be too subtle."

Hoping like hell his voice wouldn't crack on him, he said, "I think it's beautiful." And would look amazing on her with her coloring.

She slid a glance over her shoulder at him, a shy smile curving her lips. Since *shy* wasn't really a word he associated with Kate, it charmed him all to hell.

"Thank you. I've been spending most of my spare time working on designs, but now I need to get a few more models, a few different shapes and sizes. Some pieces just naturally look better on women with a certain body type. But I want to make sure I have pieces for everybody and not just flat-chested models or busty porn stars." She paused to take a breath, her mouth twisting in a grimace. "And I'm probably not making any sense at all."

"Makes perfect sense to me."

Her smile grew a little wider.

"This style"—she pointed to the camisole—"is made to enhance a woman with a smaller bust. This one"—she reached for a deep purple bra with ruffled straps and see-through lace cups and waved it at him—"absolutely needs a woman who can fill it out." He nodded, not trusting himself to speak right now.

"This is my favorite place in the whole world," she continued. "I can lose myself in here for hours. I love the texture of the fabrics. I even love the sound of the machine. It reminds me of music after a while."

She paused, but he didn't want her to stop. "How long have you been sewing?"

"Oh, I've been designing clothing since I was a kid. I started asking my parents for a sewing machine when I was seven. They finally bought me one when I was ten, when they were sure I wouldn't sew my fingers together. I'd spend entire weekends in my bedroom, making dresses for my dolls and later for my friends."

"Sounds like you knew exactly what you wanted to do with your life at an early age."

The smile she'd been wearing faded. "I did. I was going to be a costume designer." She let out a deep sigh. "And then my mom died a month before graduation."

He heard deep sorrow in those few words. "Kate. I'm sorry."

She shrugged. "It's been years but I still have that ache you talked about earlier. And I never made it to New York. I work for a dry cleaner and hem wedding dresses and suits for a living. Far cry from designing stage costumes." Her eyes flashed at him, daring him. "Are you really sure you want to take a chance on an unproven designer? Don't get me wrong. I'm not trying to talk you out of it. I know how big an opportunity this is for me. But . . ."

She was nervous. He understood that. But she couldn't let it paralyze her. "After seeing your work, I think Jed is absolutely right. Your pieces are beautiful. Sensual." He paused then decided to go for it. "Arousing."

Her eyes widened, her lips parting as if she couldn't get enough air. Blood pounded through his veins, lust driving it.

Then he froze. Was he really going to do this? Was he really going to seduce her?

It wasn't like she'd be the first woman he slept with since Mia's death. There'd been others. Okay, there'd been two. But neither of them had been anything other than a release.

And yes, he realized how that sounded. Cold. Unemotional.

But he'd been careful to choose women who were looking for the same. And the Salon—the secret play room that Jed had created at Haven—catered to several women whose tastes matched his own.

Which should be a major consideration here.

Kate had no idea what he liked, in what direction his tastes lay. Would he shock her? Would she think he was a freak?

Or, like Mia, would she be willing to experiment?

"I live in a very small town." Her voice never wavered. "And I just broke off my engagement."

He heard what she was saying. She didn't have to spell things out.

But he wasn't going to give up. Not this time. Not when, as she'd just reiterated, she was no longer engaged.

"Would you like to come back to Philadelphia with me tonight? It's still early. We have a local jazz quartet playing in the bar tonight. If we leave now, we can make their late set."

She didn't say no right away and he took that as encouragement.

"You'd be my guest. I'll have a room reserved for you." He wanted her to know he didn't expect her to sleep with him. Even though he was praying she'd end up under him somewhere in the hotel. "I'd like to spend time with you, Kate."

He could wait, would have to wait. She wasn't ready for anything more, not after breaking up with the man she'd thought she was going to marry.

He didn't want to rush her.

Silently, she weighed the situation, her gaze never leaving his.

Shit. Had he moved too fast? Maybe he should've waited. He'd be spending a lot of time at the spa. They'd have time to get acquainted. He'd make sure of it.

But, damn it, he didn't want to wait. He felt like his life had been in a holding pattern since Mia had first been diagnosed. Like he'd taken one big breath that day in the doctor's office and hadn't released it yet.

After at least thirty seconds, her chin tilted up. "I'd love to. Just let me pack an overnight bag."

He released his breath on a sigh of relief and her smile made him want to pump his fist in the air.

Nodding, he pulled out his phone. "I'll let Jed know I'm heading out."

Three

❧

The drive to Philadelphia took only an hour at this time of night, and Kate questioned her decision every other second.

When she looked out the window and saw the fields and trees flash by along the Pennsylvania Turnpike, she debated asking Tyler to turn around.

But when she turned to tell him to take her home, she knew she really didn't want to go.

She had to be honest with herself. She'd wanted Tyler since the first moment she'd met him.

And she'd be damned if she let nerves interfere with the opportunity to spend time with him. Tyler Golden drew her in a way no one ever had.

He didn't speak much but, when he did, she hung on his every word. His deep voice practically mesmerized. Hell, her panties were already damp and that was only from listening to his few and far between comments.

They hadn't kept up a running conversation but she didn't feel uncomfortable. She felt cocooned. The leather car seat conformed to her body; the soft jazz issuing from the speakers murmured to her.

As they got closer to the city, her attention focused solely on Tyler. She watched his lips as he spoke, watched his hands grip the wheel. Felt her body tense as she thought about those hands caressing her.

The amount of traffic in the city at ten at night amazed her, which then made her feel like a real hick. Adamstown rolled up its sidewalks by nine at the latest, no matter what was going on.

When they finally pulled up to the hotel and Tyler drove down the ramp into the underground parking facility, she thought she had a handle on her uncertainty.

After he'd parked in a gated area, he threw the keys to a young attendant who came rushing out of the booth.

Kate waited as they exchanged a few words, then Tyler got her bag from the trunk before he walked around to open her door and help her out.

He would have released her but she twined her fingers with his and watched his gaze narrow and his expression sharpen with intensity.

A shiver of need worked its way up her spine and she couldn't help but think how he would look at her when he took her to bed.

That was exactly what she wanted and she wasn't going to give up the opportunity.

No matter what happened in the future, she was grabbing hold of tonight and not letting go until she got what she wanted.

Tyler. In a bed. Making her scream.

Okay, she might give up the screaming for a simple orgasm that she didn't have to work so damn hard for.

Arnie had never—

No. No thoughts of Arnie tonight.

"Would you like to see your room or should I have your bag sent up so we can go to the bar?"

"Do you think I should change first?"

The elevator opened seconds after he pushed the button and they stepped inside. As the doors closed, his gaze trapped and held hers. "Absolutely not. You look stunning."

She didn't attempt to hold back her smile and was rewarded by one of his in return. "Thank you, Tyler. But this dress is probably a little much for a bar."

"Trust me, the only thing anyone will notice is how good you look in it. Besides, I have a reserved booth in the back. We won't be in the crowd. And . . . I really love the dress, Kate. Leave it on. Please."

He stole her breath with that soft "Please."

When she nodded, he turned to face the doors. And continued to stare at her in the reflection.

When the elevator stopped, Tyler ushered her out into the refined elegance of Haven's lobby.

She remembered the first time she'd been here New Year's Eve. Remembered thinking she was so far out of her league.

Her parents had never been wealthy. Well-off, yes, but they'd never spent money extravagantly. Haven qualified as extravagant and catered to a crowd that would expect it. The reception desk was cream marble, for cripes sake. Brown leather chairs and couches were grouped in small seating areas. Modern art by names even she recognized decorated the pale blue walls.

The hotel had a sleek, modern vibe without being cold and unwelcoming. The ballroom had been exquisite.

Kate hadn't been to Frank's Bar on her previous visit so she wasn't sure what to expect, but she knew it would be nothing less than amazing.

They entered the bar from a small, private door behind the registration area, after Tyler had given her bag to a bellman. A small stairway led them to a nearly invisible entrance at the back of the bar and to an elevated, u-shaped booth.

As she slid onto the black leather banquette, she had a perfect view of the stage if she sat in the center. But if she moved to either side, no one would be able to see her.

You could do all sorts of wicked things in here and no one would be the wiser.

Putting that thought aside for now, she took in the décor, which reminded her of something out of the '50s. The meticulous attention to detail would've made Sinatra and the Rat Pack feel right at home.

On stage, a quartet perfectly accompanied the singer's sultry voice.

Kate could almost imagine she'd stepped back in time.

As Tyler slid in beside her, she leaned over so she wouldn't have to raise her voice to be heard. "I love this place, Tyler. I feel like it really is the '50s."

"That's exactly what we were going for. Jed and I agreed that we wanted the bar to be swanky. We're both fans of *Mad Men* and this allowed us to play with that feeling."

"Well, you certainly achieved your goal."

Tyler started to reply but a thirtyish man in a crisp dark suit, pristine white shirt, and skinny red tie stepped up to the booth, eliciting a smile from Tyler as they shook hands.

"I figured we'd see you tonight," the man said. "I know how much you enjoy Sally and the band."

"Hey, Mike. I'm glad I could catch them. Mike, this is Kate. Kate, this is Mike Valenti, the bar manager."

Mike took her outstretched hand and gave her a dazzling smile that transformed his almost stern features into rakish handsomeness.

This one probably left a trail of broken hearts behind him though he played the perfect gentleman with her. Probably because she was with his boss.

"Nice to meet you, Kate." Then he winked at her before turning back to Tyler. "What can I get you tonight?"

"Just ginger ale for me," Tyler said. "Kate?"

Since she already felt a little drunk, she probably shouldn't push her luck. Then again, a little loosening up never hurt anyone. "Whiskey sour, please."

His smile widened. "Ah, you must have been here before to know that's the bartender's signature drink."

Tyler answered before she could. "Ignore his clumsy attempt at prying. Mike likes to stick his nose where it doesn't belong."

"And yet I've managed to keep it in one piece all these years." Mike looked unrepentant. In fact, his smile seemed even wider. "I'll be back with your drinks, boss. Kate, enjoy your evening."

Mike disappeared and she looked up to find Tyler shaking his head, his expression amused. "Mike's been one of my best friends since high school. He could be managing a fleet of restaurants around the country. When Jed and I opened this place, we brought Mike in to set up the bar. We never thought he'd stay. We're damn lucky to have him."

"Loyalty counts for a lot."

"Yes, it does. Especially when you're starting a venture like ours."

"This was a huge undertaking, wasn't it?"

Tyler leaned back into the booth, his expression relaxed and so handsome, she would've gladly sat there and simply stared at him all night.

"Any business is in this economy, but we were determined. And we figured we had a leg up because of our family history."

"Your dad owns the GoldenStar hotel chain."

"My dad *inherited* the GoldenStar hotel chain from our grandfather. My dad's a pretty savvy businessman and he thought we were crazy. He wanted us to stay with the chain."

"And you and Jared didn't want to."

"We had our own plans."

"You've created something wonderful."

That smile of his was something wonderful as well, she decided.

"We think so. It was a lot of work but rewarding as hell."

"Jared said you're the money man. He also said you helped create the plans for the hotel."

"I'm the money man because I hold an MA in business from Wharton. But Jed exaggerates when it comes to how much guidance I gave the architect."

"So you didn't sketch out the entire layout of the first three floors, including the ballrooms and conference rooms and the atrium and give that to the architect to re-create?"

Tyler leaned his head against the black leather back cushion, his smile slowly fading but the intensity in those deep blue eyes becoming more focused.

When Tyler didn't respond, she continued. "Jared also said the atrium has been your project from the beginning."

"Sounds like Jed's been talking a lot."

"Don't be mad at him. He only told me because I asked."

She realized as soon as the last word left her mouth what she'd admitted and felt a blush race to her cheeks.

Tyler's gaze sharpened. "I'm glad to hear that."

"I'm so sorry. I wasn't prying—"

"Don't be sorry. I'm flattered." His mouth quirked in an adorably lopsided grin and she forgot to be embarrassed.

Hell, she forgot everything but the way he made her feel. Lightheaded and fizzy and . . . like a teenager in love for the first time.

And she knew this wasn't love. Infatuation, yes. But love . . .
No way.

She smiled again, unsure what to say now. Small talk had never
been her strong suit and flirting . . . Well, she frankly sucked at
flirting.

So she practically kissed the waitress who brought their drinks.
Until she had the crazy compulsion to scratch the woman's eyes out
when she smiled at Tyler.

Tyler returned the woman's smile, but only for a second. Then
his attention shifted back to Kate.

Where it belonged.

Oh, God, she was going to need to have her head examined.
First thing Monday morning.

Tonight, she was going to embrace the crazy.

As if he'd picked up on her ping-ponging thoughts, Tyler took
pity on her and turned to watch the band. She took a deep breath
and did the same.

For the next thirty minutes, she sipped her drink, listened to
wonderful music, and totally enjoyed sitting next to Tyler. But
when the singer announced their last song for the night, Kate felt
excitement bubble.

She couldn't help thinking about what Annabelle had told her
about the Salon, the private room on the fourth floor. Would he
take her there?

Excitement warred with trepidation. Annabelle had said Tyler
hadn't been present during her time at the Salon. Maybe he didn't
spend any time there.

But Kate wanted to see it.

"Kate, is everything okay?"

She turned to find Tyler watching her, concern clear in his
expression.

"I'm fine. Will you show me the Salon?"

She hadn't meant to blurt it out like that, but she couldn't think of any other way to bring up the subject. And since she'd decided tonight was not going to include fear of any kind, she didn't take it back.

Not even when Tyler looked like he'd been punched in the gut.

Which he quickly covered with one of those half smiles he was so good at. And that looked so good on him.

"What exactly have you heard about the Salon?"

That Annabelle had had one of the most exciting and arousing nights of her life there.

So that's exactly what she told him.

Tyler's expression never wavered but the air seemed to thicken around them. Her sex clenched as she thought about the scene Annabelle had painted for her. The visuals had left her breathless. To think she might actually get to experience a bit of that for herself . . . Oh my.

"Did she tell you I don't typically attend Jed's games?"

"She said you weren't there that night." She took a deep breath. "So you don't use the Salon?"

Another pause. "Not regularly, no. But when we first opened and Jed set it up . . . yeah, I went."

Not wanting to appear too eager but too curious not to ask, she leaned forward. "I'm not a prude, Tyler. And I won't judge. Everyone's entitled to their own happiness, so long as they don't hurt anyone else."

"But what happens if someone does get hurt?"

She paused, because the look in his eyes made her stop and reconsider the way he'd phrased the question. And his emphasis on the last word. "I guess it depends on how. Are we talking physical or emotional? If you're talking emotional, then I guess you need to be sure you've done everything you can to *not* be a monster about it."

She'd tried so hard to minimize the damage with Arnie, but she'd known it wouldn't take the entire sting away.

"If it's physical"—just the thought made her heart speed up in a way she barely understood—"then it has to be consensual."

His smile turned just the slightest bit wicked. "I agree. On both counts. So tell me, Kate. What if I asked to tie you up? Would you let me?"

She tried hard not to be shocked. It wasn't like she'd never heard of bondage. She'd seen her share of porn. She actually loved to read romances that dealt with light bondage. The whole aspect of giving up control to someone you trusted implicitly was a strong trigger for her. Not that she'd ever told Arnie. She'd been too afraid he'd be shocked. Or repulsed.

Which should have been a huge red flag and you totally ignored it.

"I'm sorry, Kate." Tyler's voice intruded on her thoughts, the hint of self-recrimination in his tone totally drawing her attention back to him. "I never should've—"

"I think once I get to know you better"—she paused to smile—"there won't be anything I won't let you do to me. And that's a little scary."

* *

Tyler felt Kate's softly spoken words reverberate through his body with the force of a blow to the head.

He couldn't help but wonder if she was slightly drunk, but she didn't slur her words, her gaze steady on his. Her cheeks held a slight flush, but that could be attributed to lust.

The desires he hadn't fed in years began to gnaw at his gut, urging him to pull her out of the booth and into an elevator headed for the fourth floor.

"Kate . . . would you like a tour of the Salon?"

She didn't hesitate. "I'd love one."

He took her out the way they'd come in. He'd recognized several people in the bar and didn't want to get caught in a conversation with any of them.

He wanted Kate to himself.

Taking her to the staff elevator, he nodded to the few employees they passed. Most of them were too well-trained to show any indication of surprise at Kate's presence. But he knew they'd talk among themselves.

They hadn't seen him with a woman since Mia's death so the fact that he'd brought a woman to the hotel and was leading her through the inner sanctum was a huge break from protocol.

And he couldn't care less.

Jed was right. It was time to move on. He'd mourned long enough.

Being with Kate felt . . . right.

As he waved her onto the elevator, she turned and flashed him one of those mysterious, amused looks. "I never realized there was a whole secret world behind the scenes of a hotel. Reminds me of those old movies in English castles with secret passageways."

After he punched the button for the fourth floor, he leaned back against the wall and stuffed his hands in his pockets. He wanted to grab her and keep her against him but didn't want to rush her. "I haven't seen a lot of movies like that. I like movies that blow things up. Most of those aren't set in English castles."

Her smile broadened. "So you *are* a typical guy in some ways."

A typical guy? "Is that good or bad?"

She shrugged. "It's interesting."

"How so?"

"Because I don't think of you as typical in any way."

He thought about that as the elevator came to a stop and the doors opened. The fourth floor was available only to certain staff and a select group of trusted friends. His and Jed's personal offices as well as their apartments were located on this floor, as were two private suites.

The Salon occupied the other half of the floor.

The staff elevator opened at the opposite end of the building from the Salon. Jed had personally chosen the artwork for this floor so the walls held a collection of bold modern artists that didn't make Tyler cringe, even though he much preferred the pieces in the Salon.

Of course, Jed had chosen those too, but he always consulted Tyler before buying anything. Tyler did the same with any major decision involving the finances. They trusted each other's judgment in a way their father never would have.

To say their parents had been shocked when they'd announced they were going into business together would be an understatement. And when they'd told their dad their plan, the battle had turned vicious. It'd only been in the past year that he'd come around. Mostly.

They fell silent as he led her down the hallway. Her dark eyes missed nothing as she considered the artwork, studied the carpet, ran her fingers along the molding.

He and Jed had thrown every bit of the considerable fortune their grandfather had left them into making Haven the truly one-of-a-kind experience they'd envisioned.

"I remember thinking how gorgeous my room was when Annie and I stayed here New Year's Eve. You and Jared really did an amazing job with this place."

"Thank you."

Any other time, with anyone else, he would've gone on about the features the hotel offered or the accessibility to downtown

Philadelphia or some other business-related detail. Jed was the showman, but Tyler was the salesman.

Right now, he wasn't thinking about anything to do with the hotel. His entire attention was focused on Kate and getting her to the door at the end of the hall. He could have taken her through his office. Like Jed's, his had a private entrance into the Salon. But that would've required a slight delay and he had no time for that.

Finally, they reached the door. Pulling an old-fashioned brass key from his pocket, he turned the lock and pushed open the door.

Soft illumination sparked, and Kate's mouth dropped open as she entered the room.

"Oh, my God." Her voice rose barely above a whisper. "I feel like I just stepped through a time portal into Victorian England."

"Jed was involved in every aspect of designing and decorating this room. My only request was the piano but Jed had already worked that in."

She slid him a quick glance before returning to study the room. "It's amazing."

He had to agree.

But the room was no more stunning than her.

The glow from the crystal chandelier hanging dead center in the ceiling fell over her as she moved into the octagonal room. The light sparkled off her satin dress and her dark hair in a way that made him want to run his hands all over her.

Again, she studied everything, from the ornately decorated ceiling to the plush carpets on the floor.

Lush fabrics covered the chaise lounges, chairs, and ottomans set in several seating groups throughout the room while the octagonal game table with matching chairs sat directly beneath the chandelier.

Golden silk paper gleamed on the walls and a baby grand piano held court in one corner, lit by a leaded glass piano light. He'd spent a lot of time in front of that piano after Mia had died. Luckily, the room was soundproofed so no one was disturbed by his attempts at working out his grief.

Kate began walking around the room, letting her fingers brush against chairs and the heavy purple velvet drapes in front of the windows on either side of the room.

When she reached the fireplace on the opposite side of the room, she actually caressed the carved marble face and mantel.

His jaw clenched. He wanted those fingers to caress his body.

Locking the door so they wouldn't be interrupted—not that he expected to be but he wasn't taking any chances—he walked to the nearest seating group and sank into a velvet wingback love seat.

She'd made her way to the huge, glass-front walnut display cabinet that occupied an entire wall of the room before she paused.

He found he'd stopped breathing, wondering if she'd finally realize what she was getting herself into. Some of the pieces in that cabinet were sure to make a novice in certain sexual practices blush.

He wanted to reassure her that he would never push her to do anything she felt uncomfortable with. But when she finally looked over her shoulder at him, instead of surprise, he saw curiosity.

"I'm not totally sure I want to know what some of this stuff is but . . . mostly they're beautiful. Did you . . . Have you used some of these?"

He took a second to answer, knew he didn't want to lie to her. "Yes."

Her breath hitched and again, he couldn't tell if he'd put her off or turned her on.

"So you're into BDSM."

He shook his head. "No, not the whole scene. Bondage, mostly. Dominance. I'm not into the master-slave thing. I don't think dog collars look good on women." He paused, watched her lips part as she drew in a deep breath. "But there's something about giving yourself over to another person so completely . . . something about being restrained by someone you trust, that's . . . freeing."

Her eyes had narrowed, as if she were trying to comprehend what he was saying, to figure out the hidden meanings.

For him, there were none. He liked to dominate in bed. He wasn't interested in making a woman crawl on the floor or lick his feet.

But tie her to a bed—or a chair or a piano bench—and hear her beg for release?

Yeah, he got off on that.

"I'm not sure I could do that."

"Do what?"

She shook her head and that beautiful hair slid over her shoulder. He wanted to wrap it around his hand and tug her head back so he could kiss her.

"Give that much control over to anyone."

He rose then, drawn by the sudden uncertainty on her face. But instead of going to her, he headed for the bar next to one of the windows.

"Would you like a drink?"

She didn't answer right away but he heard her approach.

"Just ginger ale for me please."

He poured her a glass of soda and handed it over then poured himself a Coke. If she asked to leave because she was freaked out, he didn't want to have to arrange a ride for her. He wanted to take her himself.

They sipped their drinks in silence before she drifted off to sit on the nearest chaise.

"I know you said you don't play with Jared's crowd, but you do use this room?"

"I used to, yes." With Mia. He didn't have to say the words. She'd understand what he wasn't saying.

"So your fiancée was into the same scene?"

He shook his head, squashing a grimace midformation. "Not until she met me."

"I can imagine you're pretty good at persuasion."

"This isn't something I would ever persuade anyone to do. You have to want to experience it."

And that's where Mia had been wrong. She'd thought because he enjoyed it, he'd want her to participate. And he would have. But only if she'd actually enjoyed it and not simply put on a show for him.

He realized Kate was smiling at him and couldn't figure out why. He didn't think he'd said anything funny.

"You know, you could come over here and let me try to persuade you to kiss me."

He froze for a second as his brain processed what she'd said, then he did exactly what she wanted.

He sat next to her on the chaise, with enough space between them that she didn't feel crowded. Or persuaded.

As he turned back from setting his glass on the nearest table, he found Kate had moved closer. Their height difference wasn't as noticeable now. His lips practically brushed her forehead and her spicy scent was a stronger draw.

His heart began to pound as her gaze held his and he was glad he'd set down his glass. He might've dropped it otherwise.

Especially when she moved even closer and put her hands on his shoulders.

"Or," she said, "you could let me kiss you?"

So he wouldn't have to beg? "I have no problem with that."

He watched as she bit her bottom lip, eyes narrowing as she

closed the distance between them completely and her lips finally touched his.

He felt like a teenager at his first make-out party. Overexcited and flushed and horny as all hell. And unsure what to do with his hands.

Which was ridiculous for a thirty-year-old man.

Then Kate kissed him and left him breathless.

Four

❧

Kate didn't make a big production out of that kiss. She simply poured her heart and soul into it and took Tyler under.

Her hands came up to cup his cheeks, her fingers lightly caressing his jaw and his cheekbones. Her soft lips moved over his slowly, as if savoring the taste of him. He certainly savored her.

It'd been a while since he'd kissed anyone other than Mia and it'd been two years since he'd kissed her.

He was almost afraid he'd forgotten how until instinct took over.

One arm wrapped around her shoulders and the other around her waist. Then he drew her closer. Which still wasn't close enough. As her lips opened for the thrust of his tongue, he lifted her onto his lap. The satin of her dress made her slide across his thighs and his cock hardened even more.

Her hip pressed against his growing erection and his eyes closed at the pressure. He wanted to rub against her, to lift that dress so he could stroke his hands along the inside of her thighs. She'd be so damn soft there. And even softer between her legs.

She moaned as he slipped his tongue into her mouth then arched against him, squirming closer.

This kiss was going to get out of hand pretty damn fast. And he loved it. Lust burned in his veins, urging him to spread her out on the chaise and lick her from her toes up.

Instead he drowned in her taste, nearly suffocating because he didn't want to break away.

When he couldn't wait any longer, he slipped his lips from her mouth, heard her gulp in air and had to do the same. Then he nuzzled her hair away from her ear so he could bite the tiny lobe and felt her shiver.

Her hands had already slipped to the buttons on his shirt and were pushing them through their holes. He groaned when she reached his waistband and brushed against the tip of his cock, pressing against his pants' zipper.

She didn't seem to notice, though, because she'd already spread her hands across his stomach in preparation for sliding them up his chest.

Christ, why the hell did he have to wear a damn undershirt? He could have her hands on his skin already.

Instead, he'd have to release her to get his shirt and T-shirt over his head.

But first, he had to deal with her dress.

The zipper was carefully hidden. The tiny tab almost eluded his broad fingers. Finally, he found it tucked inside the seam at the top of the short collar.

When he began to release it, Kate froze, her cheek pressed against his, her body trembling.

He almost stopped, convinced he was going too fast, until she slid her hands to his shoulders and began to push his shirt down his arms.

Nipping at the tendon in his neck, she made him shudder, and he almost lost his tenuous grip on that tab.

As she continued to kiss her way down his neck, he drew the zipper down her back. The dress fell apart, baring warm flesh to his touch. He spread one hand across her back and wove the other through her hair, tilting her head up so he could take her mouth again.

She kissed him without reserve, putting her whole body into it. As he stroked her back, he realized she wasn't wearing a bra.

Christ.

Now he could barely breathe.

Swallowing a groan, he pulled away, breath catching in his throat as he gazed down at her.

Flushed cheeks. Red, kiss-swollen lips. Hazy, sensually dazed eyes.

Beautiful.

Holding her gaze, he reached for her shoulders and began to draw the dress down. She didn't make any attempt to stop him.

Instead, she dropped her arms to her sides so the bodice came down smoothly, revealing small, perfect breasts.

He barely restrained the urge to leave her arms trapped at her sides and pull her forward to suck on those peach-tipped mounds. They'd barely fill his palm but he bet they'd be sensitive. Maybe he could make her come simply with his mouth on her nipples.

She moved then, withdrawing her hands from the sleeves and letting the dress pool at her waist as she reached for him. He was already shaking his shirt off his wrists as she slid her hands under his T-shirt and began to lift it up his torso.

He raised his arms to help her, urgency consuming him. But she took her sweet time. And when she finally got the material bunched around his neck, she leaned forward and put her mouth on his chest, on the taut muscle of his left pec.

Yes.

Whipping the shirt over his head, he grabbed her head, tempering his response at the last second so he didn't handle her too roughly.

But he didn't want her to move. He wanted her mouth on him. Wanted her tongue licking along his skin. Wanted her teeth tugging at his nipple.

As if she'd read his mind, she opened her mouth and bit him as his free hand gripped her waist, pulling her closer. He let her torment him for minutes, let her lick and bite his nipple before stringing a line of kisses to the other, where she did the same.

All the while, he forced back the raging tide of dominance that wanted him to strip the rest of her clothes from her body and lay her out on the chaise so he could have his way with her.

He wondered what she'd do if he tried it? Would she let him? Or would she run?

They really didn't know one another well enough for him to start down that road. At least not yet. But later . . . All bets would be off.

And there would be a later. He already knew one night wasn't going to be enough to sate this lust.

Her small hands petted along his shoulders, teasing, tantalizing. Making him want more. Harder.

He realized he'd tightened his grip on her and forced himself to relax.

They had all night.

Suddenly, she straightened, pulling back to look at him.

"You do know I won't break, don't you? I can tell you're trying to hold back, and that's not what I want, Tyler. You don't frighten me."

His mouth twisted in a hard grin. "Glad to hear it. Then stand up and strip."

Her eyebrows lifted in perfect arches and her lips parted on a silent little gasp. But after a deep, unsteady breath, she twisted on his lap until her ass pressed against his cock. Then she made sure she wiggled just a little, making him nearly swallow his tongue before she rose to her feet and turned to face him.

The dress was already on its way to the floor as she turned and, when she finally faced him fully, it lay in a pale cloud at her feet.

And was instantly forgotten when he let his gaze travel upward.

Slim legs, slim hips. Her mound covered by a tiny triangle of nude silk. Did she wax? His mouth practically watered to think about sliding his tongue between smooth, plump lips.

He gripped the edge of the chaise and held on as his gaze worked its way back to her breasts. They quivered with each breath, the tips tight, flushed a beautiful pink.

As he finally caught her gaze again, he saw no apprehension or hesitation. Just plain and simple desire.

Then her lips curved. "Lie down," she said.

His heart practically thumped out of his chest.

* *

Kate watched Tyler's expression carefully, wondering if she'd pushed the man with admitted dominance issues too far.

She wanted him so badly her sex ached, muscles in her stomach tightening almost painfully as her thighs clenched, trying to ease some of that distress.

For several seconds, he simply stared at her, the heat of his gaze an almost physical caress against her body.

She wanted to hold that gaze but the sheer beauty of his naked chest was like a siren's call. She had to look.

The sudden urge to burn all of his clothing so he would have to walk around naked made her smile.

Tyler had the body of a swimmer. Broad shoulders. Wide, muscled chest. Six-pack abs and corded arms. She swore just the sight of all that leashed strength was making her dizzy.

Or it could be all the blood rushing to other parts of her body. Her breasts felt full and tingly and her sex lips puffy. And so slick. She could smell her arousal and he had to be able to, as well.

Embarrassment at her overt reaction should've caused her to shy away. Or, at the very least, not stare at him so openly.

But she'd be damned if she'd come this far only to chicken out now. Her hands practically shook with the need to touch him.

She didn't know how long it took him to comply with her demand. She only knew that when he lowered himself back onto the chaise, settling one arm behind his head and laying the other on all that lovely muscle on his abdomen, she nearly swallowed her tongue.

"Well? Are you going to stare all night?"

His voice had dropped a full octave, she swore. And it acted like gasoline on fire.

She took a step closer, bringing her within touching distance.

Holding out her hand, she didn't know what to touch first.

That chest. Those abs.

Or maybe . . .

His belt. She reached for it, managing to get the strap through the first obstacle of the buckle but needing both hands to finish the job.

Her knuckles brushed against his erection and his stomach muscles tightened as he sucked in a sharp breath.

She did it again, deliberately this time, as she released the belt then went to work on the button. That required a little more concentration, getting the small button through the hole without pinching anything . . . vital.

When she finally had it undone, his zipper began to part on its own accord.

"Kate."

His husky tone held a thinly veiled demand. And a plea.

Reaching for the zipper, she gripped the tab before glancing up at him.

"Yes?"

She asked the question but didn't really expect him to say no. She stood almost completely naked beside him, so aroused she could barely speak. His erection nearly split his pants, the outline so thick she could barely restrain herself from ripping them away to get a good look.

The hand on his stomach reached for the one hovering over him. With a gentle but firm grip, he helped her release the zipper the rest of the way.

His erection pressed through the opening, straining beneath the plain gray cotton briefs.

She loved men in briefs, either boxers or classic. Arnie had always worn cotton boxers that bagged in the ass. *So* not sexy. She had a feeling anything Tyler wore would be sexy. Tyler in nothing was going to be sexy as all hell.

She wanted to reach for his pants to pull them down but he still had hold of her hand. She tugged, but he held on.

His thumb rubbed over her knuckles then pressed against them as he drew her hand down until her palm settled on his erect shaft. The heat of him branded her through the thin cotton and she reflexively closed her fingers around him.

Tyler sucked in a breath between clenched teeth and his hand tightened around hers for a second before he released her.

And again, she had the feeling he was holding back in some way.

So instead of doing what he obviously wanted, she set out to tease him into releasing those chains.

She'd had her nails manicured earlier today, a sleek deep purple. Putting them to good use, she traced them over his abs and back to his peaked nipples. Flicking at them, she felt the tight, little nubs rise and fall with his rapid breathing.

With her thighs spread on either side of his, her pussy felt painfully exposed, even though she still wore her thong, the tiny string between her ass cheeks an arousing annoyance. Her juices drenched the miniscule patch of satin at the front and it took everything she had not to lower herself so she could rub against his cock.

Not yet. She wanted to play some more.

Without warning, she drew her nails down his stomach, letting them dig just the tiniest bit deeper than they had on the way up, leaving faint red lines on his dark gold skin.

"Kate."

His voice held a command this time, one she had every intention of obeying. On her own timetable.

When she reached the waistband of his pants, she slid her fingers beneath then started to tug.

He helped by lifting his hips, his abs flexing in fascinating motions. But even they couldn't hold her attention as she dragged his pants and underwear down, revealing the thick column of his cock.

Ruddy and smooth, the warm flesh rose toward her as she released it from the confines of his clothing.

When his pants hit his thighs, she abandoned them there, putting one hand flat on his chest so he wouldn't move and wrapping the other around that enticing shaft.

"Fuck, Kate. That feels amazing."

The obscenity, spoken in that rough tone of voice, sent shivers through her body. Her hand tightened around his cock before she could temper her response and she realized her fingers didn't meet around the circumference.

Oh. My.

Scooting farther down the chaise, she kept her grip on him as she bent to taste him.

Just a lick at first. One swipe of her tongue up the exposed side of his cock. She swore she heard him groan. Wanted to hear it again.

This time, she concentrated on swirling her tongue around the head. Keeping her hand at the base, she played with him, flicking at the slit then sliding her lips around the head. Just the head.

He groaned again and, in her peripheral vision, she saw his neck arch, his head digging into the cushion.

Though she noticed he didn't thrust into her mouth.

So much control. She wanted to break it.

She worked her way down the shaft in tiny increments, using her tongue to torment every centimeter she covered. At first, she only sank halfway before lifting back up to the head. Minutes passed as she concentrated only on those few inches and deliberately avoided taking him in totally.

And still he didn't ask her for more, didn't beg her to take it all.

A challenge. She'd been so careful to avoid them for so long.

Now she started to take more.

In. Out. Wetting him with her tongue. Letting her teeth scrape gently against the shaft.

He made a deep, guttural sound and his hand tightened in her hair. Not so calm anymore.

She drew back until the head popped out of her mouth then

looked up at him, found him staring down at her. Deliberately, she smiled, just a slight curve of her lips that made his gaze narrow.

Then she opened her mouth and slid down his shaft until she had his entire length engulfed.

And then she got serious.

She sucked on him like he was her favorite lollipop, making her cheeks hollow, his taste an aphrodisiac.

And finally, he lost his grip on all that control.

Both hands rose to cup her head, urging her without words to take him as deep as she could. He didn't hold her down or force her in the direction he wanted. Instead, he stroked his fingers along her scalp, sending sensation pulsing through her body.

She took him, enjoying the power to make him groan, loving the sharp ache between her legs.

How long had it been since she'd felt this excitement?

And whose fault is that?

No one's but her own.

Pushing those thoughts out of her head, she concentrated instead on the feel of him in her mouth, losing herself in the motion, in his scent. In the deep sounds of pleasure he continued to make.

She wasn't prepared to relinquish her hold on him when he finally eased her away.

"Kate. Stop. I don't want to come in your mouth."

The blunt words in that husky tone caused her to suck in a deep breath as she pulled away and looked up into his eyes.

But she didn't have much of a chance for more than a glimpse because he moved. Suddenly she found herself flat on her back on the chaise, blinking up at the ceiling.

The intricate molding and detail caught her eye but the second his lips fastened on to her nipple, her eyes closed, blocking out everything but him.

He curved one arm around her waist, arching her back, forcing her breasts higher. With his free hand, he cupped one breast while his lips stayed on the other.

Sucking her in, his teeth grazed the tip, sending sparks of heat to her pussy. With her eyes closed, she swore she could see those sparks as bright pinpoints of lights.

She let herself sink into the sensual vortex Tyler created with his hands and mouth. Her fingers dug into his hair, the feeling decadent. So different—

Cutting off that thought, she clutched him closer. He responded by sucking harder, then leaving a trail of stinging kisses from one breast to the other. His teeth sank into the side of her breast for a brief moment before he licked that nipple into his mouth and started the wonderful torture all over again.

She existed in a state of heightened awareness, feeling Tyler all around her. His hands on her breast and hip, his mouth teasing her nipple, his body blanketing hers in heat.

When he released her breasts and began to kiss his way down her body, she sucked in a deep breath, unaware until then that she'd been holding it. She had the vague notion that she didn't want him to move but he slipped free and continued on.

He stopped at her navel to flick his tongue in the tiny indentation, making her shiver. As he moved lower, her hands fell to his broad shoulders, brushing against the muscles there. Such strength beneath the surface. So much leashed power.

His mouth brushed against the soft, short hair on her mound. She had baby-fine hair there to begin with, so she kept it trimmed to a bare minimum and waxed between her legs. She did it for herself. Arnie had never seemed to care one way or another. At least, he'd never indicated and he'd never gone down on her like Tyler was about to.

Anticipation made her muscles tighten as Tyler pressed his lips to the soft flesh just above her clit. His breath tickled the hair there just before she felt the brush of his tongue. Just a flick against the tiny bundle of nerves and she moaned as electricity flashed through her lower body.

Her legs fell open even wider as he pushed his hands under her butt and tilted her up. So he could get a better angle

The perfect angle.

His mouth closed over her sex in an intimate kiss, sucking at her labia. The sensitive skin tingled, and an orgasm began to gather low in her body.

She'd never come from oral stimulation alone. Usually it took both penetration and clitoral stimulation to get her to the point that she shattered. Otherwise, it was a weak shimmer rather than flood. Now, she could already feel the dam begin to crack under the strain.

Her breathing rasped out in harsh gasps as he worked his tongue inside her, fucking her with it then sucking her clit and nibbling on that with his teeth.

Every move he made seemed calculated to drive her wild while he maintained total control. Forcing her eyes open, she looked down.

Naked, legs spread and a man between them.

She should have been shocked at how wanton she looked.

Instead, she felt . . . free.

A sharp spasm of pleasure caught her unawares and she moaned, trying to curl in on herself to hold the pleasure closer.

One of Tyler's hands shot to her shoulders to press her back into the chaise while the other tightened on her ass.

Her eyes opened again—she didn't remember closing them— and found Tyler staring up at her. She could barely breathe as he held her gaze while his lips sucked on her clit.

She came, a longer, sharper sensation than the one only seconds before.

Unable to keep her eyes open, she melted into the cushions and concentrated instead on the stunning feelings bouncing around her body.

Electric and all-consuming, they were almost too much to handle.

So she didn't try. She let herself ride along on the wave, which Tyler didn't seem to be close to letting fade.

She didn't know how long he played with her, licking and sucking. She only knew that when he drew back and flipped her onto her stomach, she barely protested.

She thought about turning back and reaching for him but then he put both hands on her shoulders and ran them in a rough caress down her back then up again.

Moaning at the sheer pleasure, she went boneless, only to suck in a sharp gasp when he gathered her hair in his hand and wrapped it around his fist.

He didn't tug or pull, just held the mass with a firm hand. Behind her, she felt him moving, heard a drawer open then close. He knelt between her spread legs, his knees brushing the inside of her thighs.

Yes. Hurry.

She didn't say the words aloud but he had to be able to read her body language. Her hips shifted restlessly, the ache between her legs growing sharper with every second. She reached behind her with the intention of grabbing his leg or any other part of him and urging him on.

He caught her hand and leaned over, putting his mouth right at her ear. "I want you to grab the top of the chaise and I want you to hold on tight. Don't let go. Okay?"

Swallowing hard, she nodded. Or tried to, at least.

"Kate?" His voice rubbed against her skin, raising the hair all over her body with the rich timbre. "You need to answer so I can hear you."

"Yes," she said, though the word came out as little more than a whisper. So she tried again and this time, she made sure he heard. "Yes."

"Thank you, sweetheart. I'm going to make you come so damn many times."

His voice sounded strained but his words held a conviction that made her quiver.

Oh, she was so far out of her league here, but she didn't care. Only cared that he continued to stroke her.

She held her breath until he began again. This time, his hands fell first on her thighs, kneading the lax muscles there before palming her ass. He molded her nonexistent curves as if she were the most voluptuous woman.

"Absolutely fucking beautiful."

Almost unbelievably, another orgasm began to build just from the sound of his voice. Her hands curled around the edge of the chaise and she pressed her face against the crushed velvet as his hands continued up her back to her shoulders. She felt him moving again, repositioning. His weight shifted off the cushion and he drew her legs together. She didn't have time to wonder what he was doing when he put a hand on her hips and said, "Lift up, Kate."

Obeying without thought, she lifted her hips off the chaise and felt smooth, cool fabric being shoved underneath. A pillow.

Her ass now higher than her head, she sucked in a deep breath and anticipated . . . what?

She had no idea. She only knew she wanted whatever it was.

When Tyler positioned himself behind her, she waited with

baited breath for him to spread her legs, settle his knees between hers and finally, *finally* fill her with that gorgeous cock she'd recently had in her mouth.

She wanted him to just take her already, to give her the friction she needed so badly.

Instead, he put his knees on the outside of hers, bracketing her legs. Then he pushed his hips forward and rubbed his cock in the crease of her ass.

Hot, hard, and thick. If she hadn't already been flat on her face, she would've been then.

"Oh God. Tyler . . ."

One of his hands spread across the small of her back while the other gripped her hip and kept her steady as he rubbed his shaft between her cheeks.

"Your skin is so goddamn soft." Tyler's voice held a more pronounced rasp now and it stoked her desire even higher. "No, don't move or this will be over way too soon."

She realized she'd been grinding back against him, trying to relieve some of the ache in her pussy.

"Then maybe you should start already."

Bending closer until she felt the fine hair on his chest brush against her back, he spoke close enough to her ear that she felt his breath brush against it. "When I'm ready, sweetheart. When I'm ready."

"Then be ready now, because I sure as hell am."

She swore she heard him laugh, an almost silent exhalation of amusement, before he ran the hand at her back along the curve of her ass.

"Maybe I don't think you're ready yet."

"Then why don't you check?"

She couldn't quite believe the words coming out of her mouth but she wasn't about to swallow them because Tyler didn't seem at all put off by it. He seemed to get more turned on when she talked.

He petted the back of her thigh before wedging his hand between her legs. There wasn't much room to maneuver and he didn't move his legs to accommodate his fingers. He seemed to enjoy the tight fit.

And she realized how much tighter she was going to be when he finally penetrated her.

Another moan escaped as she felt his fingers tweak her clit.

"God damn it, Tyler. Stop teasing. *Now.*"

He didn't say anything, but she heard him suck in a sharp breath. Then he pulled away for several seconds, the crackle of plastic letting her know he wasn't so far gone he wasn't thinking clearly.

Arching her back even more with one hand flat between her shoulder blades, Tyler pressed the tip of his cock to her exposed entrance and began to push inside.

Tight. Hot.

She wanted to spread her legs but Tyler would not budge. And his every move was a deliberate tease.

He made slow, shallow thrusts, tormenting her with the pace. She stayed still under his hands, absorbing each sensation as it washed over her.

The fullness of him inside her. The friction of his cock against her delicate internal tissue. The heat of his skin against hers.

As he set a deliberately slow rhythm, she felt herself drift into a state of sheer sensation. Another orgasm gathered but flirted just on the edges of her consciousness. Each harsh breath he took made her respond with one of her own until they were breathing in sync.

Her hips began to move in a slow grind, causing him to groan and his rhythm to increase. Her heart pounded as the hand on her back slid down to her shoulder.

His thrusts became more forceful, his grip tighter. Curving around her, he covered her back with his chest. Surrounded her.

The sensation became almost overwhelming. She could barely catch her breath. Her body tightened, not in fear, but in anticipation.

An anticipation that detonated in an explosive orgasm, rippling through her body with a force that left her boneless, nearly insensate with pleasure.

And with a rising sense of fear that she'd liked this way too much.

Five

When his cock finally stopped pulsing, Tyler collapsed over Kate with a rough sigh before quickly shifting to the side so he didn't crush her.

He'd couldn't remember coming that hard or feeling this . . . sense of satiation in years. Definitely not since Mia and possibly not even *with* Mia. He'd always been so careful with her, knowing he couldn't lose control and risk frightening her.

He didn't think Kate frightened easily.

She lay facing away from him, her hair a dark swath across her back. He wanted to wrap his hand around it and keep her anchored to him but figured that might be a little too much for her.

Instead, he laid his head on one bent arm and wrapped the other around her waist. She started slightly when his skin made contact with hers but wriggled back against him in the next second.

She fit perfectly. Her head under his chin, her ass snuggled against his thighs and his cock pressed against the small of her back. Rolling away for a second, he took care of the condom before rolling back to draw her close again.

She let him wrap himself around her for several minutes while her breathing settled, but he realized she was growing stiffer in his arms with each passing second.

When she finally shifted away from him, he thought she was going to get up. Now that the heat of the moment had passed, was she having second thoughts?

Instead, she rolled over until she lay facing him.

Her gaze held his steadily, but she definitely had something on her mind and it wasn't another round of sex.

"Are you okay?"

As soon as the words were out of his mouth, he wanted to take them back.

Damn it, he didn't want to treat her like a child but she definitely had something going on.

She didn't seem to take offense as she nodded slowly. "I'm fine. It's just . . . been a while since . . ."

He heard what she didn't say. It'd been a while she'd been with anyone but her fiancé. And he got that. Of course she was going to have nerves.

And now came that awkward moment as they were both naked and had no idea what to say or do or—

"Thank you."

Okay, maybe Kate was going to be better at this than he was. "For what?"

"For helping me realize I made the right decision."

It wasn't what he'd been expecting and his expression must have shown his surprise because she grimaced and her eyes closed.

"Sorry, that didn't come out the way I intended."

Putting one hand on her cheek and rubbing his thumb against her flushed skin, he waited until her eyes opened. "You can say anything you want to me, Kate. You're not going to upset me or make me angry."

Her raised eyebrows told him she didn't really believe him. But she didn't contradict him, either.

Instead, she shivered a little, and he was about to reach for her to draw her closer when she sat up. "I think I'd like to get dressed."

Disappointment bit at him, but he nodded and immediately rose to find her clothing, forcing himself not to question her.

He couldn't help but realize she was uncomfortable. And thinking way too hard. Her gaze darted all around the room, everywhere except at him.

Damn it, he'd fucked up. What the hell had he said? What had he done to make her uncomfortable?

Picking up his pants, he shoved his legs into them then picked up her dress and handed it to her. He tried not to stare at her as she dressed though his eyes kept going back to her.

She slid the dress on, hesitating only a second before she presented him with her back. "Could you . . . ?"

He'd much rather be stroking that bare skin than covering it but he pulled up the zipper before sliding his shirt over his shoulders.

"Kate, are you sure you're okay?"

She turned to face him then, nodding. "Yes. Everything's fine. It's just . . . I'm tired. It's been a long day. I've been up since five and I think I'm starting to wind down. Tonight was . . . amazing. Thank you."

Then she smiled, trying to reassure him but only managing to worry him even more.

Feeling awkward with his shoes in his hands, he nodded then led her to the door. Silence fell heavily around them as he led her down the hall to one of the two guest rooms on this floor. He'd hoped she wouldn't be using it but . . .

Pulling out his wallet, he withdrew a keycard, opened the door, then held it open for her. "I had your bag delivered earlier. If you need anything"—*give me a call*—"just let the desk know. They'll get you whatever you need."

She nodded, looking around the room before meeting his gaze. Damn, she did look exhausted. How had he missed that before?

Because he'd been too damn hot for her, that's why.

Feeling like a total heel, he leaned forward to stroke a kiss along her soft cheek. His hand clenched into a fist at his side, wanting to grip her hair and pull her close. Tumble her back into bed and wrap himself around her for the night.

Not going to happen.

When he drew back, he was really afraid he saw tears in her eyes, but the smile she gave him this time seemed more genuine.

"I'm sorry, Tyler. I'm just so ti—"

"Hey, no need for apologies. Get some sleep. When you wake up, dial star-forty-five. It'll connect you to my apartment. We can get some breakfast, if you'd like."

"That would be nice." She stopped, and he thought she might say something else but then she just shook her head and he figured retreat was his best option right now.

"Good night, Kate."

"Good night, Tyler."

Her words were barely audible as she stepped back into the room and closed the door.

He stood there for several seconds, staring at the door like some lovesick fool, before he forced himself to head to his apartment.

Once there, he headed straight for the fridge and a bottle of beer, though he knew he didn't have enough alcohol to put him to sleep tonight.

He settled himself on the couch with the remote and prepared for a restless night.

* *

Kate sat on the edge of the sleek gray couch in the living area.

The room had a definite modern vibe, with interesting patterns and color combinations. And at any other time she'd be checking out the design styles.

Tonight, she barely registered the visuals.

She'd freaked. Why the hell had she freaked?

She'd just had the best sex of her life. She could be sprawled all over Tyler in his bed and wake up at any moment to have more great sex.

What the hell was wrong with her?

Maybe it'd been too soon after the breakup. Maybe she hadn't been ready.

Which was a total joke.

She'd been more than ready, had been lusting after the man since she'd met him New Year's Eve.

Hell, she'd broken off her engagement because she couldn't get him out of her head.

And now? Now that she'd had him, was that it?

She so wanted to talk to Annabelle, but Annabelle was probably in bed with Jared and wouldn't be answering her phone anytime soon.

Those two were so in love, it made her ache to be in their proximity. And it had shown her what she'd be missing if she'd settled for Arnie.

Dropping her head in her palms, she groaned, wondering when the hell she'd gotten so far off track with her life.

She'd had such amazing plans. Finish college. Move to New York or Philadelphia or Chicago, maybe even LA. Snag an apprenticeship with one of the costume companies working for the stage. Work her way up to designer.

Have a career. Build a life away from small-town Pennsylvania.

Then her mom had died and she'd been frozen with grief.

Like tonight, she'd been afraid to move on.

She wanted to kick her own ass. She wanted Tyler to open the door and not take no for an answer.

But she knew he'd never force her into doing anything without getting her consent first.

And she'd told him no tonight.

At least, she'd made it clear that she'd needed space.

When maybe that's not at all what she'd wanted.

"Argh!"

Her frustration ate away at her fear. And she really wanted to talk to Annabelle.

Picking up her phone, she typed in Hey. What's up?

But she erased it before she hit send.

Damn it, she didn't want to be Needy Best Friend.

With a sigh, she trudged into the gorgeous bedroom, figuring if she told herself long enough she was tired, she actually would be.

Lying on the bed, she closed her eyes—

And jolted awake from a dead sleep when her phone blared "Marry You."

Fumbling around, she finally snared the obnoxious device and answered with a smoky, "Hello?"

"Oh, thank God! Kate. You gotta get here as soon as possible. It's a disaster."

The panicked voice on the other end made Kate fly up into a sitting position. "Talia? Is that you?"

"Of course it's me. Who else would be calling you at six thirty on a Saturday morning before I've had my coffee and right before *the biggest wedding of my career!*"

Uh-oh. "Please tell me it's not a problem with the dress."

Talia Driscoll laughed maniacally and Kate cringed as she threw off the covers and ran for her overnight bag.

"I could tell you that but it wouldn't be true. I need you here. Five minutes ago."

"Oh shit." Kate froze, hands tightening on her jeans as pictures of the wedding dress she'd custom made for one Margaret Mary Shanahan flipped through her mind.

Daughter of Pennsylvania senator Daniel Shanahan. Daughter of old steel money courtesy of Daniel Shanahan's wife, Tracy Carnegie Shanahan. And yes, she meant those Carnegies.

Her throat felt as dry as the Sahara and her stomach had clenched into a painful ball. "How bad is it?"

Talia didn't answer right away and Kate thought she might puke. "Not quite apocalypse but definitely Armageddon."

"Shit." Kate put the phone on speaker and put it on the bed as she threw on clothes. "I'm not at home. I'll be there in an hour. Can you deal with it until then?"

Meaning could she deal with an already jittery bride who really was a sweet girl but tended to crumble into complete meltdown at the first sign of trouble?

Talia groaned. "Oh God. I need a drink. And I don't mean coffee. Just get here as soon as you can. I will pay any and all speeding tickets or I will have Daddy Shanahan wipe them clean. Kate—"

"Don't panic," Kate jumped in, knowing exactly what Talia was about to say. This was way too big a deal for them to have something screw it up. "I'm on my way."

She hung up before Talia could say another word and reached for the bedside phone.

"Good morning, Kate. Did you sleep well?"

She shivered in response to that voice even as she told herself she didn't have the time for it. "I need to be in Reading as fast as possible."

A slight pause. "Give me five minutes."

When the phone clicked in her ear, she sat, blinking at it. Anyone else would have badgered her with questions.

Five minutes.

She sprang into action. No time to wash her hair but she could take a quick shower.

When he knocked at her door five minutes later, she was stuffing the last of her things into her overnight bag.

And even though she didn't have time to ogle him, she couldn't help the sharp twist in her gut at the dark stubble on his face, which he obviously hadn't had time to shave, and the wet and rumpled hair.

Of course, she couldn't stop her gaze from dropping lower, taking in the tight gray University of Pennsylvania T-shirt that exposed strong arms and the worn jeans that molded to muscled thighs.

She was so totally an idiot.

And he was so absolutely not. "I've got the car waiting out front."

She wanted to throw herself against that broad chest and cling for all she was worth. Instead, she straightened her spine and nodded. "I'm ready whenever you are."

He waved her out of the door then took her bag. "I hope everything's okay."

"Actually, I've got a wedding emergency."

Dark brows curving, he shot her a look as they waited for the elevator to arrive. "A wedding emergency. I thought—"

"Oh, God! Not mine!" She waved her hands like she was guiding in a plane. "No, I made a dress for a girl but something happened to it and the wedding planner called me in a panic. I don't even know what's wrong yet and . . . Damn, I just realized I won't have my box. *Shit.*"

The elevator doors opened and she hurried inside, as if that would get her to Reading any faster.

"What box?"

"My sewing kit. I'll need that to repair whatever happened to the dress."

"Why don't you call Annabelle and have her bring it to you?"

"I would, but I don't want to disturb her." The elevator took them directly to the parking garage and they headed for Tyler's car. "I guess I'm going to have to. She's gonna hate me."

"Do you want me to call Jed?"

She gave him a smile as they got into the car and got on their way. God, she really was an idiot or he really was too good to be true. "No, that's okay. I'll call Annabelle."

As she pulled her phone out, her gaze brushed by his big hand on the gearshift. Long fingers that had brought her so much pleasure. She wanted those hands on her again.

And now was definitely not the time to be thinking about that because she had an emergency.

Annabelle didn't pick up until the third ring. "Kate! Are you okay?" Then her voice dropped into an almost-whisper. "Did you really leave with Tyler last night and go back to Haven with him? Where are you? Did you have fun?"

"And good morning to you, too." Kate felt a blush flare and

hoped Tyler couldn't hear Annabelle's overly exuberant voice. "Hey, I need a favor and I'm so sorry to have to ask—"

"What's wrong? Is everything okay? Do you need me to come get you?"

Kate couldn't help but smile. "Nothing's wrong. Yes, I did. I'm on my way to Reading, and no, I don't need you to come get me. But I do need you to bring my full kit to Reading for me."

"Whose— Oh no." Dread filled Annabelle's tone. "The Shanahan wedding's today, isn't it? And there's a problem with the dress? Ooh, that can't be good."

"No, probably not. I didn't get a lot of detail from Talia because she was already freaked out, so that's not a good sign. It must be bad."

"I'll get your kit and meet you— Where should I meet you?"

"At St. Catherine's in Mount Penn. I'm so sorry to interrupt your, uh, morning."

Annabelle laughed and Kate heard the rumble of a male voice in the background.

"No worries," Annabelle assured her. "We can't stay in bed the entire day."

A pause and Kate definitely heard Jared say, "And why not?"

Annabelle laughed again. "I'll be there with your kit. See you soon."

Annabelle hung up, and she set her phone back in her purse, sighing.

"I like Annabelle," Tyler said after a few seconds of silence had passed. "She seems like a great friend."

"The very best. We met in college and have been best friends ever since. When my mom died, I don't think I would've managed without her."

"I'm sorry about your mom. Was she ill?"

She really didn't want to talk about her mom but she didn't want to be rude either. And in her current state, she might just snap off his head. "She had an undiagnosed heart defect. Went out for a run one day and never came home. She had a heart attack, fell over, and hit her head on a rock. She was dead before anyone found her."

He paused. "I'm so sorry. How old were you?"

"Twenty."

Please God don't let him ask any more questions. She hated talking about her mom because it always made her cry. And that made her angry. It'd been more than seven years since her death. Most people figured she should be over it by now. Or at least have moved on.

Which she had. Really.

As if he'd picked up on her silent pleading, he changed the subject.

"So this dress, is it your first custom gown?"

Breathing a hopefully silent sigh of relief, she shook her head. "No, but it is the first I've designed for one of Talia's clients."

"And Talia is . . . ?"

"Talia Driscoll, event planner. This is her first major wedding and she's been running on Red Bull and dark chocolate for the past week. I was kind of afraid she wouldn't be able to hold it together until the actual wedding day, but so far she's managed. Talia's brilliant. She was able to pull this wedding together in record time."

"Why the rush?"

"The bride's fiancé is about to ship out with the Peace Corps for a two-year stint in Africa and the bride didn't want to wait to get married until he came home. When the Shanahans couldn't find anyone else to take over the wedding on such short notice, Talia's mother offered up her daughter's services. It's a great opportunity. It'll make her career if the day comes off without a hitch."

"But that can't happen unless you fix the dress. Will you be able to?"

She couldn't afford to believe otherwise. "Unless the thing got dumped in a sludge pile and shredded, I can fix it."

"You sound pretty sure of yourself."

She was, actually. "The dress is pure Cinderella. Lots of tulle, big puffy skirt. The bodice is fitted, but even if I have to resew a few seams, it shouldn't be a problem. I guess I should've asked Talia what happened but I'm almost afraid I'll psych myself into a panic before I get there."

His mouth quirked into one of those smiles she couldn't seem to get enough of. "Sounds like you've got this all worked out."

"Yeah, except now I'm wondering if I shouldn't have had Annabelle pick up some extra fabric and the bolt of tulle . . ."

Even as she spoke, she reached for her cell to text Annabelle.

"Better safe than sorry."

Tyler's voice hit that spot deep inside that made her shiver. Her thumbs fumbled the message and she had to retype it before she hit send.

Then she noticed the tremble in her hands and her racing heart.

Damn. She couldn't afford to panic.

"So, Tyler. Tell me *all* about the hotel business."

Tyler turned to look at Kate, noticed the shaking hands and the tremor in her voice.

And realized he didn't know enough about her to know what to say to calm her down because she was about to lose it. He figured that wouldn't be a couple of sniffles and a tear or two.

He knew just where to touch her to make her shiver and he knew that if he sucked on her breasts a certain way, she moaned.

But heading off a meltdown?

Shit. Jared handled women much better than he did. He knew

what to say to calm them down, to get their minds turned in another direction.

Tyler had known that when Mia dissolved in tears, he could pull her into his arms and let her cry it out against his chest.

He hadn't pegged Kate as a crier and, as he watched her struggle to maintain her composure, he realized she didn't want to cry. Was fighting against it hard.

Her bottom lip trembled but she bit down on it as she took a deep breath. She stared straight out the window, her hands held tight in her lap.

Strong. Battling.

He liked that.

So he talked about zoning laws and union workers and waste management contracts, figuring if nothing else he would bore her into a state of numbness.

Except she surprised him. She asked questions. Questions that told him she was actually listening to him instead of just nodding her head when he paused for a breath.

So they discussed aspects of the company he never discussed with anyone other than Jed.

Mia had never wanted to know details about hotel management. She'd been content to let him handle all financial aspects of their relationship. Anything having to do with money or business had been off Mia's radar.

She'd been more concerned with their impending marriage, which had still been six months in the future at the time of her death. They'd seen no need to worry about when they held the actual marriage, but Mia had wanted the whole royal wedding deal—big church, ten bridesmaids, ten groomsmen, ring bearer, flower girls, huge dress, ice sculptures, ten-piece orchestra and an entire warehouse of flowers decorating the hotel ballroom.

He'd gone along with everything because he'd loved Mia.

"Tyler? I'm sorry. I don't mean to bombard you with all these questions. It's okay if you don't—"

"No, Kate." He shook his head and reached for her hands, twisted into a knot on her lap. He wrapped his fingers around hers and squeezed. "Sorry. I just kind of zoned out there for a minute."

"What were you thinking about?"

He paused. "My fiancée."

"Do you want to talk about her?"

No. Not at all. "Would you like to talk about your ex-fiancé?"

He wanted to take back the words as soon as they left his mouth. Damn it, he hadn't meant to sound so damn defensive, especially in the state she was in.

Mia would have broken down in a hysterical mess if he'd said the same to her

Kate laughed, a short burst of sound that hit him low in the gut. "Touché. Okay, so no talking about former partners. How about you tell me the story behind the Salon? That should take my mind off of other things."

For a second, he couldn't believe she'd let it go so easily. Mia— Kate wasn't Mia. And he had to remember that.

"I wasn't really involved in the inception of the Salon, but I know Jared's inspiration comes from his interest in Victorian erotica."

"Not something you typically hear guys get worked up about."

Tyler slid a grin in her direction. "Have you met my brother? He's not exactly the poster child for typical."

"No, Jared definitely is not typical. But then neither is Annabelle."

"They suit each other."

He glanced over and caught Kate's smile. Damn, he really liked making her smile.

"Yes, they do. Seeing them together helped me realize what I'd be giving up if I married Arnie." Her smile disappeared. "I decided I didn't want to live half a life."

Something in her voice made him want to dig a little deeper. "What do you mean?"

She paused so long he wasn't sure she was going to answer.

Finally, she said, "My mom . . . She was never really happy. When you're a kid, you know how you pick up on things that you know aren't right but you can't really figure out what's going on?"

He nodded, his jaw tightening as images of his own mother's troubled past crowded to the forefront. "Yeah, I do."

"I didn't realize until I was about thirteen or so that my mom wanted to be a photojournalist. I thought she'd always wanted to teach college. Then one night, I heard her and my dad arguing. That wasn't unusual. My dad was born in Reading, but my grandparents are from Korea. He's never been a real affectionate person. It just wasn't how he was raised. But my mom was Italian." She stopped to shake her head, her smile bemused. "They met at college and, according to my mom, it was love at first sight. My dad defied his parents to marry my mom, and Mom gave up her dream of traveling the world for him.

"My dad's parents have been gone for years and we didn't see them much growing up. My mom's parents got over the fact that their daughter married a guy who acted like he had a stick up his butt and I think they were relieved that she wasn't going to fly off to some foreign country and never return."

"Sounds stressful."

She nodded, gaze fixed on a point in the distance. "Yeah, I guess it was. But when you're in it, and you're a kid, you don't really understand it. I mean, you know it's going on but you can't really do anything about it. I only figured out what was really going on when

I was in college. I knew my mom was unhappy and I thought it had to be my dad's fault."

Pausing, she sighed before looking up at him with a rueful smile. "But nothing's ever that simple, is it?"

Considering his parents' problems, he knew that for a fact. "No, it's not."

She must have heard something in his voice because she paused again, staring up at him. But she didn't press him on it. "After she died, I blamed my dad for a lot of stuff that probably wasn't his fault."

"But you still returned home after college."

He didn't phrase it as a question but she had to know he'd meant it as one.

She shrugged. "I love my dad."

As if it was that easy. And maybe it was.

Jed had had a tough time forgiving their father for his indiscretions. Tyler had realized at a much younger age that their parents' marriage had gaping wounds that might never be healed.

He'd never wanted to go through that with his own wife.

Which had made Mia perfect for him.

The perfect doll who never talked back.

And that was totally unfair.

"So do you still want to be a costume designer?"

"Yes." She spoke without any hesitation. "But I have to be realistic. The time for that might have come and gone. It would've been easier to get an apprenticeship right out of college, when I had the contacts with my professors."

"But it's not like you're over the hill. You've been working in the field—"

Her short, sharp laugh cut him off. "I don't think hemming pants and suit jackets qualifies as working in the field."

"And the lingerie and wedding design don't either? I think you're selling yourself a little short."

He snuck a quick glance at her—traffic was getting heavier the closer they got to Reading—and did a double take at her smile. Holy shit. That one could cut him off at the knees.

"I appreciate the vote of confidence. But all you've seen are little bits of lace and satin so far."

"And two beautiful fairy costumes. And the dress you wore last night was stunning."

Another pause. "Thank you. I don't . . . Thank you, Tyler."

She laid her hand over his on the steering wheel and he wanted to twine their fingers together and bring it to his mouth, but that seemed like a gesture a lover would make.

He wasn't sure they were at that stage yet. But he was fast realizing he wanted to be.

And that kind of scared the shit out of him.

* /*

The knot in the pit of Kate's stomach tightened as they stopped in front of the church less than an hour later. For all that Tyler seemed like such a steady-as-he-goes guy, he had a lead foot.

Which she *so* appreciated at the moment.

She had the door open before the car came to a complete stop behind another car she recognized. Jared and Annabelle were already here.

Kate had a quick moment to panic over where to go. She didn't figure anyone was in the church yet. The bride-to-be was probably in one of the ancillary rooms in one of the wings off the church but—

"Kate! Thank God! Over here."

Talia stood in an open doorway to the left of the church entrance, waving at her frantically.

Kate had almost expected to see the normally unflappable event planner with her hair standing on end and her shirttails hanging out, but she should've known better.

Talia's dove gray suit hung perfectly, every line immaculate. Every strand of wheat blonde hair remained in place in an elegant twist on the back of her head.

It was only when she looked in Talia's wide turquoise eyes that Kate saw panic.

Shit, this was bad.

Forcing down her own fear that wanted to eat her alive, Kate ran for the door.

"Where's Annabelle?"

"With Maggie trying to keep her calm."

"How bad is it?"

Talia's lips flattened until they almost disappeared and Kate's stomach flipped.

"That bad."

"Bad enough." Talia took a deep breath and Kate found herself following suit as they hurried down a long hall. Kate tried not to let images of a torn bodice cloud her mind.

She had to keep her head, no matter what.

But by the time she walked into the room where the bride sat in a mound of tulle and satin, she could barely breathe.

Annabelle stood beside her, hand on Maggie's shoulder, her expression almost apologetic.

Wow. Really not good.

The bride's mother stood on the other side of the room, wringing her hands while talking to someone in clerical robes.

Hope he isn't here to do last rites on the dress.

Maggie's head had popped up as soon as she and Talia walked

through the door and Kate saw such utter despair on the other girl's face, she almost thought someone had died.

And that was enough to snap her out of her funk.

Straightening her back, Kate stopped in front of the bride, propped her hands on her hips, and stared down at the girl. "Alright. No more of that. It's not the end of the world. Let's see what's wrong."

Kate thought she heard Talia literally sigh in relief. But Maggie's lower lip continued to wobble.

"The dog . . ."

Then she stood and Kate's gaze immediately went to the form-fitting satin bodice covered in hand-sewn crystals.

Oh, God, please not the bodice.

She saw nothing on the bodice . . . until Maggie turned to the side.

Kate's breath caught in her throat, and when she tried to breathe past it, she almost choked.

Something—a dog's claw, she guessed—had ripped through the bodice and torn the fragile material, leaving a gash at least three inches long.

Her lungs tightened to the point where she thought she might actually suffocate.

She'd never understood the term *blind panic* until that moment.

She couldn't fix this.

A smack on her back made her suck in air and got her heart started again.

"Kate." Annabelle's voice snapped her back into the moment. "I brought everything I thought you'd need. I also grabbed a few more things you probably don't but I guess they can't hurt."

Kate turned toward Annabelle, her hair pulled back in a makeshift bun with curls escaping all over the place. Annabelle stared back with total confidence.

Okay, she could do this. Taking a deep breath, Kate nodded. "Thank you."

Annabelle's answering smile bolstered confidence further. "Do you need me to stay and help?"

Kate hugged her. "No offense, but I'd be afraid you'd sew your fingers into the dress. No, but thank you for bringing my stuff. I really appreciate it."

"What are friends for?" Then Annabelle whispered into her ear. "But I have a price. I want to know all about your night. I'll talk to you soon."

Annabelle left on that note, and Kate turned to the trembling bride-to-be.

"Alright, Maggie, take off the dress. When I'm done, you won't be able to remember where it was ripped."

She could do this.

Just like last night with Tyler, she only had to take the first step and the rest would follow.

* *

"So. How was your night?"

Tyler turned at the sound of his brother's voice. Kate had disappeared into a room down the hall and he'd stopped just inside the door.

Jed wore a bland expression but the gleam in his eyes didn't bode well for Tyler's piece of mind.

"My night was fine. Where's Nana?"

"Probably still sleeping. We got her a room at the B&B up the street from the shop. Belle introduced us to the owners at the party and they hit it off with Nana right away. I'll make sure she gets home."

"And you and Belle? Everything okay?"

"Yes. So what hap—"

"I don't know when I'll be back to the hotel today," Tyler cut in, not wanting to go there with his brother. Not now. "I need to make a few calls, let Betsy and Mark know I won't be back today."

"So you're—"

"When do you think you'll be going back?"

He stared back at his brother with a look Jed should know and understand.

Then again, his brother typically never listened to him.

"So I guess that means you're staying with Kate."

When he didn't respond, Jed grinned.

Tyler gritted his teeth and his damn brother started to laugh.

"No need to break your jaw. Lighten up, big brother. The hotel will survive without you for a few days and—"

"I'll be back tonight. I don't want to leave Kate here without a ride home."

"Uh-huh." Jed lost his smile and moved closer. "You know it's okay to move on, right? It's been almost two years."

He didn't pretend to misunderstand what Jed was talking about. "Are you saying I haven't?"

Jed shook his head. "Nope. Not buying your denial. You're so damn good at deflection. You should've been a lawyer, you know that, right?"

They'd had this talk before and Tyler had his response down pat. "Then who would manage all that money you like to think you make on your own?"

Jed raised one hand in surrender. "Alright. Fine. We won't talk about it."

Because there was nothing to talk about. Mia was gone. He wasn't.

And one night with a woman—even one as exciting as Kate—did not make a relationship.

"We need to decide on a contractor and— Why are you laughing?"

After Jed calmed down enough to speak, his brother sighed and got out his cell. "I've got the list right here. Why don't we go over a few of the possibilities now?"

Yeah, that should take his mind off last night. *Right.*

* *

Thirty minutes later, Jed and Annabelle left, but only after Tyler assured Annabelle he'd stay until the bitter end and make sure Kate ate something. And that he'd get Kate home safely. And make sure she didn't obsess over what she couldn't fix. And that he didn't let her get depressed or drink too much at the reception.

That last one caught him off guard.

Kate hadn't said anything about being invited to the wedding. And she definitely hadn't said anything about attending the wedding.

He'd assumed she wasn't going.

He'd also assumed she'd want to spend more time with him. Tonight. Maybe Sunday night as well.

Then again, maybe she'd thought last night had been once and done.

Just thinking about that made him tense.

When Kate walked through the door a minute later, he had himself back under control. Or so he thought.

When he saw how tired she looked, he wanted to grab her, put her in his car, and take her back to the hotel. He'd feed her, put her to bed and, when she woke, he'd show her why she should let him take care of her.

Luckily, he had enough sense to realize that was probably a bad idea.

Instead, he met her halfway and waited for her to make a move. She stopped only inches away but didn't reach for him.

She smiled up at him. At least, he thought she was trying to smile. "Thank you for waiting. You didn't have to, but I appreciate it."

Not exactly the response he'd expected. His gaze narrowed as he watched her bite her bottom lip and take a deep breath before meeting his gaze. Almost as if she was nervous. Or worried.

"Is everything okay? Annabelle said you were able to repair the dress."

Her mouth twisted in a grimace. "Not exactly repair. More like camouflage."

"So the damage was extensive?"

"No, just bad enough. I'm hoping no one looks very closely at the side of the dress."

"Kate . . . what's wrong?"

Because he could tell something was eating at her.

Again, all he wanted to do was fix it for her.

And that could become a habit he figured she wouldn't appreciate. Still, it was damn hard to simply stand there and watch her worry and not know what to do to make it better.

"Maggie begged me to stay for the wedding and the reception. In case she needed additional repairs. I'm going to stay, but you don't have to. I'm sure Maggie's father can arrange for someone to take me home."

Did she not want him to stay? Was this her way of getting rid of him without having to tell him to go?

And there he was. Back in high school.

"Would you like me to stay, Kate?"

Now she looked him in the eyes and he saw fatigue.

"Why don't you let me take you home so you can get some rest?"

She raised an eyebrow at him. "No way am I leaving while she's still in that dress."

His mouth quirked at the force behind her statement. "Okay." But where did that leave him?

Her teeth worried her top lip for a second. "Would you mind staying with me?"

He answered without having to think. "Not at all."

Was he mistaken or did she look relieved? "Okay. That's great. Thank you." Then she looked down at her clothes. "I realize neither of us is really dressed for this but I figure if we stay in the background, no one will pay much attention to us."

The only person he'd have his eyes on would be Kate and he honestly didn't much care what other people thought of him. There was the possibility that he'd know a few people at the wedding besides the bride's family. The Shanahans moved in the same circles as his parents, and he'd met Maggie several times. She and Mia had gone to the same college and shared a circle of friends.

Who hadn't liked him much.

But Kate wanted him with her so he was staying.

Maggie would probably be too busy to even notice he was there.

And Kate's smile was all the reason he needed to justify his presence.

* *

By the time Kate slipped into the very last church pew in the back right corner next to Tyler, she felt like she'd run a marathon.

Tyler watched as she took a deep breath and tried to relax, but he knew that wasn't going to happen.

As long as Maggie wore that dress, Kate had to be prepared to jump at a moment's notice. She wasn't too worried about the wedding but the reception . . . Photos, eating. *Dancing.*

She shuddered. God, what if the stitches didn't hold? She'd never sewn so fast in her life but she had to admit, even close up, it was difficult to tell where she'd made the repair.

But *she* knew it was there. And she couldn't stop obsessing.

"So what happened to the dress?"

Tyler leaned down and spoke directly into her ear because the organist had amped up her efforts in preparation for the bridesmaids' entrance, causing her to shiver.

His voice sank deep into her body, heating her from the inside out. Even with all the stress, she realized she wanted him. If he asked her to leave right now and follow him back to a bed, any bed, she'd have a hard time saying no.

And that was wrong. Of course it was wrong. He shouldn't have that kind of control over her.

Not now.

Not ever.

She suppressed a shiver and fought the desire to glance up at him because she knew if she looked into those beautiful eyes, she'd ask him to leave.

"She had an unfortunate encounter with her dog. Who lets a dog anywhere near her wedding dress? Especially on her wedding day. It ranks right up there with getting too close to the unity candle and having your veil go up in flames."

The organist was really getting into it now, the volume increasing as the tempo picked up as well. Since she couldn't see the musician from where she was sitting, her brain supplied images of a woman in a pale pink suit with a pillbox hat rocking out as she banged out "Trumpet Voluntary."

Kate had the totally inappropriate urge to laugh and had to literally bite her tongue so the sound wouldn't escape.

"Kate, are you sure you're okay?"

Since she was afraid if she opened her mouth, her laughter would escape, she nodded but couldn't look at Tyler. She knew he continued to watch her and then she couldn't stop thinking about what they'd done last night.

The organ music overlaid those erotic images and the laughter tried to surge.

Oh my God, she was about to lose it.

She caught a flash of white and knew she couldn't watch. If anything happened to the dress, she figured the gasp from the audience would alert her.

Still, she couldn't overcome the urge to laugh. Her chest rose and fell at an ever-increasing rate.

Crap. She was totally going to lose it.

Tyler wrapped his hand around hers and laced their fingers together. The warmth of his skin threw her back into the memories of last night. How he'd used those hands on her body. How she'd lost her inhibitions. How he'd made her feel.

"Kate, look here."

She took a few shallow breaths before she obeyed.

And when she did, she fell into that dark gaze. He anchored her. Calmed her.

"Breathe in and hold it a few seconds. Everything's okay."

It certainly seemed that way now, didn't it?

And that's what she was afraid of. That she'd let him take her over.

But, God, he was so beautiful. In a totally masculine way.

Those blue eyes. That perfect mouth. That strong nose. She wanted to lift her hand and run it along his jaw, dark with scruff.

He hadn't had time to shave this morning and, as much as she liked seeing him decked out in a tux or a suit or tailored slacks and a shirt, there was something about a guy in well-worn jeans and a tight T-shirt that made her heart speed up.

Or maybe it was just this guy. Arnie had lived in jeans and T-shirts, and she'd never looked at him the way she looked at Tyler.

He leaned in and spoke into her ear. "Good. You're okay."

She shivered. "Yes. I'm fine." *Now.* "Thank you."

The music stopped and Tyler pulled away, gave her a nod, then turned his attention to the front of the church. Hers lingered for a few seconds more before she forced it front.

Another deep breath and she finally managed to relax. At least enough that she didn't feel like she was going to puke.

* *

Since they weren't exactly dressed for a wedding that had to have cost upwards of fifty thousand dollars, Kate and Tyler slipped away from the crowd as they lined up to greet the bride and groom.

As they headed back to the room where she'd fixed Maggie's dress, Tyler watched her for another breakdown.

He knew the signs. He'd had enough practice growing up with his mother. Not that he thought Kate was bipolar, like his mom. Then again, he didn't know her well enough to know if she was prone to breakdowns at the slightest provocation. Like Mia.

And how the hell many times was he going to compare this woman to his dead fiancée before he got it through his head that Kate was not Mia.

She wouldn't have the same faults. Wouldn't have the same likes and dislikes.

As soon as the door closed behind them, Kate let out a huge sigh of relief and slumped into a padded chair, eyes closing as her head leaned back.

"I need a drink."

Tyler smiled at the dramatic tone but saw stress lingering in the lines of her beautiful face.

"Isn't it a little early to start drinking?"

She cracked open one eye and glared at him for a second, which just made his smile widen. "Considering I feel like I've been running a marathon for the past ten hours, no, I don't think it's too early to start drinking."

"Would you like me to run you home so you can change before we head to the reception?"

"No time. They're taking pictures in a few minutes then heading straight for the reception. I'm not leaving that dress. We'll sit in a dark corner and hope no one notices us."

Of course people would notice them. And he figured Kate would hate being at a fancy affair like this wedding not looking her best. "I'll call Jed. He and Annabelle can get a dress for you and pick up a pair of pants and a shirt for me."

She didn't bother to open her eyes this time. "Are you always this bossy?"

Usually, yes. He chose not to answer. "Where's the reception? I'll have them meet us there."

She didn't answer right away. "Hidden Pond Farm. It's only a few miles from here. But I really don't need—"

He'd already pulled out his phone and dialed Jed. "Hey, I need you and Annabelle to do us another favor."

As he gave Jed a detailed list, he saw Kate open her eyes. She watched him, her expression unreadable.

"I take it you're staying for the reception?" Jed asked in a tone that caused Tyler to frown.

"And there's a problem with that?"

"No. No problem. So I guess you won't be back to Haven tonight to greet Greg?"

Shit. How the hell had he forgotten that? His mind went blank for a full five seconds, time enough for Jed to laugh.

"I guess that's my answer. No problem. I'll handle it."

Greg Hicks was a regular, a Hollywood producer who rented a suite year round for when he returned to Pennsylvania to visit his parents. Greg had been one of their first recurring clients and had become a friend. They shared several common interests and had become close.

Tyler couldn't believe he'd forgotten Greg's arrival.

At any other time, Tyler would've dropped whatever he was doing and headed back to the hotel. The hotel always came first, sometimes even before Mia, though she'd understood.

Now . . .

"Thanks, Jed. That's great. Tell Greg I'll see him tomorrow."

Six

❧

"I can't believe I'm still conscious. I should be crashing but I'm so wired, I don't think I'll be able to sleep for hours."

"Stressful day will do that to you."

Tyler watched Kate kick off her shoes and drop onto the couch in her living room. The silky skirt of her blue dress flared around her legs for a brief second before it settled above her knees.

Way above her knees.

And she didn't bother to adjust it, so he had a damn good view of her beautiful legs. He wondered if she knew about the view or if she just didn't care.

She did look exhausted as she leaned her head against the cushions at her back and closed her eyes.

"I feel like I was in constant motion but all I did the entire time was stress. I can't believe the repairs held up the entire day. I kept waiting for the stitches to pop and Maggie to run screaming."

"Screaming would have been bad."

"Screaming would've been *awful*."

"But you saved the day."

Her eyes opened and she gave Tyler that half-rueful, half-sarcastic grin he was fast becoming addicted to.

Every time she leveled it in his direction, he felt his muscles tense in preparation.

For what, he wasn't sure.

Well, that wasn't entirely true. He knew what he *wanted* to do to her.

He wanted to push that dress farther up her thighs, spread her legs, and kneel between them.

He wanted to lick her to orgasm and make her scream while she sat there with that dress around her waist. He wanted her hands in his hair and his hands on her thighs holding her open.

"Just call me The Amazing Seamstress. My needle is mightier than my . . . Hmm. My pen? Oh, wait. My scissors!" She laughed, the sound barely audible but still able to make his cock throb. "Wow. I need to rethink that whole standup comedy routine."

Sighing, she twisted around on the couch until her legs were drawn up onto the cushions and she lay lengthwise, staring at the ceiling. "I can't believe I'm not passed out already. But I don't even feel tired."

Still standing by the door, he leaned his back against the wall and watched her. "Adrenaline will do that to you. You've been running on it all day. Are you hungry? You didn't really eat much at the wedding."

She turned to look at him. "I wasn't that hungry. And I'm not really thinking about food right now."

Her expression left him in no doubt as to what she was thinking about. Naked sexual hunger made her eyelids fall as her mouth curved in a slight smile.

Good thing they were alone, because if she'd looked at him like this in a room full of people, he wouldn't have cared who was watching. He would've done exactly what he planned to do now.

Shoving away from the wall, he walked forward until he stood over her. She never took her eyes off him and, by the time he reached her, she'd already stretched her arms over her head as if he'd told her to.

Her eyes were half closed and her lips curled in a bare semblance of a smile.

She couldn't have looked more enticing, even if she were naked.

He wasn't sure if he wanted her to remove the dress or not. For now, he'd leave it on. It'd only take a couple of tugs on the bow at the side to unwrap her like a present. He knew because he'd watched her put it on and taken notes on how to get it off.

"So what are you thinking about?"

He wanted her to say it. Not because he wasn't sure of her answer, but because he got hard just hearing her talk. And when she talked about sex . . . Hell, he almost felt like she was stroking his cock.

The corners of her mouth lifted in a beguiling grin. "I'm thinking about having sex with you."

"Good to know we're on the same page."

She swallowed hard, the sound audible over the heaviness of his own breathing.

Reaching for the hem of her skirt with one hand, he brushed his fingers up her thigh, dragging the skirt with it.

Inches of ivory thigh were revealed until he finally exposed the triangle of lace barely covering her mound.

The tips of his fingers swept across that triangle and she drew in a sharp breath. "Sit up, sweetheart."

She moved slowly, keeping her eyes on his the entire time. He had the sense she wasn't obeying his demand so much as allowing him to think she was. The dominance issues he tried to keep under control with her roared up and he had to reign in the impulse to pull her upright and make her submit to his demands.

The fact that she was doing what he wanted wasn't enough.

And was exactly why he wouldn't say anything.

Instead, he watched her reposition herself into a sitting position, her hair falling over her shoulder like a dark, silk waterfall.

Standing, he was at the perfect height to open his zipper, pull out his stiff, aching cock, and bring her mouth forward to suck him.

He wanted it so badly, he could almost feel her lips wrapped around his dick.

Again, he reined in the impulse. Instead, he went to his knees.

And looked into her eyes.

Hers were still half closed, but now her lips had parted and he heard the increased labor of her breathing.

His hands fisted at his sides so he didn't just grab her legs, spread them, and put his mouth on her.

She blinked before her gaze narrowed and her head tilted slightly to the side. "Why do I get the sense you've just shut down on me?"

He couldn't help the momentary shock that jolted through him. She was so damn perceptive.

"I don't know what you're talking about."

Her expression perfectly said, "Yeah, right," without her uttering the words.

She leaned forward until their eyes were level. "What do you want, Tyler? Just say it."

"I want to rip off your panties and put my mouth between your legs. I want to play with you until you come. I want to fuck you wearing that dress."

Her eyes widened with each word until his last statement. Then he saw startled confusion. "You want me to keep the dress on?"

His lips quirked into a grin and he leaned forward until their noses almost touched. "I'll take it off later. Right now, I want you to know you're wearing it while I put my mouth between your legs."

For several seconds, she simply looked at him. "Then what's stopping you?"

That's my girl. "Not a damn thing."

He kept his gaze on hers as he put his hands high on her thighs. The warmth of her skin made his fingers clench convulsively and her lids lowered for a second before lifting again.

Good. She'd remembered he liked her to look at him.

Or maybe she just liked watching him.

At this point, he didn't really care. He'd been lusting after her all day. He couldn't wait any longer.

While one hand moved up her thigh, the other lifted to her cheek, drawing her forward so he could kiss her.

Their lips met, harder than he'd planned, but he didn't ease up. As he pried open her lips and let his tongue sink into her mouth, his fingers slid beneath her panties and found her wet.

He groaned, the hand between her legs twisting so he could cup her mound before pushing two fingers into that wet channel.

Kate squirmed, her hips pushing forward, pushing his fingers farther into her.

Her hands clasped his shoulders, not pushing him away but not pulling him closer. Just a tight grip that sent heat crashing through his body.

His cock throbbed against the zipper, his balls a tight ache below. He kissed her, stealing her breath as her hips began to twist against his hand.

He stroked into her with a steady pace, until his fingers were coated with her moisture.

Then he released her head and let that hand fall to her waist.

When he pulled away from her kiss, she gasped a little, a tiny sound that made him grit his teeth in conquest.

He nipped at her jaw before moving lower, pressing kisses along her throat to her sternum then down the center of her chest. He let his lips linger over her rapidly beating heart before he continued down. He didn't touch her breasts. Instead he rubbed his lips against the material of her dress, right where the two pieces of fabric crossed, before he continued.

Her sharp inhale made his cock throb and, as he moved, her hands transferred to his head, sinking into his hair. They clenched and unclenched with the same rhythm that his fingers moved inside of her.

Perfect.

As his lips moved lower, he put his other hand beneath the skirt and pushed against her thigh.

He spread her legs open another couple of inches before he withdrew his fingers from her.

She responded with a moan and tightened her fingers in his hair. The need to push her harder, faster, was a constant battle, one he was afraid he was going to lose.

Grabbing at his unraveling control, he forced himself to slow down even more.

Instead of pushing his fingers back inside and getting her off as fast as possible, he reached for her panties and began to drag them down her legs.

She responded immediately, drawing her legs together to help him. In seconds, her panties lay on the floor and he had her legs spread again.

The hem of her dress fell just enough to cover the top of her mound and the sight made him bare his teeth in a feral grin.

Her sharply drawn breath drew his gaze up and he found her looking down at him, her bottom lip caught between her teeth.

He didn't see fear so he didn't stop.

"So pretty."

Looking down again, he moved his hands up her thighs until he could touch her labia with his thumbs. Catching the petals, he gently pulled them back to expose her completely.

Her breathing increased as her hands sank back into his hair. Not pulling him closer. Not pushing him away.

When he moved, he heard her gasp in a sharp breath then freeze as the tip of his tongue flicked out at her exposed clit.

Her thighs quivered beneath his hands as he teased the little nub. Her scent made him want to rush, to use his teeth and have her writhing in ecstasy.

So why the hell not?

She hadn't balked at anything he'd asked of her. Why continue to hold back?

Gripping her legs a little tighter, he nipped and sucked. Her juices coated his tongue. The warmth made his muscles tighten with lust, the drive to possess her completely a hot ball of lead in his stomach.

As she moaned, her fingers clenched into his hair, tugging until the slight pain penetrated his senses.

Yes.

Stiffening his tongue, he fucked her with it, licking inside her, lapping up her taste. Delicate inner muscles clenched, tightened around his tongue.

Heat blasted through him and he gave himself over to the red haze of pleasure.

Moving his hands to her hips, he tugged her closer. Heard her breath hitch as his teeth fastened on to her clit. He bit, his hands clamping down on her thighs so she couldn't squirm away.

She wanted to move. Her leg muscles tensed and flexed.

He held her tighter as he teased her mercilessly, learned how to use his tongue and teeth in ways that made her sigh and gasp.

Using the flat of his tongue, he swiped against her clit before coming back to fuck her again. Just that tiny bit of penetration seemed to make her wild.

"Tyler."

She tugged on his hair to try and get his attention, but he was focused and wouldn't be deterred.

Since she seemed to enjoy the dual sensations on her clit and her sheath, he released one of her legs and slid two fingers inside her.

Her back arched off the couch and her moan reverberated through him, straight to his cock.

With his years of practice, he was able to control his immediate response to rip open his pants and sink deep.

Instead, he focused on getting her off. At least once, if not twice.

When she was practically liquid in his arms, he'd flip her over and fuck her hard and fast.

With the promise of that in mind, he increased his efforts. He shafted his fingers higher, stroked the tips higher until he heard her gasp.

Right there.

Then he used his tongue on her clit. Licking, biting, flicking.

Until, finally, she broke. She cried out, the moan sounding ripped from her throat.

"Oh my God."

She released his hair, her arms reaching out to her sides to hold on to the cushions. He drew back to watch her, keeping his fingers firmly inside. Her sheath pulsed around him, her face a study in passion.

"So fucking gorgeous."

He drew out her orgasm as long as he could before he withdrew his fingers from her clutching channel.

Just as she began to relax and sink back into the couch, he leaned back onto his heels and grabbed her by the hips.

Her eyes barely fluttered open but he knew she could see him. Her lips parted to draw in a deep breath as he pulled her toward him.

The sultry look that appeared on her face made his own breathing deepen and roughen.

"Are you looking for reciprocation?"

The words made him feel like he'd been sucker punched. Christ, yes, he wanted her mouth on his cock.

But even more so, he wanted to be inside her.

"Not right this second. What I want is for you to stand up, walk over to the dining table, and bend over."

Her eyes widened with each word but he didn't give her an out this time. If she wanted one, she had to know she could take it. Stand up to him and say no.

If she couldn't . . . then there was no way this would work.

He and Mia had—

God damn it. When the hell was he going to stop?

Apparently as soon as she got up and did as he asked.

Which was now.

Drawing her legs together, she stood, so close to him the hem of her dress brushed his cheek as she turned and headed for the table.

It was only big enough for four people and that was pushing it. But it was the perfect size for her to lie across and grab the other side.

Fuck, she looked so damn hot, even though her dress had fallen to cover her to her knees.

He'd remedy that soon enough.

Pushing to his feet, he followed her, his hard cock rubbing against his zipper and making him even hotter.

When he reached her, he flipped the skirt up over her hips, exposing her rear.

Her skin gleamed in the low light from the table lamp across the room. He wanted to make her ass burn, watch it turn red.

He stopped himself from fulfilling that one. Again, too soon. Didn't want to rush her.

He settled for pushing.

She shivered as his hands made contact with the backs of her thighs, rubbing the skin, massaging her tight muscles. When she began to relax, he shoved her thighs farther apart.

Her gasp sounded harsh but she didn't pull away. At this point, he didn't know that he would have let her. At least not right away.

"Hold there and don't move."

Her eyes closed this time as she laid her cheek against the wood top.

"Good. I want to fuck you just like this."

"Then do it. Don't just talk about it."

Her arch tone brought a smile to his face. He really wanted to give her a swat for that but, again, he stopped, gritting his teeth.

Another time. And there will *be another time.*

When he opened his belt and lowered his zipper, she trembled. But her legs didn't close.

And when his cock finally escaped the confines of his pants, he couldn't help but tap it against one rounded cheek. The sensation made him groan, the zip of electricity shooting from his balls to the tip of his cock.

He pulled a condom from his wallet and sheathed himself, unsure if he'd remember to do it later. Or even care.

Christ, he hoped they got to the point in their relationship where they didn't need one.

What relationship?

He shut off the voice and concentrated on her.

She couldn't exactly lay still—her breathing was too heavy. But she didn't arch her back toward him when he moved closer. Maybe she did have a little submissiveness in her.

He placed one hand low on her back to hold her down. Let her feel the weight pinning her.

He kicked her feet out several more inches, opening her even more.

When he looked down, he saw the evidence of her desire slicking her pussy.

Taking his cock in one hand, he angled it straight ahead. Rubbing the head in that moisture, he made sure he was coated.

They were both breathing like track stars after a four-minute mile. The urge to take her felt like a fever in his blood.

And still he took the time to bend down and bite the curve of her hip.

Hard enough to leave a mark and make her flinch.

"Jesus, Tyler, do you want me to have a heart attack? I need you to fuck me now."

He loved hearing that obscenity come out of her mouth. He never had before, but from Kate . . . it lit him up.

She wiggled her ass, rubbing against his cock until he thought he might explode before he got inside her.

Grabbing her hips, he held her still, using just enough force to ensure she knew what he wanted.

He wasn't sure she'd obey. He wasn't sure he wanted her to. He almost wanted her to fight him.

But when she stilled, he knew nothing would ever be easy, or uncomplicated, with Kate.

He couldn't go slow. He had enough sense to wrap one arm around her hips so she didn't get hurt. Then he thrust, hard and deep.

So fucking tight. She clenched around him, her grip as tight as a fist. He felt his orgasm building already and took a few seconds to stave it off. And to absorb the feel of her rippling around him.

So damn good.

With his cock hard inside her, he ran a hand up her back, along her spine, and into the dark silk of her hair. She'd twisted her head to the side and lay with one cheek against the table. Eyes closed, lips pursed. Waiting.

Watching her face, he withdrew only to push back in hard.

Her lips parted and a soft sound emerged. Almost a gasp.

He did it again, and she moaned this time. The sound hit him in the gut, made his cock twitch. His fingers curled into her hair, rubbing the strands between his fingers as he began to thrust, slow and steady.

He didn't pull her hair. He let it slide through his fingers as he slid in and out of her body. The color and texture ensnared him. Like mahogany silk, such a deep, rich color.

Against her skin, it looked even darker. And her skin was so soft.

Bending even farther, he let his forehead touch her back as his hips picked up the pace.

His heavier weight kept her pinned, the edge of the table biting into his arm and keeping him grounded, but each time his thighs slapped against her ass, the sound brought him closer to climaxing.

"Do you like being under me, Kate? Do you like having my weight pin you down?"

She didn't speak. She wriggled against him, making his cock move inside her, hitting different nerve endings and making him grit his teeth.

With a hard tug, he pulled her tight against him, stuffed as far inside her as he could go.

"Answer me."

After a short gasp, her mouth curled into a smile. "Trust me, if I didn't like it, you'd know."

He thrust again, smiling when he heard her moan this time.

"I'm going to keep you under me all night."

"Sounds like a challenge to me."

The catch in her voice made her tone breathy and brought out the part of him that wanted to own her.

The part he was afraid would never want to let her go. Even though he'd sworn not to fall so hard for a woman that his entire life was wrapped up with hers.

Sex. This is only sex.

Right. He knew there was a hell of a lot more going on here. And he didn't know if he had it in him to make it work.

He only knew he needed to make her understand that right here, right now, she was his.

"Not a challenge. A promise." He felt a tremor run through her body, causing her sex to clench around him. "One you're going to love. Starting now."

He withdrew until the tip of his shaft barely kissed her labia, maneuvered until he rubbed against her clit, then sought her entrance again. He followed this pattern for several minutes, feeling her body tighten just a little more with each thrust.

His own body throbbed with the need to release, to ride her until he exploded. Each retreat and return pushed him closer to that edge. Lost in a haze of pure animal sensuality, he put one hand on her shoulder to hold her steady and finally let go.

He rode her. Hard. Each time he thrust, he felt like she parted a tiny bit more for him.

Moving the arm around her waist so he could get his hand nearer her pussy, he speared two fingers between her thighs and trapped her clit between them.

She cried out and tried to move her legs closer together. "Oh God, yes."

With his legs between hers, she couldn't move. "Come on, Kate." He tightened his fingers then released. And repeated until she was gasping for breath, squirming against him.

Her every move inflamed him and he gave her clit one last pinch, which set her off.

She practically screamed his name, her sex clenching around him, squeezing.

He tried to hold off, tried to ride it out so he could continue to fuck her, but she was too much.

He thrust one more time then held himself deep inside her as he came.

Seven

❧

"So, Tyler, are you ever going to loosen up enough to ask me if I want to be tied down?"

Kate felt Tyler start beside her.

They'd made it to her bed a few minutes ago, and she still felt slightly drunk from the amount of champagne she'd consumed at the wedding after finally loosening up enough to have some.

She hadn't eaten much, though Tyler had made sure she had just enough not to get sloppy stupid on the alcohol.

Now, she still felt pleasantly buzzed and totally triumphant.

The dress had held together. And she'd gotten a damn nice bonus check from Senator Shanahan.

Still riding the high of the day and the alcohol, she figured she might as well say what was on her mind while she felt uninhibited enough to do it.

Hell, she'd just had sex on her dining room table. What was a little baring of the souls between them?

"Are you sure you're not too drunk to want to know the answer to that question?"

She wanted to laugh at the totally tight-assed way Tyler said that.

Lifting her head, she propped her hands on his chest then rested her chin on them so she could stare up at him.

With his hair mussed and his five-o'clock shadow even darker than it had been earlier, he took her breath away. The phrase *stunningly masculine* didn't do him justice, she decided.

And his body . . . She wanted to lick him from head to toe and tie him to her bed so he couldn't leave.

But that wasn't what he'd said he liked.

No, he'd told her he was into dominance, and right now, her inhibitions were low enough for her to try just about anything. Or at least entertain the possibility of trying anything.

"I'm not drunk enough not to know what I want."

His mouth quirked into a devastatingly sexy grin. "I think I understood that. And I didn't have near as much alcohol as you did."

"Are you avoiding the question, Mr. Golden?"

The grin disappeared into an intense stare. "Not avoiding. Just wondering what your answer would be if I told you exactly what I wanted to do."

Ooh, that sounded naughty. She shivered even as her sex clenched.

Jeez, a little decent sex and she turned into a deviant.

And now she sounded like her dad. Shit. She quickly shoved away that thought. It had no place here.

"Why don't you try me?"

He paused again and she could tell he was debating just how much he wanted to say. Just how kinky was this guy?

"Have you ever been tied down?"

The question, asked in that whiskey-dark tone of his, made her sex go even wetter.

She felt a blush creep onto her cheeks but refused to drop his gaze. "No. But I've thought about it."

"What else have you thought about?"

Hmm, where to start? How much to reveal?

It felt like a delicate dance. Say too little and he'd be afraid he'd scare her off. Say too much and possibly bite off more than she could chew.

Not that she'd mind taking a bite out of him like he'd done to her.

"Tell me your fantasies, Kate. You can trust me with them."

Oh, it wasn't that she didn't trust him. Tyler seemed nothing if not trustworthy. Stable. Steady.

All the things she'd wanted in a man. All the things she'd thought she'd found with Arnie.

And yet with Tyler, it all felt different. Maybe because she sensed the darker side he typically kept hidden.

Could she deal with that side? Did she have it in her?

"I've thought about having my hands and feet tied to the bedposts. Of being blindfolded. Of being taken and having no control over what happens to me. Of being forced to accept pleasure."

She watched his expression tighten with each word, felt his body tense beneath her.

When he didn't say anything right away, she thought maybe she'd said too much. Damn her mouth. It almost always got her in trouble.

She closed her eyes, but when he cupped her face and rubbed his thumb along her cheek, she opened them again to find him looking at her with undisguised lust.

"Will you let me tie you up?"

"Do you want to?"

"I've wanted to tie you to my bed since the moment I met you."

It made her even wetter to hear him say that. If she hadn't been sure she wanted to at least try it up until that moment, she certainly was now.

"I'm willing to give it a shot."

He didn't move right away, just stared at her until she thought maybe he'd changed his mind.

"Can I borrow a few things from your workshop?"

"Sure."

He slid out from beneath her and headed out the door. She got a quick glimpse of his very fine, naked ass before he disappeared down the hall. God, the man was gorgeous coming and going.

She tried not to let her brain run wild while she waited for his return. Tried not to let her nerves get the best of her. She wasn't frightened. She knew Tyler wouldn't do anything to harm her.

So why did she have such a knot in her stomach?

She didn't have enough time to think about it because Tyler returned, his hands filled with various colors and fabrics.

She saw black and red silk she used for underwear, black lace she'd used to overlay a satin corset, and some purple velvet she had plans to use in a peignoir set.

"On your back, Kate."

Oh, baby. The command in his tone made it hard for her to breathe, but she obeyed.

And that little kernel of doubt pinged in her brain again. That one word—*obey*—hit a sore spot she wasn't sure she understood.

But she pushed that aside and concentrated only on Tyler.

The man was built like a piece of art. He didn't have a typical businessman's body.

A light coat of fine, dark hair covered his muscled chest and arrowed down to his groin. His erection bobbed almost flat against his rippled abdomen, the tip nearly reaching his belly button.

Her mouth watered and she thought about sitting up and taking him in her mouth, but she didn't want him to think she didn't want to play this game.

If this even was a game.

He stopped by the side of her bed and crossed his arms over his chest. "Arms out. Spread your legs. And don't move."

"Am I allowed to speak?"

"Only to tell me no or to tell me how much you like it."

Okay, this was going to require a lot of tongue-biting because usually her mouth ran nonstop.

But she nodded and did as he'd said.

The urge to pull her arms back in and close her legs hit her almost immediately but she swallowed hard and kept her eyes on him.

"Perfect." He lifted his hand to run his fingers down her cheek, along her neck and to her breasts, where he rubbed his thumb over a nipple. The sensation was so sharp, it made her gasp.

"I'm going to tie your wrists to the posts," he said as he dropped the pile of material next to her on the bed. The piece of velvet rubbed against the outside of her thigh, the roughness enticing.

She bit her lip against the urge to squirm.

"Good. Control the need to move as much as possible. Part of this process is trust, Kate. You need to trust that I won't hurt you. That I only want to bring you pleasure."

She did trust him, even on their short acquaintance.

Nodding, she let her gaze drop to his hands as he fingered the pile of cloth.

He picked up the red silk, ran it through his hands, then looped it around her closest wrist.

The material felt cool against her skin but heated fast when he tied it securely around her wrist. Her shoulder bent as he tugged her arm up closer to the bedpost, the sensation of being vulnerable increasing.

Still, she managed to keep her mouth closed even though she wanted to say something, anything, to relieve just a little bit of the tension building in the room.

Although, why she wanted to do that . . .

Just call her contrary.

And a little out of her comfort zone.

But isn't that what she wanted? To step out of her comfort zone?

Tyler moved to her ankle, pulling a length of peach satin from the pile. This time he gave a little tug as he tied the piece to the post, stretching her body just a little farther.

More air evaporated from the room, and now she knew she wouldn't be able to take her eyes off of him, even if she tried.

On the other side of the bed, he picked a matching piece of peach satin to tie off her other foot. His fingers lingered on her ankle for a few seconds before he began to drag them up her shin. Light enough to raise goose bumps. Her legs instinctively tried to close, and the fact that she couldn't increased her desire.

Her sex, still sensitive from earlier, felt almost painfully so now. She needed something to fill it, whether it was his finger or his tongue or his cock.

"Tyler, I need—Oh!"

He did exactly what she wanted, stuffed two fingers inside her sheath. No warning. No hesitation.

"No speaking, Kate."

He removed his fingers just as quickly, leaving her panting with lust. And when he continued to trail those two fingers up her body, she felt her own moisture, wet against her skin.

She bit her lip, trying to hold in the whimpers. She refused to be reduced to a pile of quivering flesh so soon. She was stronger than this.

He made fast work of her other wrist with the black satin then stood back, as if to admire his handiwork.

She felt tight all over but in no pain from the bindings. Even so, she tugged on them. The air felt cooler than it had, but that was probably her imagination. Or the fact that she felt like she was burning up.

Then he picked up the black lace.

"Now I want you to close your eyes. This will only affect your vision. It won't block it completely. You can open them when I'm done. Trust me, Kate."

That was *so* not the problem right now. She wanted him to hurry. She felt like a bottle of pop he'd shaken for hours, corked and ready to explode.

It should've embarrassed her, how fast she snapped her eyes shut.

But she couldn't be bothered to care because he was tying the knot at the back of her head now.

"You look beautiful. You can open your eyes or you might want to keep them closed for a little while yet and just feel."

The bed shook and she felt his knees brush her hips just before his hands landed on her breasts.

Cupping them, he plumped the small mounds, pinching the nipples, making her arch off the bed, at least as far as she could. She only had so much leeway with the bindings.

He played with her breasts for several long minutes, as if he were fascinated by them. When he bent and put his mouth on her, she choked out a sigh.

Yes. There.

His lips closed around one hard tip, sucking it into his mouth and flicking at it with his tongue. The sensation lit through her like a steady pulse of electricity. The heat from his mouth then the cool of his breath as he pulled back to blow on her wet skin drove her closer to achieving something she never had before—an orgasm simply from having someone suck on her breasts.

She knew, somewhere deep in the part of her brain that was still capable of thought, that it was almost more mental than physical. Sure, the sensation was necessary, beyond pleasurable. But the mental stimulation from knowing it was Tyler and the deprivation of her sight combined to make her nearly frantic.

Almost as if he could read her mind—more likely, he could read her body language—Tyler spent several long minutes at her breasts, alternating his attention between them. His tongue felt like wet sandpaper, her nipples peaked and throbbing beneath it.

She tried not to writhe too much, didn't want to dislodge him, but she needed more.

Needed—

Yes.

He bit her, hard enough that she felt it between her legs. Hard enough to give her that orgasm she'd been reaching for.

She moaned as her sex clenched with tiny contractions then nearly jumped out of her skin when Tyler tapped her mound, catching her clit with one finger.

"So beautiful. You're so fucking beautiful, Kate. I'm gonna make you come again, sweetheart."

She opened her mouth to tell him to hurry up but before she could get the words out, he tapped her again, harder this time.

And she came with a strangled cry. Short and sharp and still not enough.

Vaguely, she realized he was moving again, his knees now shifting between her legs.

"Lift up." He tapped her hip and she moved without a thought. A second later, he shoved a pillow beneath her hips.

The feeling of exposure intensified and she could barely hold in a moan.

"Kate. Are you okay?"

She had to take in a breath before she could speak. "I'm fine."

"Good. Because I'm going to fuck you now. Open your eyes."

She did, immediately. And blinked at the distortion of her sight by the lace.

Just as Tyler began to work his cock inside her.

As she sought to make out his form above her, her body fought his intrusion, even though she wanted it so desperately.

His cockhead breached her lips, lodging in the narrow channel that desperately tried to pull him deeper. She felt so empty.

But instead of thrusting hard and fast like he had before and as she needed, he worked himself inside centimeter by centimeter.

Her hands twisted until she had her fingers wrapped around the material at her wrists, trying to leverage herself closer, force him deeper.

He retreated immediately. "I didn't say you could move." Grabbing her hips, he forced her to hold still. "I promise if you stay still, you'll get what you want. On my terms. But you will get what you need."

His words only made her burn hotter, made her pant with the intensity of it. But it also made that doubt surge forward as well. That little hint of fear that she couldn't quite rid herself of.

She felt like she was being pushed closer to an edge she might never come back from.

"Kate. Are you still okay?"

"Yes." Or she would be. "I'm fine."

She felt him pause, but only for a few seconds. Finally, he breached her again, deeper this time but still just as slowly.

Staring up at him through the lace, she could barely make out his features. But it was enough to push her back from that edge.

"Move, damn it. I need you to."

"I'll move, sweetheart." And he did, so slowly, she thought she felt every square inch of his flesh against her own. "But I'm taking my own sweet time. No way will I rush this when I have you right where I want you."

His voice stroked over her, in concert with his hands that caressed her hips. Relentlessly, he pushed inside, filling her until she felt she couldn't stretch any more.

The slight burn only enhanced her pleasure.

He thrust a few times, each more deliberate than the last.

She didn't realize she was bucking against the restraints until Tyler leaned forward, planting his hands on each side of her torso, pushing himself even farther inside.

"Stay still or I don't move."

His voice held a note of steely command that made her breath catch and her pussy clench around him. And her body go still.

"Good. Now I'll fuck you."

His hips began to move at that same steady pace but his mouth covered hers for a heated kiss that stole what little breath she had left. Forceful yet gentle enough that she actually wanted him to kiss her harder. She hadn't realized she'd closed her eyes until she opened them again and found him much closer.

He looked nothing like the steady businessman now.

He looked hard, determined. And totally in control.

Of her and everything else.

His cock rubbed high inside her, at that mystical spot that had to begin with a *G*. And every time he pushed forward, he scraped against her clit, wracking her body with shivers.

She was going to come again. The only question was how hard. And would she survive it.

"That's right. Let go, Kate."

He didn't increase his pace and she couldn't tell if she needed him to or if she was the one holding back. Couldn't decide if her pleasure was in her hands or his.

Most definitely his.

Yes. She had to let go, had to—

Shutting off the voice in her head, she blanked her mind and sank into the sensation of his cock inside her.

And let the fire burn her from the inside out.

Eight

❦

"So, I guess you have to get back to the hotel today."

Tyler had just finished his coffee and was putting the mug in the dishwasher when Kate finally spoke.

He'd woken this morning to find Kate already out of bed, showered and making coffee. He couldn't believe he'd slept through all of that. Then again, he'd been wiped out last night.

Kate, however, still seemed to be running on adrenaline. Or maybe this was her normal speed—full-steam ahead.

He wanted to stick around long enough to find out.

But, "Yeah, I do. We've got a client staying with us that I need to talk to."

Curled onto the overstuffed chair in her living room, she looked so damn sexy in a hot pink silk robe as she stared at him over the rim of her coffee cup. Those huge dark eyes watched his every move, but he couldn't decide if she had regrets about last night.

No way did he want her to have regrets. In fact, he wanted her to want more but he knew he shouldn't push her.

"A business client?"

"A possible investor in the spa. And a friend."

Interest sparked as her gaze sharpened. "So the spa . . . Tell me a little more about your plans."

His first inclination was to give her the glossy overview and leave it at that. He wasn't used to discussing business with anyone but Jed and Greg, who'd become a trusted advisor. Greg had a cut-throat way of looking at business that Tyler appreciated. While he trusted Jed as he trusted no one else in his life, he and Greg shared a business sensibility Jed just didn't have.

Then he remembered that Kate was not only a bed partner but a potential vendor. And a smart woman.

She'd realize he was blowing her off.

"Jed came up with the idea. Actually, I think he came up with it because he wanted to go to a place like the one he had in his head but couldn't find."

Her expression showed her disbelief. "Seriously? There are spas all over the world and he couldn't find one he liked?"

Settling back into the couch, he realized he liked having her across from him so he could watch her. She was a stunner, with her hair still rumpled and no makeup and that robe hanging open just enough that he could see the soft curves of her breasts in the neckline. "Jed may seem to be the easygoing playboy but he's really damn hard to please. He knows what he wants and he knows how he wants things to be. He's got a deeply ingrained sensuality, and I don't mean that in a strictly sexual way."

Her head tilted and ribbons of hair fell over her shoulder, reaching nearly to her nipples. An image of her sitting there naked flashed through his mind and his cock began to throb. With another woman, he might have tried to hide it or will the erection away.

Not with Kate. He wanted her to see how she affected him.

"Then what do you mean?"

"I mean he knows what makes people feel good, whether it's visual or tactile. The art he collects is a perfect example. Yes, most of it's erotic but he chooses the pieces because they evoke an emotion, a response. That's what he wants to do with the spa."

She nodded, her lips curving in a smile. "And what do you bring to the table?"

"You know that already. I handle the business angles. The money, the staff. All those finer details Jed doesn't want to be bothered with."

"And you didn't offer anything at all to the feel of Haven?"

He considered saying no, but that would be a lie. Still, his contribution to the aesthetics of Haven had been relatively small. And for the spa it would be even less. He just didn't have the time. "I designed the atrium."

Her smile told him she'd already known but was pleased he'd confided in her. It wasn't something he bragged about. Not that he wasn't proud of it. He was. But his work in the atrium had been one of the things that had gotten him through Mia's death and he really hated to talk about that.

"Tell me about it. Where'd you get the idea?"

Setting her coffee cup on the nearest table, she let her head fall back against the chair cushion, her body relaxing. He wondered what she'd do if he walked over to her, slid her to the edge of the chair, and brought her off with his mouth. She'd certainly seemed to enjoy it last night.

Or would she think he was trying to avoid her questions? That he only wanted her for sex?

Better to stay where he was.

Later, he'd see if she'd be interested in riding him right here on the couch.

"My grandmother. My mother has been . . . ill most of her life, and Jed and I spent a lot of time with my grandmother at her home on the Main Line. Nana would spend hours in her gardens. And when I say gardens, I mean at least two acres of cultivated beds. Yes, she had help, but she was in charge of every aspect. What to plant, when to plant, where to plant. She should have been a landscape architect. Those beds are works of art."

"And you helped her with those."

He grinned. "Under protest, at first. I remember when I was ten, Nana had to drag me out of the house to help her. I used to think she loved torturing me by having me deadhead and weed. I mean, gardening was for girls. Or the hired help."

"Not for a mighty Golden." Her raised eyebrows held a challenge.

"Yeah, I guess you could say I had an oversized ego back then."

"Don't all ten-year-olds? But somewhere along the line, yours got deflated. How did that happen?"

He'd learned that life didn't always go your way. "When I realized my mother would never be completely healthy or mentally stable. It was reinforced when my fiancée died."

"I'm sorry to hear about your mother. I didn't realize she had problems."

"Neither did I until I was thirteen. I knew she had violent mood swings, and I realized pretty early on that her personal assistants were really private nurses. But we didn't talk about our problems in my house. Jed became our mom's jester. He was the only one who could put a smile on her face sometimes."

"And you were the one who took care of everything else, weren't you?"

"Why do you think that?"

She gave a short, little laugh that went straight to his balls. "Because that's who you are. You take care of things. And you always expect things to go sideways so you're not surprised when they do."

It shook him to realize she'd seen that part of him so easily. Yes, he worked damn hard to present an unruffled appearance. Jed always said Armageddon could be happening and he would be stockpiling cases of water and caviar for the aftermath.

Which was probably true.

"So," she started without waiting for his response, "tell me what you'll expect from me and the boutique."

"Does this mean I can have a contract drawn up?"

He hadn't realized until now how much he wanted to tie her to him. At least through the boutique. Did that make him a bad person?

Her lips quirked into a wry little smile. "No. Not yet. I'd like to know a little more about what I'd be getting into. What my liabilities will be. What I'll be expected to do."

He appreciated that she wanted all her ducks in a row before she signed on the dotted line. "The way we work the boutique at the hotel is that Jed and I own the space. We hire a manager for the shop and she decides on the clothing she wants to stock. Then we work a deal with the designers. Every deal is different. Some of the pieces we take on consignment. Some we buy outright."

"So I'd be just one of several designers in the boutique?"

He couldn't tell if she liked the idea or not. "No. Because of the size of the boutique and the nature of the merchandise, we're only planning to feature one designer. And from what I've seen, I think one will be more than enough. Your designs are beautiful, Kate. Sexy and sensuous, but they still manage to be tasteful. What I've seen is more than enough to make me confident your designs are perfect for what we're looking for."

Her cheeks blushed with the barest hint of color. "Thank you, Tyler. And I can't deny that this is a major opportunity for me. I'd be a fool to pass it up."

"Then say yes." He wanted her to say yes. Wanted to work with her on this, help her build this.

Until now, he'd only ever trusted Jed to be his business partner. He'd even kept Mia on the sidelines about the hotel.

But Kate . . . He wanted Kate to want this, to *want* to work with him. Wanted it with a teeth-grinding need that shocked the hell out of him.

He trusted her judgment. Trusted her ability. Trusted her.

She drew in a deep breath, like she was preparing to take a plunge into deep water. "I need just a few more days to decide. Is that okay?"

No. But he couldn't say that. "That's fine. Now come over here and let's not talk business."

There was that half smile of hers again. "I still have a lot of questions—"

"And those can all be answered later. Right now, I want you."

He barely reined in the urge to demand she get off the chair and come to him. Turned out he didn't need to.

With her chin stuck in the air, she rose from her chair . . .

And turned toward the kitchen.

"Would you like some more coffee?"

He was on his feet and only steps behind her when she stepped into the tiny kitchen. Leaning against the wall, he watched her pour another mug for herself then held up the carafe at him.

"Did I frighten you last night?"

He needed to know. Needed to know if he had to curb his appetite if he wanted to continue to see her.

Because he *really* wanted to continue seeing her.

She didn't answer right away and, for a few seconds, he wasn't sure she was going to. Then she sighed and set the pot back into the machine.

"No, *you* didn't scare me."

Her emphasis on that one word made him hesitate and take a mental step back. "Then what did?"

She didn't answer right away as she set her mug on the counter. Crossing her arms under her breasts, she stared up at him for several seconds before shaking her head. "I'm not sure I'm cut out for that type of lifestyle."

What was he missing? "I'm not asking you to change the way you live, Kate. I'm not looking to take over your life or put a collar on you."

Her expression showed nothing of her thoughts, and he wondered how she'd gotten so good at that. "I'm just not sure I enjoyed how it made me feel."

Now, he knew that was bullshit. She'd enjoyed the hell out of it.

Why would she not want more of that pleasure?

His first inclination was to argue with her, but he bit back the urge. He could push her away and that's exactly what he didn't want to happen.

"Okay." He shrugged as if he wasn't beating back the very dominance that she found so distasteful. "Would you like to discuss terms for the boutique instead?"

For a moment she looked stunned, as if she hadn't expected him to give in so easily. Then she nodded and gestured toward the tiny table against the wall. "Why don't we sit down? Let me get a pad and pen to take notes. I've got lots of questions."

Yeah, he was sure she did. Just not all of them were about the boutique. But it didn't seem like they'd be talking about those anytime soon.

* *

"So do you want to talk about it or are we just going to ignore the elephant in the room?"

Kate made a face at Annabelle as she pressed the hem on Mr. Morrissey's new suit pants. The retired banker had to have the most expensive wardrobe of anyone in town. And she'd know because she'd been doing all of his alterations since she'd taken this job at Parisi Dry Cleaning.

His suits were Hugo Boss and his shirts custom made in Italy and shipped to his home for final fittings. He owned a huge horse farm outside of Adamstown and bred racing stock. He also dabbled in stocks, according to the town gossip mill, otherwise known as Cuppa Joe, Tracy Tate's coffee shop on Main Street.

"There's no elephant. Yes, we had amazing sex. Then he gave me details on the boutique at the spa to think over and then he left."

No, Kate didn't think there was an elephant. It was more like a voracious black bear, waiting to rise up on its hind legs and bite her in the ass.

She didn't think anyone had seen Tyler leave her apartment Sunday morning but she'd dreaded coming into work in case someone had.

And of course, that person would *not* be able to keep it to themselves. No, they'd head to Tracy's for their morning coffee and someone would say, "Did you notice that sweet Mercedes sitting in the lot behind Schmidt's apartment building?"

Then someone else would say, "No. Did the Harrisons get a new car?"

And because no one believed the very nice Harrisons, the couple who lived on the first floor of Kate's apartment building and had two kids in college, would spring for an expensive foreign car, it wouldn't take long for someone to say, "You know, I think I saw that car parked at Annabelle's for the party."

And someone else would say, "And did you see who left with Mr. Tall, Dark, and Handsome that night? Kate Song practically dragged that man out of the building—"

Annabelle snapped her fingers in front of her face, startling her out of her thoughts.

Shit. She looked down to make sure she hadn't scorched Mr. Morrissey's pants. Luckily, the iron stood upright at the end of the board.

"Hey, you winked out there for a minute," Annabelle said. "If last night was so amazing, why are you scowling just like your boss? Could you stop? You're kinda freaking me out."

Since she had a love-hate relationship with Joe Parisi, who'd hired her straight out of college with no experience whatsoever but had the patience of a gnat and an Italian temper to go with it, she gave Annabelle one of Joe's favorite hand gestures.

Then she sighed and shrugged. "It was amazing. I just don't know that we're going to repeat it. Why are you here anyway? Don't you have a playboy fiancé to keep happy and a business of your own to run?"

Annabelle gave her the don't-even-try-it face. "It's Monday so the shop's closed, which you would remember if your brains weren't addled by Tyler. Jared had to go back to Philly to meet with some big client at Haven, and I remembered Joe took the day off to visit his mother in Delaware so you're alone all day. Now, spit it out. What happened?"

Since she didn't want to screw up Mr. Morrissey's pants beyond repair, she switched off the iron and cocked her head for Annabelle to follow her to the break room.

After she'd poured herself her fourth—or fifth—cup of coffee for the morning, she set her mug on the tiny table along the wall and flopped onto one of the chairs.

"You have to promise me you won't judge."

Annabelle's eyebrows curved into serious arches. "How kinky are we talking?"

"That's just the thing. How kinky is too kinky? I'm not even sure I know. And I don't know if I'm freaked out because I'm a prude or because I have a preexisting hang-up. And if I do have a preexisting hang-up, can I get over it before I completely push him away?"

Annabelle shook her head, an amused grin starting to form. "Maybe you should start by telling me exactly what happened and we can go from there."

Kate took the plunge and let it spill out. "I let him tie me to the bed." Ignoring Annabelle's suddenly huge eyes, she pressed on. "I liked it in the moment but, of course, Sunday morning, I started to question everything. And now I think Tyler thinks I'm not into it and he won't want to see me again. The problem is, I think I might be into it, but should I be? I mean, I'm supposed to be a strong woman, right? I shouldn't want to be dominated by a man. I shouldn't want to feel all helpless and 'oh, save me, big strong man.' Right?"

Annabelle blinked, looking totally confused. "Um, I'm still at, I let him tie me to the bed. I'm not shocked," she rushed to add. "And I'm not judging. I'm just . . . Yeah, wow. That must have been a huge leap of faith for you."

And this was why Annabelle was her best friend. She got her.

"It was. But what do I do about Tyler?"

"Well, what do you *want* to do about Tyler?"

Kate threw her hands in the air. "That's just it. I don't have a clue."

Annabelle scrunched her face into a grimace. "Have you considered maybe it's too soon after your breakup with Arnie to be with anyone else?"

"No, not really. I mean, breaking up with Arnie was the right thing to do. I just don't love him like I should to make the commitment to marry him. I should've realized that months ago."

"I think you did realize it months ago. When you first met Tyler. Do you think that has anything to do with how you're feeling now?"

She took a sip of coffee and pondered that. "Possibly. Probably." Then she sighed. "But what do I do about it? I want to see him again, but I'm not sure I'm ready to jump into that lifestyle. Hell, I'm not even sure I really approve of the lifestyle."

"I'm sorry." Annabelle offered her a lopsided grin. "I just don't know what to tell you. You're the only one who can know what you're comfortable with. But maybe you're not giving Tyler enough credit. Talk to him. Tell him what you're thinking."

"I know, I know. You're absolutely right. It's just not that easy when you don't really know the guy."

Annabelle shook her head. "Honey, you probably know him better than you realize. I think you learn a lot about a guy when you allow him to tie you up."

Okay, when Annabelle put it like that . . .

She sighed. "I really like him."

"Then don't scare yourself away from him." Annabelle reached for her hand and squeezed. "I say go for it."

* *

"Are you going to mope the entire time I'm in town? Seriously, I thought we were gonna have some fun this week and you're acting like a fucking robot. What the hell's wrong? And don't give me any bullshit. I've known you for years, Tyler. What's going on?"

Greg Hicks held out his hand for the glass of whiskey Tyler had just poured him then sat back in the leather club chair in the Salon.

A dreary Monday afternoon cast shadows throughout the room, perfectly matching Tyler's mood.

He'd tried to throw off this serious funk because he was happy to see Greg, but not even last night in the bar, listening to some great, live music, could he dredge up a smile.

Dropping into the chair opposite Greg, he took a long pull from his own drink before he spilled his problem onto his friend's shoulders.

"I met a woman. We spent a few nights together. Not sure it's going to work out."

"But you like her."

The shock in Greg's tone didn't make him feel any better. Hell, did everyone think he was going to pine away for Mia for the next twenty years?

She was gone. He'd come to grips with her death, for Christ's sake.

"Yeah. I do."

Greg broke out in a smile that had been known to make women throw themselves on his casting couch without any hope of landing a job.

The guy looked like a SoCal surfer, with his sun-streaked brown hair and killer green eyes, and he towered over most men at six three.

People outside the film industry saw an easygoing dude with a ready smile and down-home charm. Industry insiders knew that outward charm hid the tough-as-balls producer who got films made on time and within budget and didn't take shit from anyone.

"Well, now, I'm glad to hear that. So what's the problem?"

Tyler wasn't exactly sure, and that pissed him the hell off. "I think I scared her."

And that really didn't sit right with him.

"So what happened? Come on, now. Tell Father Greg all about it."

That coaxed a smile out of him. Greg was barely six years older but he constantly razzed Tyler about his youth and inexperience.

Of course, Tyler reciprocated by telling him he was old, so it all evened out.

Tyler gave him the finger as he took another swallow and let the whiskey's warmth sink into his blood. He'd been feeling pretty damn cold since he'd returned on Sunday.

"We're gonna be ducking lightning bolts if you don't watch your mouth." Tyler set his empty glass on the table, figuring it was too early to finish the bottle. He and Greg had plans for tonight that required him to be coherent.

"Trust me, if I haven't been struck by now, it ain't happening. Start with the girl. Who is she?"

"You don't know her."

Greg's gaze narrowed, as if Tyler had just presented him with an interesting puzzle. "Okay, so someone new. Someone who doesn't know about your preferences?"

"She knows now."

"Ah. And that's the problem."

He remembered word for word what Kate had said Sunday morning. "Yeah."

"So what? You've been through this before. Mia had no idea what you liked when you first met her. Hell, Mia was practically an innocent when you brought her in. She adapted. What makes you think this girl won't?"

Good question. "She's stronger than Mia."

Greg nodded. "No offense intended to Mia, you know I thought she was a sweet girl but . . . Hell, a thin sheet of ice was stronger than Mia. You had the perfect little submissive there."

He knew that's what everyone thought about Mia, at least those who knew his predilections. He still wondered, though, if Mia had been submissive. Or just afraid to refuse him.

There was a difference.

"So this girl didn't like it. Or she was truly frightened?"

"That's the problem. I'm not sure."

"Did you talk to her about it?"

"A little. Mostly we discussed business."

He'd shocked Greg again. "I thought you didn't discuss business with anyone but Jed and me."

"I don't. Usually." He grimaced. "We're talking about opening a lingerie boutique at the spa. She's the designer Jed chose."

"Well, damn. Another rule broken. Business and pleasure. Now that's a slippery slope."

Yeah, Tyler wasn't happy about it either. But he wanted Kate and, for the first time in his life, he was willing to bend some of his long-held rules.

"So what are you going to do?" Greg asked.

"I'm not sure."

Greg lifted an eyebrow at him as he sipped his whiskey. "Another first. I think I need to meet the lady who makes you more human."

More human? "What the hell are you talking about?"

"Since Mia died, you've been going through the motions. I've been waiting for you to snap out of it. Seems like you might be ready to do that."

With a start, he realized Greg was right. He *had* been going through the motions. Waiting . . . He hadn't known what for.

"So," Greg prodded, "what are you going to do about her?"

He didn't have to think very long on that one. "I'm going to call her and see if she wants to have dinner with me later this week. Take it slow."

"Slow's never been your strong suit, Tyler."

"I think you're mixing me up with my brother. Jed's the impulsive one."

Greg just smiled. "I didn't say you were impulsive. But when you make up your mind to do something, you're like a freight train gathering speed as it heads down the hill. Now, since I haven't met the girl, I don't have any pertinent advice. But why don't we correct that. Invite her down for dinner Friday night. I don't have plans. We can make it a double with Jed. I'm anxious to meet his girl too."

"That should make things easier. Kate is Annabelle's best friend."

"Interesting. I look forward to it." Greg took a deep breath then set his glass on the table, his expression settling into serious lines. "All right, enough small talk. Let's get down to business."

* *

"Dr. Malinowski, this is Kate Song. I was a student of—"

"Kate! Oh my God, it's so nice to hear from you. How are you?"

Kate swallowed an audible sigh of relief as she caught up with her former professor for several minutes on the phone.

Since she couldn't make this call from work, she'd taken her lunch break at home Wednesday afternoon. But she hadn't eaten yet. She'd been too nervous.

She didn't know why. Dr. Dinah Malinowski was as personable as she'd been at college. They talked for several minutes before Kate worked up the nerve to get around to the real reason she'd called.

"Dr. Mal—"

"Oh, please call me Dinah, Kate. You're not in college any longer. And I can't believe you called me, today of all days. I was actually planning to call you. There may be an opportunity for you to work in New York with me on a show. Would you be interested? I wanted to talk to you before I throw your name into the pot."

The question took her by complete surprise and left her speechless for several seconds as her brain tried to process.

A show. An actual New York show?

Before she could think of anything to say, Dinah continued on. "It would be off-Broadway but for an established company. Their longtime costume designer is retiring and, since I've been working with her for years, she suggested me for her position. And the first person I thought about bringing with me was you."

"Congratulations, Dinah. That's a wonderful opportunity for you. And I'm flattered that you thought of me."

"I know it might be a huge leap of faith for you, considering I have no idea what you've been doing since graduation, but that doesn't change the fact that you were one of my most gifted students and I want you to consider it. What *are* you doing now?"

She almost didn't want to say. Not that there was anything wrong with her job. It was a solid use of her skills. But working in a dry cleaners wasn't exactly the life she'd had planned.

But this . . .

This was her dream.

And totally not what she'd called about.

"I'm working as a tailor and designing on the side," she said, then rushed on before Dinah could ask more questions. "I'd love to hear more about this."

"Great! That's just what I hoped to hear. Are you free later this week to meet? I guess I should ask if you're still in the area. I know you always talked about heading for New York but . . ."

Her mother had died. "I'm still in Adamstown, so I could be in Gettysburg any night."

"Actually I'm living in New York City now but I'll be in the area tomorrow night to visit my folks. How about I give you a call? We can meet for drinks and talk. Now, I guess I should ask why you called."

Kate assured Dinah they could discuss it at dinner and they hung up after a short round of good-byes.

When her phone rang again only seconds later, Kate almost expected it to be Dinah calling back, telling her she'd made a horrible mistake, that she hadn't realized who she was talking to and that she didn't really want to talk about a job in New York City.

And when she picked up the phone and realized the call was from her father, she nearly put it down without answering.

Of course she couldn't do that.

Deep breath. "Hi, Dad. How are you? Is everything okay?"

His sigh rang through the connection, loud and clear. "Why do you always assume something's wrong when I call? I'm not that old, am I?"

She had to laugh. Her dad had an extremely dry sense of humor, when he had any at all. It'd taken her years to figure out when he was making a joke.

"No, Dad, you're not that old. Sorry. What's up?"

"I haven't heard from you since last week. I'm simply checking in. I called the shop but Joe told me you'd gone home for lunch. Are *you* feeling okay?"

She wasn't sure how to answer that without divulging more than her dad would probably want to know so she simply said, "I'm fine. The wedding dress I made for Maggie Shanahan survived the day despite being ripped by a dog. I had to repair it before the wedding but it held."

"I have no doubt it did."

Was that pride she heard in his voice? It would be nice if she could tell. But that was something to ponder another day. She had way too much stuff in her brain now.

They talked for another few minutes. Her dad asked questions. She responded. A normal conversation for them.

It was all so . . . civilized. Which was a sucky way to characterize her relationship with her father. But true.

"I heard Annabelle's grand opening was quite the event."

Shit. Had he heard about her leaving the party with Tyler? Would she get his infamous "You should have more respect for yourself" speech? Or would it be the "Don't disgrace yourself" speech? With her dad, there was always a speech.

"Um, yeah. It was."

"Please let her know how sorry I was to miss it. I understand she made an announcement about her parents. That must have been difficult for her. Please tell her I wish her the best with her new endeavor."

And once again, her father had surprised her. "I will. I'm sure she'll appreciate it."

"I understand you left with a man. Is there someone new in your life?"

And there it was. The zinger.

Way to bury the lede, Dad.

There was no way she going there, not with him. "No, Dad. There's not. The man is Annabelle's boyfriend's brother. His name's Tyler Golden. He's simply an acquaintance."

An acquaintance she'd had mind-blowing sex with.

Yeah, really not going there.

"Kate." He paused, and she braced herself for the speech, whichever one it might be. "Do you think that's wise? You've only just broken off your engagement with Arnold. People will talk. I don't want you to be the center of people's conversation."

"I know, Dad. That won't happen."

He fell silent and so did she. She was an adult and she wasn't about to offer up any more information. Though he might still consider her a child, there were things he didn't need to know about her life. Such as the fact that she had sex. He could go on thinking she was a virgin until she married.

He sighed. She heard it loud and clear and she fought the urge to cave and tell him what he wanted to hear.

"Well, I should let you get back to work. Maybe we can schedule dinner soon. If you have the time."

She held back a sigh. Her dad had mastered the art of the guilt trip a long time ago. "Sure. I'm, ah, meeting an old professor tomorrow night but I'm free every other night." And yes, that was totally pathetic. She had no hope that Tyler would call. At least, not to ask her out.

She didn't think she'd ever see him outside of business again. "Why don't we plan on Sunday night? I have plans Friday and Saturday."

Gee, her dad had plans for the weekend and she didn't. How pathetic was that? "Sure, that's great."

At least she'd have all weekend to sew.

* *

"Kate, it's Tyler. How are you?"

Shocked was the only word that came to mind Friday night around eight as she sat at her machine, eyes nearly crossed.

She'd been here close to five hours, sewing together tiny bits of lace and satin and chewing over last night's conversation with Dinah. Her former professor had offered her a great opportunity, practically gift-wrapped and on a silver platter. She should've jumped at the offer immediately.

Instead, she'd smiled and said she had to give it some thought.

She'd been expecting a call from Annabelle to tell her how stupid she was being when she'd answered her phone without looking at the number.

Now, she rescued her latest design from the machine before she could totally ruin the fabric then she sat back in her chair and tried not to feel like a tongue-tied teenager.

"I'm fine. And you?"

Oh, look how polite we're being.

She nearly snorted.

"I'd like to see you," he said. "I know I should have called earlier, but we had a situation at the hotel. This is the first chance I've had to call and I'd really like to see you."

Okay, maybe not so polite.

And possibly a little drunk? Had he slurred his words? Or was she hearing something that wasn't there?

Or maybe the entire conversation was a dream. Maybe she'd fallen asleep, which would account for the strange vibe.

"Are you okay, Tyler?"

"I'm fine." And he did sound fine. Absolutely controlled. "I'd simply like to see you."

That was the third time he'd said that. A shiver of anticipation ran up her spine. She'd wondered if he was going to call her again. But as Thursday and today had passed and he hadn't, she'd thought maybe he never would.

And yeah, she'd been a little pissed off about that.

Which was totally irrational because she could've called him.

Only she hadn't.

"Would it be okay if I came in?" he asked.

Oh no.

She shot out of her chair and headed for the window at the back that overlooked the parking area. Sure enough, there was Tyler's Mercedes.

Her heart thudded like a bass drum and she could barely breathe. She'd never had a man do this to her before. She wasn't entirely sure she liked it.

"What are you doing here, Tyler?"

"I want to see you."

The low tone of his voice made her heart pound even faster. "You don't call first?"

"Aren't we talking on the phone right now?"

And people thought she was a smart-ass. "But you're sitting in my parking lot."

"I called first."

"But . . ."

"If you don't want to see me, we'll go."

She paused. "We?"

"I had a friend drive me. I had a little too much to drink."

"So you're drunk."

"No. I didn't drink enough to be impaired. I'm just cautious."

Which she should be, too. Trouble was, she wanted to see him. She'd missed him. Which totally sucked because she'd been determined not to break down and call him.

But here he was. Practically gift-wrapped.

"May I come in, Kate? Or should I leave?"

"No. I mean, come up. Is your friend . . . joining you?"

A pause. "He'd like to meet you, if it's okay with you."

"Um, sure. That's fine."

He didn't miss the hesitation in her tone. "I'm sorry. We shouldn't have barged in like this. We'll—"

"No. No, it's fine. Please, come up."

She hung up before she could say any more then ran for her bedroom. She managed to tear off her old sweats and pull on a pair of worn jeans and a long-sleeved T-shirt before she heard the knock on her door.

Taking a deep breath as she covered the few feet to the door, she didn't give herself time to second-guess. Instead, she braced for impact.

And still couldn't manage to completely control her response to him.

Tyler nearly filled the narrow doorway, all broad shoulders and wide chest. She looked up into his face and noticed how intently he stared at her.

"Hi."

Her stomach actually fluttered as the sound of his deep voice penetrated. "Hello, Tyler. Please come in."

Gosh, what manners. Dad would be so pleased.

She moved to the side so he could enter then felt her gaze catch on the man behind him.

She'd thought Tyler was tall but this man had at least a few inches on him. But where Tyler had that dark and brooding vibe, this guy had a loving-every-minute-of-it smile. One of those completely confident, devil-may-care smiles that made people want to be in his presence.

And totally screwed with her sense of balance.

Tyler had already knocked her for a loop. If she got any more off-kilter, she'd simply fall over.

"Kate Song, this is a good friend of mine, Greg Hicks."

The name sounded familiar but she couldn't say she recognized him. She held out her hand after she'd closed the door behind him. "Nice to meet you, Mr. Hicks."

Tyler and his friend exchanged a quick glance she couldn't interpret before Greg turned his smile up a notch. "Great to meet you, Kate. Tyler's told me a lot about you."

He had? Like how he'd tied her to her bed and fucked her until she nearly passed out?

She almost tripped over her own feet as she led them toward her tiny living room.

"I told him about your designs for the boutique and your wedding gowns." Tyler's hand touched her elbow, as if to steady her. Or to reassure her he hadn't divulged any other secrets. "Greg's been a friend of mine for years."

Directing her to the couch, he sat beside her, while Greg sat in the armchair that seemed to shrink beneath his bulk.

Yet, even though she obviously acknowledged the man's appeal, he didn't make her want to strip him down to the skin and run her hands all over his body.

But then she couldn't help but wonder what Greg looked like naked.

Oh wow.

She forced herself to smile at Greg. "And how did you meet?"

"I was one of Haven's first customers. I live on the West Coast, but my parents still live in Philly so I travel back East a lot."

She nodded, her brain too scrambled to come up with any more small talk. After the meeting with Dinah Thursday night, she'd felt torn in five different directions. But one look at Tyler and she only wanted to know why he was here. What did he want?

She hoped it was her.

And talk about further complicating your life . . .

Switching her attention back to Tyler, she noticed how intently he stared at her.

"Is everything okay?"

He nodded. "Everything's fine. Greg wanted to see the new property, and since we were in the area, I wanted to stop and see you. How was your week?"

She'd learned the fine art of lying with a smile at a young age. "Fine. And yours?"

Tyler's expression darkened and she knew he'd seen through her. She readied herself for the second degree.

"I missed you." Tyler's stark words made her gut clench. How did he manage to do that with only three little words? "I decided I'd waited long enough for you to call so I made the first move."

Her mouth dropped open but she couldn't think of a damn thing to say. Across from them, Greg choked on a cough she was pretty sure started as a laugh.

"You know you could've called me."

"I did. Tonight. Are you telling me you wanted me to call earlier?"

That was a pretty personal question to answer in front of a total stranger, who watched them like they were engaged in a fierce tennis match.

And how should she answer that? If she said yes, she'd sound petulant. If she said no, she'd be lying. And apparently he'd be able to tell.

"What are you really doing here tonight, Tyler?"

"I told you. I missed you. Spend the weekend at Haven with me. Greg and I have some business to take care of tomorrow morning but there's a reception tomorrow night I'd like you to attend with me."

"A reception for what?"

He didn't answer right away and she wondered if this had to do with the Salon. She couldn't decide if she was disappointed when he said, "A fund-raising event for Greg's new film."

"Greg's a director?"

"I'm a producer," Greg answered, drawing her gaze toward him once again, forcing her to acknowledge his presence.

"Would I know anything you've produced?"

Greg's smile grew, and the quick look he exchanged with Tyler said something she couldn't interpret. "Probably a few."

Then he rattled off three huge blockbusters even a person who didn't follow mainstream movies would know.

She blushed, feeling like a rube and not liking the feeling at all. "I'm—"

"Kate." Greg reached for her hand, shaking his head. "If I wanted people to fawn over me, I'd wear my Oscar around my neck, sweetheart. Put Tyler out of his misery and say yes."

She turned back to Tyler, who continued to watch her with that intent gaze. "What should I bring?"

His smile barely registered on his face but his eyes shone. "Why don't you show me what you have, and I'll help you choose?"

He wanted to pick her clothes for her? If any other man had suggested that, she'd think he was weird. But with Tyler . . . "Okay."

She stood, but Tyler was already on his feet, reaching for her hand. She took his but when she tried to pull away, he wouldn't let her. He threaded his fingers through hers and led the way to her bedroom. When she'd crossed the threshold, she nearly lost her breath when he put his hands around her waist, lifted her off her feet then held her back against the door.

He leaned in close enough that she could smell the faint, seductive hint of alcohol on his breath. "I wasn't lying before. I missed you this week."

Then he kissed her.

And not a hey-happy-to-see-you kiss. This was an I-want-to-devour-you kiss. She barely sucked in a breath before he took it away again with the force of his lips on hers and the thrust of his tongue in her mouth.

He didn't hold anything back, and she realized she didn't want him to. She wanted to know how much he'd missed her, how much he needed her.

Because she'd been pining for him too.

Shoving her hands in his hair, she caught the short strands between her fingers and tugged. Not to pull him away but to feel him resist.

He slid one arm beneath her ass so he could hold her up then let his free hand stroke up her side to her breast. Cupping her, he kneaded the soft flesh until she moaned into his mouth and lifted her legs to wrap around his waist.

His groan echoed through her small bedroom and sank deep into her body, making her thighs tighten and her hips thrust forward to press his erection into her clit.

Ah, God, just a little more pressure, a little movement, and she swore she'd come.

As if he'd read her mind, he pressed forward, catching her clit on the seam of her jeans until she thought she'd scream.

And when he pulled away, she muttered a frustrated sound that made him smile against her lips before he set her on her feet.

"Glad you're happy to see me too."

She wanted to glare up at him but it dissolved under the sexual need driving her crazy.

Hell, for those few minutes he'd been kissing her, she'd forgotten another man sat in her living room waiting for them while she wanted to rip off Tyler's clothes and throw him on her bed.

"You didn't call."

Damn it, she *did* sound like a petulant teenager.

"I wasn't sure you'd want to hear from me."

His expression indicated it wasn't something he wanted to talk about, so she let that slide. "I *did* miss you, Tyler." More than she wanted to admit.

"Then why didn't *you* call?"

She crossed her arms over her chest and raised her eyebrows. "Why didn't you?"

His lips curved in that half smile that made her knees weak. "An impasse. I can deal with that. For now."

Turning, he walked to her closet, opened the door, and just stood there.

She walked over to stand next to him. "Are you really going to tell me what clothes to wear?"

He gave her a wry look. "Of course not. But if I stood like that any longer, I might've had you naked and pinned to the door with my cock inside you. I'm not sure you were ready for that with Greg sitting out there."

Oh.

Images flashed through her mind, making her hot and breathless. My God, it just wasn't fair what he could do to her with only his voice. But two could play that game.

"Maybe I would've been okay with that."

He turned to face her completely. "Would you?"

She knew he was asking about what had happened last Sunday. And since she'd had some time to think about it, she'd realized she didn't want to give up on Tyler quite so fast.

She didn't want to lie to herself. She'd enjoyed it. And she didn't want fear to rule her life.

Smiling, she turned to her closet. "Tell me a little about this party."

* *

Since Greg couldn't fit comfortably in the back of his Mercedes and Tyler had sobered up enough to drive, Kate sat in the back.

He'd wanted her beside him but she'd laughed when Greg had grudgingly offered to fold himself into the backseat then slid into the backseat herself.

He could see her in the mirror and he knew she watched him as much as he watched her.

He knew she could tell he had something weighing on his mind. His father's bombshell earlier today felt like a concrete block on his shoulders.

The bastard was going to sell the GoldenStar chain unless Tyler took over chairmanship of the board.

Tyler still felt like he'd been punched in the gut. He'd left his father's office in a seething rage that he'd only managed to douse with a trip to the gym to punch the bag for an hour and a bottle of Patrón before dinner with Greg.

Dinner had helped sober him but nothing had erased the need to see Kate.

When he thought of her, all the other shit in his head settled.

Greg had offered to drive and Tyler wasn't far enough gone to not realize that was probably a good idea. His head wasn't on straight.

But he'd known exactly what he needed to take his mind off everything else.

He needed *her*.

After that kiss, he'd managed to keep his hands in his pockets, even though she tempted him with each article of clothing she pulled out of the closet.

A dress for tomorrow night's reception that looked like nothing more than a tube of black velvet with two straps to hold it up. A pair of black slacks and a baby blue blouse he assumed she'd wear with it. A T-shirt and a pair of jeans.

Then she'd opened the chest of drawers and threw tiny bits of silk and lace on the bed. Underwear and bras.

His mouth dried and his hands curled into fists in his pockets.

He wondered what she was wearing right now. Although, if he had to guess, he didn't think she was wearing anything under that T-shirt.

It didn't take her long to pack a bag though she'd probably spent more time picking out her shoes and jewelry than she had her clothes.

She'd also stopped just before they were ready to walk out the door and said she'd forgotten something. He had no idea what but she'd taken her overnight bag with her and when he'd picked it up again, it was heavier.

"So, Kate." Greg turned so he could address her after they'd reached the turnpike. "Tyler tells me you're considering taking a boutique in the spa. I gotta say, it sounds like a great opportunity for you."

She surprised him by saying, "I think so too."

"So you're going to do it?" Tyler caught her gaze in the mirror for a few brief seconds.

She smiled. "I've had a lot of time to think about it this week but there are a few things I need to figure out before I say yes."

He wanted her to say yes but knew he couldn't pressure her into making this decision. He settled for a restrained, "I'll answer any question you have."

Her smile did weird and wonderful things to his insides, and he knew he should probably be worried about that. He knew what happened when he let himself get out of control and he didn't want to ever feel like that again.

"I know. I just . . . need a little more time."

Greg steered the conversation away from the subject after that, drawing out Kate and keeping her engaged. Tyler added a little here and there, though he was more than content to listen to Kate.

Who didn't seem at all attracted to Greg. He couldn't help feeling superior about that. Yes, it was juvenile. He'd have to watch that.

What she was interested in was costume design. He knew that's what she'd studied in college and what she'd hoped to pursue after graduation. Until her mother's death had interrupted those plans.

When he finally pulled into the garage at Haven, she and Greg were laughing about a recent Broadway production they'd both seen and the amazing costumes.

"Her use of color to show character was brilliant," Kate said as Tyler helped her out of the car. "It was amazing how much emotion a simple blue handkerchief in his pocket could convey."

Since Tyler hadn't seen the show, he had no idea what they were talking about. And he didn't care. He simply enjoyed listening to Kate and watching her talk about something she obviously loved.

When they reached the fourth floor, though, the conversation came to a halt as the elevator doors opened. Greg was staying in one of the suites and he nodded at Tyler and said good night to Kate before he disappeared into it, leaving them staring into each other's eyes.

"Would you like your own room, Kate? Or will you stay with me this weekend?"

He heard no hesitation in her voice when she said, "I'd like to stay with you."

Which was exactly what he wanted so he didn't bother to hide his smile. "Good."

Opening the door to his apartment, he waved her in then headed to his bedroom to drop off her bag.

He hadn't realized she'd followed him until he turned and found her standing in the doorway, her gaze taking in everything.

"You decorated this room yourself, didn't you?"

How did she know that? "Pretty much, yes."

Her gaze returned to him and she smiled. "I like it."

"I'm glad. But how could you tell I decorated it?"

"It feels like you."

Navy blue walls decorated with the framed conceptual drawings he'd made of the atrium. Sky blue silk drapes at the windows. Cherry mahogany furniture, including a king-size bed, a double chest, and a night table.

No clutter. No mess.

Not much personality.

"So I'm boring."

She laughed, her eyes crinkling at the corners until they almost disappeared. "I don't think you're boring, Tyler. Not at all. You've got hidden depths. You're straightforward. I like that."

Closing the distance between them, he stopped only inches away, close enough that she had to tilt her head back to look at him.

He wanted to reach for her but kept his hands to himself. For now, anyway. At the moment, he wanted to know why she'd agreed to come. Before, it hadn't mattered. Only that she had.

"I'm glad you came. I believe you'll have a good time at the party. I believe Annabelle will be there, too, at least for a little while."

Her eyes widened slightly in surprise. "She didn't say anything. Then again, we didn't get to talk much this week."

He saw that didn't sit well with her. "Did you have a busy week?"

She sighed and nodded. "Yeah, busier than normal. And I spent most nights working on designs."

Heat began to build low in his gut. "Lingerie designs?"

A mysterious look crossed her face. "And others."

"More wedding dresses?"

She shook her head. "It'll probably be easier if I show you."

"Are you going to model?"

"Would you like me to?"

Her expression had turned flirtatious and the way she stared up at him made his cock swell. The remnants of alcohol in his system burned away from the look in her eyes.

"I guess it depends on what you're going to model."

With that same mysterious smile, she walked to the bed, where he'd set her bag on the floor next to it.

"Lingerie and wedding dresses aren't all I've been working on. I was trained as a costume designer. I've had a few requests recently for costumes." She paused. "Role-playing costumes."

His heart began to pound. "Like the fairy costumes you made for you and Annabelle."

Her smile turned wicked. "Kind of, yes. But not the kind you can wear outside of the bedroom. Unless it's down the hall in the Salon."

Oh, hell yes. He definitely wanted to see whatever she had in that bag.

He'd never really considered the idea of dress-up before. It wasn't something Mia had ever suggested, and it'd just never popped up on his radar. Some of the women who attended Jed's Salons did dress up, but he'd been there so infrequently in the past several years that it had never really registered.

Now, he couldn't think of anything he wanted more.

Kate picked up the bag and set it on the bed. "Why don't you go sit in the living room and I'll be out in a few minutes?"

He nodded. "Would you like a drink?"

She took a deep breath and he saw the slightest hint of nerves hit her. But then she nodded and the nerves disappeared. "Sure. Something light."

"Champagne?"'

"Okay."

He forced himself to leave slowly, not run for the other room like a horny teenager. Shutting the door behind him, he stopped to take a deep breath, trying to rein in the excitement roiling through his gut. He didn't want to rip the clothes off her the minute he saw her. But his control was pretty damn shoddy at the moment.

And that was the one thing he couldn't lose.

Nine

❧

Kate watched the door close behind Tyler and breathed a sigh of relief.

She couldn't believe she was going to go through with this. Couldn't believe she'd actually had the nerve to stuff the clothes in her bag.

It'd been a last-minute idea and she had no idea where it'd come from.

Okay, maybe she had a little bit of an idea where it came from.

She'd done a lot of thinking after her meeting with Dinah about the job in New York. Actually, all she'd been doing was thinking. So much so, she'd been fending off a headache since last night.

Now, she wanted to play so she pushed everything out of her mind except Tyler.

And the pleasure she wanted to experience with him.

Opening her overnight bag, she pulled out the pieces she'd brought.

Am I really going to do this? Dress up in these clothes and parade in front of that man?

Yes, damn it. She was.

Because she wanted to.

Stripping her T-shirt over her head, she tossed it on the bed, quickly followed by her jeans and undies. Standing there naked, she caught sight of herself in the cheval mirror in a corner.

She had her share of body issues, same as any other woman. She wished she wasn't so flat-chested and she definitely wished she had anything in the way of hips. She knew other women would kill to look the way she did, but truthfully, she wished she could put on a few pounds. But only in the right places, of course.

And since that wasn't going to happen, she figured she should be grateful for what she did have.

Decent legs, for one. And beautiful hair. The perfect combination of her mom's mahogany color and her dad's sleek shine. It set off her pale skin perfectly.

And Tyler seemed to love it. He always had his hands in it.

Now, what to wear first?

Should she start tame and work up to raunchy?

Pulling the French maid costume out, she held it up to her body. And caught back the laughter trying to break free.

How corny could she get?

She'd originally designed this for a college play. Of course, the one worn on stage had actually covered the actress's ass. This one was made to expose the bottom half of her cheeks. And the little white lace apron that attached to the frilly black skirt with concealed Velcro left most of her breasts exposed.

She'd even remembered to toss in the feather duster.

It only took her seconds to put it on, but when she did a final check in the mirror, her lips curved in a smile.

Okay. You can do this.

The one thing she didn't have were the right shoes. She hadn't brought the black patent stilettos sitting in her closet gathering dust.

Hopefully, he wouldn't notice.

Taking a deep breath, she opened the door.

And had to work hard to control her smile when Tyler turned away from the window where he was standing and his mouth dropped open for several seconds.

Yes. This was exactly the response she'd been looking for.

It gave her the courage to saunter out into the living room. The air brushed against her exposed skin, pebbling her nipples until they peaked beneath the lace.

He held a glass in his hand, though the clear liquid appeared to be water. She noticed how his fingers flexed around the glass before he set it on the closest table.

As his mouth closed, his gaze made a leisurely trip from her bare feet up to her eyes.

"Do you like this one?" She posed with her feet together and her hands clasping the feather duster just below her breasts, looking at him from beneath her lashes. "I got the idea from a costume I made for a play in college."

As she breathed, the feathers brushed against her breasts, the sensation intensifying the lust pulsing through her body.

A flush spread across Tyler's cheeks and his eyes glittered in the dusky light of the room. Without saying a word, he lifted his hand and drew circles in the air with his index finger.

She complied with his request—at least, she chose to think of it as a request—and did a slow spin. "So what do you think?"

He walked forward, and she thought he'd come to her. Instead, he stopped at the couch and sat down.

Sprawled would be more like it. He slung one arm on the back of the couch and let the other rest on the cushion next to him. With his dark hair tousled, as if he'd been running his fingers through it, and the casual jeans and tight T-shirt that clung to his broad chest, she wanted to go over and sit on his lap and lick him. Everywhere.

"I think I'd like to see what else you have in that bag."

His voice had deepened to a low rasp and she was glad she'd added a thong to the ensemble. It would be soaked by the time she was finished but that was okay.

She pouted and put one hand on her cocked hip. "Don't you like it? I would have thought this would be right up your alley, being in the hotel business and all."

The corners of his mouth barely moved in a smile but she knew he was. "I'm all for letting you design the next round of service uniforms, sweetheart. But I think I'd have a riot on my hands."

She sighed dramatically and turned on her heel to head back to the bedroom. But just before she closed the door behind her, she looked over her shoulder. "Then I guess we'll just have to try something a little less . . . frilly."

With the door closed, she practically skipped back to the bed and the pile of clothes she'd laid there.

Shimmying out of the maid's costume, she let it drop to the floor as she picked up a leaf-green piece of chamois deliberately made to look torn and jagged. She tied that around her breasts then tied a slightly larger, dark brown chamois piece around her waist.

She didn't bother with the headband. He'd get the general idea.

"I always did want to be Tarzan when I grew up," he said as she stopped just in front of him this time.

"He certainly has that beauty-and-the-beast thing going for him. What do you think of this one?"

"I think it's sexy as all hell. And I think you should come over here and let me take it off you."

Right then she realized she wanted him to come after her. Wanted to break his rigid control and entice him off the couch and to her.

"Hmm, no. I don't think you're all that interested in this one. I guess we'll just have to try another."

When she returned the next time, she swore he turned a deeper shade of red.

She hadn't been sure what he'd make of this one.

"I'm missing the boots but I think you get the general idea. What do you think of this one?"

He didn't say anything right away, his gaze glued to her body. He stared so long, she wondered if she'd actually shocked him.

Finally, he stood, closing the few feet between them.

He towered over her, hands at his sides as he circled around her.

"What was your inspiration for this one?"

She actually shivered at the sound of his voice, couldn't control it. "I had a huge crush on Keanu Reeves in *The Matrix*. I wanted to be Trinity."

"I think her clothes were a little more . . . concealing."

He still hadn't touched her, yet she could feel the heat of his body like a caress against her skin. Her fingers curled into her palms to keep from reaching for him when he stopped in front of her again.

"I took a few liberties."

"I see that."

Yes, this costume was made of leather, but it probably only used the same amount of fabric as one pants leg of Trinity's outfit.

The black shorts were no more than six inches at the widest point and, though he couldn't see it, the crotch was missing. Well, not missing, she just hadn't made one.

Her breasts were mostly bare, although her nipples were covered by crisscrossing, two-inch strips of leather that attached at her neck and behind her back.

Another intricate pattern of straps crossed her stomach and attached to the shorts.

"Is *The Matrix* the only inspiration you had for this?"

She knew what he was asking. "I had a personal request for this one."

His gaze finally connected with hers. "From someone who wanted you to wear it?"

Was that jealousy she detected in his tone? "From someone who wanted to wear it herself."

He nodded, and she knew he'd totally dismissed the thought. "Do you have any more?"

"Only one."

"Am I going to get to see it now?"

"Do you want to?"

"Do you have other designs at home?"

"Yes."

His lips barely moved but she could tell he was smiling. "Then let's see the last one."

She'd saved her favorite for last. Wondered if he'd realize why. The man seemed to be able to read her mind.

As she changed, she drew in a sharp breath as the leather pulled away from her oh-so-sensitive nipples. At least when she drew the shorts down nothing rubbed against her clit. Though she wanted something to.

God, if he didn't grab her and throw her on a flat surface soon, she swore she'd spontaneously combust.

Which didn't make a lick of sense considering she'd spent half the past week worrying about losing herself to him.

Of course, she'd spent the rest of it pining after him.

She needed to get out of this circular thinking pattern. It wasn't helping at all.

Picking up the pieces of the last costume, she smiled. She'd made this one for herself.

The tiny, see-through white blouse gaped open to expose the neon blue bra, barely covered the bottom curve of her breasts, and left her entire midsection exposed. The seven-inch-long, pleated plaid skirt barely brushed her hips at the top and almost covered her ass in the back. The blue thong that matched her bra left her ass exposed but its strings were visible above the skirt's waistband.

The line of tiny buttons up the side required concentration to work through the holes. Though if you were in a hurry, you really didn't need to remove the skirt at all.

Damn, she was going to soak through the panties in seconds.

Speaking of which . . . She pulled the thong on first, nearly moaning at the feel of the silk string between her cheeks and against the lips of her pussy. All he'd have to do was touch her and she'd explode.

Next, the bra. The lace felt almost abrasive against her skin, heightening her already burning lust. By the time she'd pulled on the skirt and shirt, she wanted to run back to Tyler and let him rip it all off of her.

She was going to need a shrink by the time this relationship came to an end.

Which she refused to even think about right now.

At the mirror, she gathered her hair into two ponytails over her ears, leaving a few strands to brush her cheeks.

Stepping back, she checked her appearance. And nearly chickened out.

It might actually take more strength for her to walk out to Tyler wearing this than it would to go out naked.

Did she look ridiculous? Would he find her sexy dressed like this? Some men had hang-ups about stuff like this. She didn't think Tyler was one of them, but how did she know for sure? They didn't really know each other all that well, did they?

And you're making excuses because you're scared. Now or never.

She went to the door and walked through.

* *

She'd been in there longer than she had for the other costumes and Tyler couldn't help but let his imagination run a little wild.

He'd been shocked speechless when she'd walked out in that first outfit. Not because he didn't like it but because he hadn't expected her to do anything like that.

Obviously, he didn't know Kate as well as he thought he did.

And he wanted to, so badly he could see it becoming something of a problem in the future.

A future he hadn't imagined with anyone since he'd lost Mia.

One that—

The door opened and his brain stuttered to a stop for a full thirty seconds.

Holy shit.

He wasn't sure he was going to be able to breathe without choking.

She looked . . . so fucking hot. And he'd never before been one for the whole naughty schoolgirl thing.

But holy hell, he was beginning to see the appeal.

At least on Kate.

The skirt made her legs look amazingly long and the top and bra accentuated her somewhat meager attributes. Not that he'd ever complain. He was more a big-picture guy than a breast or ass man.

And this picture . . . Christ, put a bullet in him now. He was done.

As she strolled over to stand in front of him, she had one hand on her hip and twirled the end of one ponytail with the other.

All she needed was a lollipop to suck on and he might as well just melt into a puddle right here.

Then he'd give her something else to suck on.

Very soon.

First, he forced himself to lean back into the couch though he never took his eyes off of her.

Her expression held the perfect mix of boredom and sexuality. He wanted to lay her over his lap and smack her ass. There were paddles down the hall in the Salon. He'd take a few minutes and go get one.

He wouldn't hurt her. He only wanted to see her skin flush red before he sat her on his dick and fucked her until she went limp in his arms.

Then he'd lay her out on the bed and do her again.

Overkill?

Hell no.

She let him look for a few more seconds before she spoke. "So what do you think?"

He swallowed first, afraid his voice would crack. "I think someone watched a little too much MTV as a teenager."

He saw her smile just before she affected that bored expression again. The one he wanted to kiss off her face. "I was more into manga. Sailor Moon, HunterX, Naruta. I was very aware of how different I was from most of my friends, and those characters looked like me."

Yes, he could understand the appeal that would have to a teen-ager with her heritage.

Her expression turned coy and she looked at him from beneath her lashes again. That look incinerated his remaining control.

Sliding to the edge of the couch, he stood, enjoying how her gaze followed him all the way up.

From this angle, her cleavage looked even deeper and he could see the shadow of her nipples beneath the lace and the almost sheer fabric of that little white blouse.

"So was this modeled after a character in a book?"

"No." She paused and he heard her clear her throat. "Not really. I just liked the fabrics and the colors."

"Good choices." He was having a hard time regulating his breathing. His lungs felt starved for air. "Can I touch you, Kate?"

She shrugged. "I guess."

Bored insolence looked good on her. He swallowed a laugh and circled around to her back.

"I'm not going to take this off." He stepped closer, until his chest nearly touched her back, gratified to hear her breathing become labored. "I'm going to fuck you with it on."

She flinched and he cursed himself for his language. He'd have to watch that—

"Maybe"—she flicked her hair over her shoulder, the ends brushing against his jaw—"I'll be the one fucking you this time."

Guess he didn't have to watch his language. Leaning closer, he spoke directly into her ear. "You can try."

Would she take the bait? He hoped like hell she did.

For several seconds, he simply listened to her breathe and watched the increasing pace of her rising and falling breasts. A man could get hypnotized like that.

Slowly, she turned, though she didn't put any space between them.

"I'm going to start with your clothes," she said, "but I don't want you to do anything unless I tell you to."

She didn't ask permission but he swore he heard her silent question. Would he allow her to have the upper hand here?

Yes.

To a certain point.

He'd figure out what that point was when they got there.

He gave a short nod and her smile spread, a hint of sin in her eyes. "I'm going to unbutton your shirt. I want you to stand still."

Her fingers traced their way up the front of his shirt until they reached the open vee at his neck. She stroked the hollow of his neck with her fingertips before she plucked open the first button.

The button-down shirt was one of his favorites, the cotton faded to a pale blue and soft as butter. He had the sleeves rolled up to his elbows and had left the tails untucked.

Kate worked her way down the row of buttons with an unhurried ease that made the muscles of his stomach tighten. As she neared the bottom, where the tails brushed nearly to his thighs, her knuckles bumped against the thrust of his erection.

He swore he'd have the imprint of his zipper on his dick forever.

When his shirt finally hung open, she didn't push it off as he'd expected.

She brushed it aside as she scraped her fingernails up and down his abs. The sensation fired his nerve endings but wasn't hard enough to do more than tease.

And when she leaned forward, he held his breath as she leaned close and flicked her tongue at one taut nipple.

Christ, that felt amazing, like liquid fire. He bit back a groan and clenched his hands into fists, keeping them locked at his sides. Otherwise he would've had his hands wrapped in those ponytails.

Later, he'd do just that. But not now. Not when she was driving him to distraction with only her tongue and her fingertips.

"I want you to keep the shirt on, Tyler."

"Whatever you want, sweetheart."

She gave him a doubtful glance. "I'm going to remind you you said that later."

"You do that."

Turning her attention back to what her fingers were doing, she watched as they traced the line of dark hair that arrowed from his belly to his groin. She brushed it, petted him, and made his cock strain even harder against his zipper.

As she traced the waistband of his jeans from the front to the back, she raised all the hair on his body by the time she returned to the button and worked it free.

The head of his cock leaped at the chance to escape and, when she tugged down the zipper, he practically burst out of his boxers.

He waited with baited breath for her to touch him, to take his cock in her hands and jerk him off. He wanted to tell her what to do but he remembered his earlier words. "Whatever you want."

Apparently what she wanted was to drive him crazy, because instead of touching him, she grabbed the sides of his jeans and pushed them down his legs.

Since he'd already taken off his shoes, he didn't have to fumble around when she said, "Kick those off."

With his jeans in a pile by his feet, he felt strangely exposed, which didn't make a bit of sense. But the feeling fled when he saw how she stared at him—with enough heat in her eyes to blister paint.

"Now I want you to sit on the couch, arms across the back."

He didn't obey right away, couldn't force himself to blindly follow her commands. It just wasn't in him.

But when she raised one curved brow at him and crossed her arms over her chest, he realized this was a game to her. Not a dominance play.

He crossed the few feet to the couch and sat back down, just as she'd asked.

"There now, that wasn't so hard, was it?"

Her voice held a sweet-as-sugar tone that made him grin as he held her gaze.

"I guess we'll just have to see if the reward is worth it."

With deliberate steps, she approached the couch. "Spread your legs."

Again, he waited until she raised her eyebrows.

"You know"—she put her hands on her hips, making that tiny white shirt gape even more—"if you don't listen, I'm not going to reward you."

"Reward me for what?"

"For being a good boy."

He did smile then, which she returned with a sly grin. "Then it better be one hell of a good reward because I am being one hell of a good boy right now."

"I'll be the judge of that."

He couldn't stop grinning at the pleasure he saw on her face. She was having a good time and he didn't want anything to get in the way of that.

With a slight dip of his head, he spread his legs.

Hell, it was reward enough to watch her go to her knees between his. Then she moved closer.

He held his breath as she reached for him, praying this time she'd give his cock some relief. Instead, she reached for his underwear. She tugged and maneuvered until she'd exposed his shaft.

The heat of her breath brushed against the ultrasensitive tip, making his cock quiver. He grabbed hold of the cushions with both hands so he didn't grab for her.

She didn't do anything other than sit there for several seconds, staring at his straining erection. He swore if she didn't touch him soon, he'd come just from the anticipation.

Finally, she reached for him . . .

But only to splay her hands on his chest.

He bit back a groan as she kneaded his pecs then sank her fingernails lightly into his skin and dragged them down his body.

He nearly came off the couch when she scraped along the sensitive area on either side of the root of his cock. And with his underwear still caught around his thighs, he couldn't widen his legs any more to silently beg her to scrape those nails on his balls.

"Kate."

Her name emerged as a groan, making her grin widen.

"Don't worry, Tyler. I won't leave you high and dry."

"Then suck me."

"Ah, ah, ah. Let's not get ahead of ourselves."

She did lean forward though and blew a cool stream of air over the head of his cock. He bit back another groan and nearly ripped the cushions to pieces.

With her nails and her breath, she whipped him into a frenzy without touching that vital organ. Fluid seeped from the tip, a drop that rolled down the shaft.

He closed his eyes—

And her lips closed around the head.

Christ, that mouth. He groaned, low and deep.

Heaven. Absolute heaven.

She sucked on the tip with delicate greed, one hand wrapping around the shaft, the other working its way between his legs to cup his balls.

As her fingernails scraped at that tender flesh, goose bumps rose all over his body and even more blood rushed to his cock.

She focused on the head for long minutes, licking and sucking, until finally she couldn't seem to hold back and took him all the way to the back of her throat.

His hips came off the cushions, seeking more depth. He couldn't help himself. She didn't seem to mind.

Her rhythm picked up now, her head bobbing faster and faster until he thought she'd make him come in her mouth.

At the very last second, she pulled off, nearly gasping for air.

With passion-glazed eyes, she scrambled to her feet before crawling onto the couch, one thigh on either side of his. Pulling a condom from God-knows-where, she covered him quickly, her hands trembling.

But there was no fumbling as she positioned his cock straight into the air and sank down on it in one, smooth motion.

She was so slick, he felt no resistance at all.

"Fuck, you're wet."

She leaned in to rest her forehead against his. "You do that to me, Tyler. Only you. Now *move.*"

Buried deep inside her, he almost didn't want to. He could come just from the tight grip of her pussy.

But she needed friction.

Gripping her hips, he lifted her up then let gravity take its course. She slid down with a moan, her fingers digging into the muscles of his shoulders. He let her stay there for several seconds, not wanting to rush.

But Kate obviously had other plans.

She rocked forward then rolled back, making his eyes roll back in his head. "Jesus, Kate. You do that again and I won't be responsible for not getting you off before I come."

She slid one hand into his hair and tugged. "Then you'd better learn a little self-control, because this time I'm in charge."

Her words felt like an erotic slap against his senses and his body responded with a surge of blood to his cock.

Clamping down on his instinctive urge to take over, he let his head fall back so he could look at her.

Her eyes were half open and glazed with lust though he knew she watched him. Her teeth clamped into her bottom lip and she did that rock-and-roll again and nearly made his eyes cross.

Forcing his eyes to remain open, he watched her work herself into a higher state of ecstasy with each movement.

And watching her sharpened his attention to a laser's precision. He noticed every breathless sigh each time his cock pressed against a particularly sensitive area inside her. Noticed how she'd hitch in a short breath when she sank down on him and took him deep. How her movement increased as her eyes closed.

She appeared lost in her own world, but her fingers kneaded his shoulder and his scalp, and when she leaned forward, she licked at his earlobe before nipping it.

"You feel so amazing inside me." Her words, whispered in his ear, felt like she'd wrapped a fist around his lungs and squeezed. His balls tightened and he couldn't hold back any longer.

On her next downward slide, he grabbed her hips and pulled her down. Hard.

She gasped, her eyes flying open to stare into his.

When he was sure he had her complete attention, he gripped her hips even tighter and slowly drew her upward. Not far enough that his cock slipped out, but to the point that she was stretched around the widest part of him.

Then he held her there while he started to thrust. It took some effort on his part but it was worth it. The position hit different angles inside her and one in particular made her gasp.

With his control beginning to unravel, he worked with a single-minded purpose—to make her come.

If he gave himself a raging case of blue balls until then, so be it.

Every gasp she made, every time she tried to wriggle out of his hold made him that much more determined.

The balance of power had shifted and she seemed to know it.

She didn't say a word as she held on while he pounded into her, both of them reaching for something they hadn't known they needed.

Something still just out of reach.

"Tyler, oh, my God. Just—"

He shifted her a half centimeter forward.

"Yes!" she cried out, her fingers biting painfully into his shoulder as she came.

He couldn't stop, continued to thrust until she practically melted around him.

When she finally released his shoulder and lay limp against his chest, he brought her down one more time, sank as deep as he could go, and came with a deep groan and a sense of pure satisfaction.

Ten

❦

Kate needed a shower but was too wiped out to move.

She knew if she asked the man who'd made her like this to clean her up, he'd be on his feet and have her in the bathroom in two seconds flat.

She wasn't sure she wanted to move just yet.

Lying here, she felt his cock continue to twitch deep inside and it brought a smile to her lips. Beneath her ear, she heard his heart thundering and his chest rose and fell like he'd just finished sprinting up twenty flights of steps.

That she'd been able to rouse him to this condition made her feel like a conquering heroine.

That is, if the heroine was too tired to do more than breathe afterward.

Which she was.

And sated. She felt completely and utterly satisfied.

She couldn't ever remember—

"Kate. Are you still awake?"

Was she? She had her doubts. Could this blissful state be considered sleeping?

"Mmm."

It was really all she could manage to say at the moment and perfectly expressed the way she felt.

After a few silent minutes, as his heart slowly reverted to a normal rhythm and she could breathe more easily, he shifted beneath her.

"Alright, sweetheart. Enough lying around already. Time for a shower."

Since that sounded good, she draped her arms around his neck and nuzzled her face into the curve of his neck. "Okay. But you have to carry me since my state of . . . whatever state this is, is all your fault."

He chuckled, a deep rasp of sound that, amazingly, made her pussy clench with desire.

She couldn't believe after that last orgasm that she could even think about having more sex right now.

This must be what obsessed means.

Lying against him, she thought about that as he maneuvered her into his arms with minimal effort then stood as if she didn't weigh more than a sack of potatoes.

She felt warm and boneless against him and she wondered if she'd seen a bathtub in his bathroom.

Then couldn't remember if she'd seen his bathroom at all.

She became sufficiently curious to lift her head from his chest when he stopped moving. Opening her eyes, she looked around. "Wow. I didn't realize how much of a hedonist you really are."

He paused before pulling back so he could see her expression. "What do you mean?"

"I mean this bathroom. It's amazing. You designed this too, didn't you?"

His lips twisted in a crooked smile. "What makes you think that?"

Where his bedroom was decorated in shades of light and dark blue, the bathroom was black and white. But it wasn't at all cold.

The walls appeared to be covered with black moiré silk and the black marble shower took up nearly a third of the floor space. A clear glass door hid nothing from view and she saw several shower-heads protruding from the walls and the ceiling.

A sunken tub that could hold a party of four occupied the other side of the room, and she nearly started to salivate over that.

"It's masculine and bold but understated enough not to be pretentious."

"Glad you like it."

"Oh, I do. That tub is amazing."

"Then I guess we'll have to christen it."

"You've never used it?"

He shook his head and something crossed his expression, some old pain. "I'm not really one to soak for hours on end."

Setting her on her feet next to the massive tub, he bent to twist the taps. Water immediately gushed forth and, seconds, later, steam heated her skin.

"I think it's finally time for this to come off."

He reached for her shirt as she stared up at him. His expression had sharpened again. It gave her a thrill deep inside to know he continued to find her sexy, even after he'd screwed her senseless.

Standing still, she stared at his face as he watched his fingers undo the two buttons holding the shirt together. He took his time, his knuckles brushing against her tight nipples, teasing them into even harder peaks. When the shirt gaped open, he brushed it off her shoulders and watched it fall to the ground.

Then his gaze and his fingers returned to her bra. "Turn."

She obeyed, presenting him with her back. It only took a second for her bra to join the shirt.

Since he didn't say anything else, she stayed as she was and nearly jumped out of her skin when his fingers trailed down her spine. Her head dropped back, her hair brushing against her spine for a few seconds before he gathered it in one hand and twisted it around his fist.

She felt him bend close and rub his cheek against the top of her head as he tugged on her hair.

A second later, he released her, and she sucked in a sharp gasp of air at the almost overwhelming urge to grab him and make sure he was coming back to her.

This man was going to give her a heart attack.

Next, she felt his fingers at her waist, undoing the buttons on the skirt until that fell to the floor as well.

He paused before removing the thong, plucking at the string between her ass cheeks, sending sharp jolts of lightning zinging through her.

"I know I didn't say anything earlier"—he brushed his lips against her nape, causing her to tilt her head to give him more access—"but I really admire this design."

He tugged again, a little harder this time, and the seam at the front caught her clit at just the right angle. As she'd designed it to do.

She swore she *heard* him smile. "Such a simple design and yet so . . . ingenious."

Slipping his fingers between her legs, he stroked the bare lips of her sex, sensitive, slick, and puffy from their recent play.

"It's a shame I have to take them off, but I know I'll see them again."

He sounded awfully sure of himself and she wanted to have a

snappy retort, but her brain simply didn't have the necessary cell power left to come up with something.

Instead, she bit back a moan as he slid one finger inside her and stroked.

His fast withdrawal left her aching. She barely noticed as he stripped the thong down her legs.

"Let's get you in the tub. I'm sure you're ready for a good soak."

He swept her off her feet and the next second, she found herself submerged up to her shoulders in perfectly hot water.

She glared up at him, determined to tell him off for treating her like a rag doll, but the words died in her throat as she caught him in the act of pushing his boxer briefs off his hips.

My God, a naked Tyler would be enough to give the most devout nun second thoughts about her vows.

He left his boxers next to her clothes then climbed into the tub behind her.

Leaning into the curve, he drew her back until her head rested comfortably on his chest.

He didn't wrap his arms around her this time but rested them on the ledge of the tub. His chest rose and fell on a deep breath and she swore she felt every muscle in his body relax.

Encouraged to do the same, she let her mind drift, knowing he wouldn't allow anything to happen to her.

The silence wasn't uncomfortable but she felt Tyler shift and do something behind her just before soft music filled the air.

Jazz.

"Is that okay?" he asked. "I can turn something else on if you don't like it."

"No, that's fine, though I don't really know a lot about jazz. My parents listened to a lot of blues when I was a kid. And they were both heavily into Springsteen."

"My grandfather got me started on jazz. He was into big band, Sinatra and the Rat Pack, music like that. As I got older, I started listening to more Coltrane, Stanley Clarke, Wynton Marsalis."

"I like it. It's soothing."

"Are you going to fall asleep on me?"

"What do you expect? You wore me out." She punctuated that with a yawn that caught her off guard.

His husky laughter rumbled through her back. "So I shouldn't do this."

He shifted again and pressed his stiffening erection between the cheeks of her ass.

She moaned, because, yes, she did want him to do that. But she wasn't going to be able to keep her eyes open much longer.

"So not fair. But I'm warning you. I may fall asleep in the middle. Just saying."

"Then I guess I should get you back to bed. Just to sleep, of course."

"You don't have to be too hasty." She paused. "So what prompted your visit tonight, Tyler? Not that I don't appreciate it, but I was a little surprised to find you there. After you didn't call all week."

If she was expecting an apology, she should've known better. "I wanted to see you."

"So you were horny."

He didn't answer right away. "Is that a problem?"

"No. Unless that's all you want from me. Then I'd prefer you to be honest."

"Do you only want a relationship based on sex?"

"I'm not sure. Do you?"

Another pause. "Can I answer that honestly and say I'm not sure what I'm looking for?"

She told herself that pang in her gut was relief. It had to be, because she couldn't allow herself to believe it was anything else.

She'd only recently broken off a long engagement. She wanted to change her life and that could include moving away from her home, possibly to New York City. If she was lucky, it would be New York.

She wasn't in the market for a relationship that sank emotional hooks into her.

And if she was lying to herself just a little . . . well, she could ignore that too.

She scooted back just a little, wriggled her ass just a tiny bit more and smiled when he hitched in a breath.

"Honesty works for me."

"Then, honestly, I want you again, Kate."

It was a wonder the water splashing over the side of the tub didn't flood the room.

*   *

"So this reception . . . How many people are going to be there?"

"About a hundred."

Watching Tyler expertly do his tie while she put in her earrings, she wondered if the reason she wasn't nervous about this event was because she couldn't think beyond the fact that Tyler in a suit scrambled her brain or that she wasn't going to know anyone so she'd probably be mostly invisible.

It was pretty much a toss-up.

"And Greg's looking for investors, so they're all going to be rich?"

"Pretty much, yes." Turning away from the mirror, he let his gaze roam over her. "You look amazing. I'll be careful not to rip that dress off of you later before I spread you out on a flat surface and fuck you."

She figured she should be used to the things Tyler said that made her wet between her thighs and so damn horny she couldn't think straight.

From the outside, Tyler looked as straitlaced as any nine-to-five businessman. But she knew now that façade hid a relentless sexual appetite that threatened to devour her whole.

But she was determined to enjoy it while she could. It brought out a side of her she hadn't realized she had. A slightly raunchy side that liked to give as good as she got.

Closing the few feet between them, she stopped with barely an inch to spare so she had to look up into his face and into those navy blue eyes. "Maybe I'll back you into a corner instead. Maybe I'll take you in my mouth and get you off before I allow you to put me on that table and make me come with your mouth."

As the words spilled from her, she felt a blush creeping into her cheeks. Combined with the flush of heat originating from between her legs and working its way through her entire body, she probably looked like she was running a high fever.

She didn't know if she'd be able to tell the difference right now.

A taut silence stretched between them, broken only when someone knocked at the apartment door. Even then, it took Tyler a few seconds to lift his hand to brush his fingers across her lips, making them tingle. Then he dropped his hand to brush across her nipples.

Kate silently congratulated herself for remembering to bring a bra that wouldn't show her nipples every time they got hard, which was all the time around Tyler.

"I guess we should be going." Tyler sighed. "Greg's already worked himself up over this. He doesn't need me to be late."

She couldn't imagine Greg getting nervous over anything. The man seemed perpetually relaxed. They'd had lunch with him around noon, after she and Tyler had finally rolled out of bed around eleven. He hadn't seemed any different than he had last night.

But when they joined Greg in the hall to take the elevator to the fifth floor, she noticed a few cracks in his composure. His smile wasn't as wide and he didn't laugh as much.

Tyler kept up most of the conversation, though Greg did contribute. Kate listened, not really up on the current Hollywood gossip. She did recognize several names that made her shake her head in bemusement a few times. The circles Greg ran in were those that magazines like *People* and *Entertainment Weekly* made a living covering.

"You look beautiful tonight, Kate."

Greg's serious tone caught her attention just as they arrived at the entrance to a room she'd never been in before.

Smiling up at him, she noticed how his gaze traveled from her head to her toes and back up again. His smile held an appreciation she'd not seen there before.

A quick glance at Tyler showed no jealousy. "Thank you. And you look amazing. These people won't know what hit them."

Greg bowed his head then looked at Tyler with a raised brow, though he didn't say anything. The men apparently knew each other well enough that they didn't need words to communicate.

Kate wasn't sure she wanted to know what they'd been thinking, especially if that look had anything to do with her.

As Greg pushed through the doors, she realized they weren't the first to arrive. A few couples mingled at the bar on one side of the beautifully decorated room.

Less than half the size of the ballroom, this room had a breathtaking view of the atrium garden.

She knew Tyler had personally designed the indoor garden, so when he excused himself to handle a question from one of the staff, she wandered over to the glass wall.

Though it was still technically winter outside, the atrium burst with color. She had no idea what most of the plants were, but they looked tropical.

"You'd never realize Tyler had such a flair for the dramatic, considering how conservative the man appears."

Startled, Kate looked up.

The man standing next to her had a slim build, fair hair, and a handsome face.

And a smile that made her think he had an ulterior motive for talking to her.

Before she could say anything, he stuck out his hand. "Mark Vasser. Nice to meet you."

She took his hand with a smile. If this was a friend of Tyler's, she didn't want to get off on the wrong foot. "Kate Song."

"Beautiful name. I don't believe we've met before. I'm certain I would have remembered. Where are you from, Kate?"

"Adamstown. And you?"

"Right here in Philadelphia. My family's company is considering investing in Greg's film. Do you know Greg?"

"Only casually. What business is your family in, Mr. Vasser?"

"His family enjoys eating up companies and spitting them out, doesn't it, Vasser?"

Behind her, she felt the solid heat of Tyler's body. Turning to look at him, she could tell he didn't like the man standing in front of her.

Not that Tyler showed any outright disdain. His expression was pleasant, though he wasn't smiling. But when he put his arm around her shoulder, she felt the stiffness in his body.

She took another, closer look at Mark. And knew there was something going on here that she had no idea about.

* *

Tyler couldn't believe the bastard had the balls to show up in his hotel.

But then Mark had always had enough bravado to get him through any situation. That had never bothered Tyler before. In fact, he'd admired the man for it.

But now, with Mark's father pressuring Tyler's father to sell the GoldenStar chain of hotels to him, it made him want to strangle the man.

Mark's smile held only a trace of snark as they shook hands, though he watched carefully as Tyler tucked Kate into his side. She fit as if she belonged there and he had a momentary caveman moment when her arm curved around his back.

Which Mark didn't miss, if Tyler read his grin correctly.

"Actually, our company gives options to corporations that have become bloated or have overextended themselves. We can buy the entire company or we can buy pieces."

They were corporate raiders, in Tyler's opinion. They came in and sold off bits and pieces of companies, no matter the cost to the individuals.

Which wasn't exactly true or fair.

Tyler didn't have a problem with Mark. The person he had an issue with was his own father. Mark just happened to be the nearest target at the moment.

"Well, that sounds like something that would go straight over my head." Kate laughed, giving his waist a squeeze as if she thought he needed comfort. What he needed was her.

"In that case," Mark said, "I'll change the subject. How long have you and Tyler been seeing each other?"

"We've known each other for a few months," Kate answered before he could think of what to say. He wasn't sure what she'd want him to reveal. Which is how he knew his brain was totally messed up. "We met at the New Year's Eve party."

"Lucky man. I was at that party. Too bad I didn't see you first."

"I wasn't exactly looking for a man that night. Tyler happened to be too interesting to ignore."

"Interesting, huh?" Mark's grin widened. "Now I really am fascinated. You'll have to tell me more about it after our meeting next week, Tyler."

He bit back what would have probably been a profane and anatomically impossible suggestion. "I doubt we'll have time then. I'll see you around, Vasser."

Mark nodded, his expression still cocky, but Tyler knew he should cut the guy some slack. It wasn't his fault Tyler's father was playing head games to get what he wanted.

With Kate tucked to his side, he made his way across the room to a quiet corner where he tried to stuff all those out-of-control emotions back into a deep hole. He didn't want to think about business now. He had Kate for the weekend and he didn't want anything to screw with that.

"Tyler, is everything okay?"

He didn't want to lie to her, but there were too many ears listening to anything he might say.

"I'm sorry, Kate."

"For what?"

"For Vasser dragging you into the middle of business."

Her eyes widened. "That was business?"

He gritted his teeth. "That was an ambush."

She paused. "Do you want to talk about it?"

"No." Grimacing, he shook his head. "Not now."

With a sigh, he raised a hand to run it along her hair hanging in a sleek sheet down her back. Just the feel of it against his skin managed to calm him.

Probably didn't want to think about that too closely.

"And I'm sorry again. Kate." He waited until she looked up at him, dark eyes solemn, then he leaned down to speak into her ear. "I can't get into it now. And tonight, I plan to devote to enjoying you. But I promise I'll explain. Later."

He felt her shiver, saw the way her gaze warmed when he talked about later.

And hoped like hell later came a lot sooner.

* *

"Would you like to come to the Salon with me for a little while? I need some time to unwind."

Two hours later, Tyler felt like a pull toy that'd had its string yanked a few too many times.

Vasser's presence at the reception had put him on edge.

Considering the events of the past week, he felt justified in feeling unsettled. But the only way he knew how to bring himself back into balance involved methods he wasn't sure Kate would be comfortable with.

But he was sure as hell going to ask.

With a slight smile and a nod, Kate agreed. They took the elevator in silence to the fourth floor.

He could tell she knew something was bothering him, but so far she hadn't pushed.

Growing up with his mom, never knowing what kind of mood she'd be in, had taught him to always expect the unexpected. He'd managed to hold it together most days, but there were some he couldn't. It hadn't been until he'd been older that he'd found a way to cope.

And a woman who allowed him to use her to cope.

Damn, that made him sound like a total asshole.

But Mia had understood, he thought as he opened the door to the Salon and ushered Kate inside. Mia had known about his innermost fears. The ones he'd been able to conquer with her help.

You mean with her submission.

"Would you like another drink?"

"I could do with some water." Kate's voice sounded a little rough, a little deeper than normal. "I don't think I've made as much small talk in the past year as I did tonight."

At the bar, he shot her a glance over his shoulder as he put ice in a glass then poured water into it. "I have to say, I think you might have turned a few people into investors who might not have been. You're extremely compelling."

"When I believe in something, I have no problem promoting it. And Greg's idea for the documentary is impressive. I really like the way he wants to use the proceeds to fund the foundation to get more arts education into schools. It's something that's sorely lacking."

He should've known she'd find Greg's proposal worthwhile. And he would have if he didn't have all this other shit clogging his brain.

Christ, how self-absorbed was he?

Since he'd already had enough alcohol, he got a 7UP for himself and then returned to Kate, sitting by the fireplace on the love seat. Since the fireplace burned actual wood, he squatted down to light a match to the kindling and paper already set beneath the logs and watched until he was sure it'd caught.

When he looked up, he found her watching him, an intent expression on her face.

"Are you going to tell me what's going on with you? If you don't want me to know then say that. But don't lie and tell me nothing's wrong."

Her straightforward approach made his lips curve in a slight smile as he sat next to her on the love seat. He didn't reach for her and drag her onto his lap like he wanted. Instead, he turned so he could rest his back against the armrest and look directly at her.

"My father is considering selling his shares in the GoldenStar chain to Vasser's company. The deal would include the original hotel my grandfather built here in the city. Dad told me if Jared or

I don't take over his seat on the board, he has no reason to keep it. I thought he was beyond playing these games."

And there was the fury he couldn't keep contained. It rose up like bile, threatening to choke him.

"Maybe he wants to retire." Kate's eyes had narrowed, watching him closely. "I've never heard you mention any cousins or aunts or uncles. Isn't there anyone else to take over?"

"No. My parents were only children. No cousins, no aunts, no uncles."

"So you and Jared are his only heirs?"

When she put it like that, he saw how it looked from her side. That Glen Golden wasn't really manipulating his sons into doing what he wanted. That this could be the only logical solution to a problem that didn't have an easy answer.

But his father was only in his midfifties. He still had at least ten years to go before he even thought about retirement.

But Mom's health hasn't been great lately, has it?

"Yeah, we are," he answered. "And my mom's had some complications with her medication recently."

Or was there something else going on that neither of his parents wanted to tell them? Either way, Glen Golden was playing an angle. He had to be. There's no way he would have ever sold the chain out of the family.

"Is her condition life-threatening?"

Kate's quiet question had his spine straightening, but he didn't hear avarice in her voice. Many women in Philadelphia society would love to get their greedy nails into whatever gossip they could uncover and spread through their circles. Some women prided themselves on how much pain they could cause.

Kate's tone held genuine compassion.

"It depends on the day." He took a deep breath and allowed her

into one of his deepest-held secrets. "She's bipolar. Has been as long
as I can remember. Growing up, it'd get so bad, she'd be confined
to her bedroom for weeks. Then she'd go months without an epi-
sode. And then she'd break again and be out of touch for a month."

"I'm sorry." Two simple words, but they eased something inside
him. "But she's doing well now?"

"As far as I know. Which is why this move of my dad's seems
like a ploy. He's always wanted me to take over the chairmanship.
Hell, I was groomed for it for years. And then Jared came up with
the idea for Haven and we knew this is what we wanted to do."

"But you don't want to lose your grandfather's legacy, do you?"

"Granddad left Jared and I enough money to build this place.
We own the majority of the stock, although we do have a few investors. But no one can take it away from us. It's ours. Still . . ."

He'd never considered that his dad would sell the chain. It'd
never even occurred to him.

"You don't want to see the chain get sold off, but you have your
life, your own properties."

"The spa is a huge undertaking. I don't even think Jared knows
how big. In this economy, we could lose every cent we stick into it."

"Or it could be a huge success as people begin to spend again.
You and Jared made a success of this hotel in one of the worst economic climates. I have no doubt you can do the same with the spa."

His lips curved in an unexpected smile. He never really thought
of Kate as having an optimistic streak. Her snarky attitude had led
him to believe she was a pessimist.

And yet, here she was, trying to lift his spirits.

And making his cock stiff.

"Do you want to be chairman of the board, Tyler?"

He thought about his answer for several seconds, not really sure
he wanted to talk business right now. He wanted to strip her naked,

bend her over the double-sided, black leather horse in the far corner of the room, and fuck her until he couldn't think straight.

But that wasn't all he wanted to do with her.

He wanted to talk to her, have her listen to what he said, and hear her opinions. He and Jed had way too much history with their father to see this situation clearly. And as much as he appreciated Greg's advice, his opinion would be colored by his knowledge of the situation.

The horse wasn't going anywhere and they still had hours before daylight.

"It was all I wanted as a teenager. It was why I got straight As in high school and college so I could go to Wharton."

Her smile had a mischievous curve to it. "Wow, I knew you were smart but . . ." She shook her head. "All you need is a cape and a pair of black-rimmed glasses to complete the image. And little red tights."

He snorted in amusement. "I'm no one's image of Superman."

"Don't sell yourself short, Clark. You know, I do have some red and blue silk at my apartment. I could whip you up a nice little costume—"

His laughter cut her short, the sound bouncing off the walls. "Thanks, but I don't think you'd ever be able to look at me without laughing after you see me in tights."

Her eyebrows curved and there was that smart-ass grin again. "Oh, I don't know about that. Those tights don't leave much to the imagination and, trust me, you'd fill them out. Nicely."

Damn, she managed to crank his lust even higher. His cock felt as stiff as a bat and his balls ached for release. But he wasn't finished with their conversation yet. And he refused to be rushed.

It's what made him a damn good businessman. Patience really was a virtue. In business and pleasure.

"I don't think there are many board chairmen who wear red tights under their suits."

"But I think you'd fit right in on that board, Tyler. I guess what it comes down to is this—do you really want the GoldenStar to go to someone who isn't family? Could you live with yourself? And if you can't, can you find a way to do it all?"

That was the million-dollar question, wasn't it?

Could he manage Haven and the spa and a multinational company comprising ten hotels?

Yes, he had Jared, and together they made a great team.

But the board had six other members, men his father had butted heads with over the years. The chairman position came with more than its fair share of headaches.

And did he really want to add more responsibilities to his plate right now, when his attention was fractured enough as it was? A lot of that due to the woman sitting close enough that he could reach out and touch her.

"Right now, I only want to do you."

Color rushed into her cheeks but she didn't drop his gaze. "And how do you want to do me?"

He watched her color deepen as he stared at her. "There's a black leather bench in the corner. I don't know if you've noticed it before. You might not have. Jared had it specially made to fit in with the rest of the room. If you don't know what you're looking at, you wouldn't realize what it's used for."

"And what is it used for?"

"Are you willing to let me show you?"

She didn't answer right away. Instead, she continued to stare at him, as if searching for answers. Before, when he'd asked her to trust him, she'd almost immediately agreed.

"I'm not sure I should be," she finally said. "Willing, that is. It's taken me years to feel like I have control of my life. Growing up, my dad had an image of me that I never quite fit into and it was . . . stressful trying to be that person he expected me to be."

Tyler could tell "stressful" didn't exactly do the situation justice. He wanted to push her for more, dig out her secrets, but managed to hold his tongue as she continued.

"And when you ask me to give up so much of my control to you, my brain automatically says, 'No.' But there's part of me that wants to."

"We're consenting adults," he said. "There's nothing wrong with sex between consenting adults."

Her smile had a wicked edge to it. "I know that, Tyler. But . . ." She stopped and her smile faded into a slight scowl.

"But?" he prompted.

"There's still that little piece of me that keeps saying, 'This is bad. You shouldn't want this.' That we don't really know each other that well yet. But there's a bigger piece egging me on."

He liked the sound of that. "So where does that leave us?"

Finally, she sighed. "I want you to relax enough around me to stop asking me if I'm willing. I want you to be comfortable with me."

Frowning, he shook his head. "Why do you think I'm not comfortable around you?"

"Because you stop and ask my permission every time you want me to try something new. I want you to stop treating me like I'm going to freak out every time you want to introduce me to something new."

He opened his mouth to say . . . something. "So if I tell you to take your clothes off and kneel on that bench, you'll do it?"

She gave him a considering look before turning toward the bench.

With a flick of her head, she tossed her hair over her shoulder.

He loved watching the fall of her hair down her back. It turned him on in ways he'd never known were possible.

He wanted to see it brushing against her naked back, feel it wrapped around his hands as he thrust into her from behind.

Which was exactly what he had planned for tonight.

Kate had reached the bench and stood beside it with her head cocked to the side.

As if she was dissecting it.

He was about to ask her if he could show her what they could do with the bench but stopped before he opened his mouth.

She wanted to know how he truly responded in this situation?

Fine. Let the games begin.

He walked over to her, stopped next to her. He watched her gaze trace the padded hump separating the benches, the three silver loops embedded on each side of the hump and the loops on each side of the base of the four legs.

"So many possibilities." He kept his tone deliberately level. "So many different positions."

"Did you design this?" She didn't turn to look at him, kept her gaze on the bench.

"I sketched out a basic design. Jared found a furniture maker to create it."

"It's simple. Elegant. Ingenious."

"And versatile."

She nodded, and he heard her take in a deep breath.

"Take off your dress and lay it over the chair. Leave your bra and panties."

Eleven

Tyler's demand poured over Kate like heat in a sauna, filling her with lust . . . and tearing through her doubts.

God, she loved the hard command in his voice. She'd only caught a hint of it before, the night he'd tied her up in her room. Now, she was pretty sure she was hearing the true nature of the man.

It made her burn.

And brought up a host of other feelings she didn't want intruding right now. Turning off that train of thought was harder than she'd expected. She knew he wouldn't hurt her, but she also knew this went beyond play for him.

Could she handle giving over that much control to him?

She was damn sure going to try.

Turning to face Tyler, she looked up into his eyes and reached for the side zipper on her dress. He held her gaze as she loosened the dress enough to shimmy it off her shoulders and let it drop to the floor.

Stepping out of it, she bent to pick it up, remembering, barely, that he wanted her to put it on the chair. When she turned back from laying out her dress, she lifted her right foot to remove her shoe.

"Leave those on too."

The heels weren't her highest but they were black patent leather and went well with the sheer stockings held up by a cream lace garter belt.

She watched his expression as his gaze dropped, noting the tic in his jaw as he took in the strapless bra that matched the garter belt and the panties.

Her nipples pushed against the lace of the bra in stiff points and her panties were already soaked through.

"Take off the panties and give them to me."

His voice sent pulses of electricity through her body. Anticipation made all the oxygen in the room disappear, and she took a deep breath because she wasn't sure she'd remembered to breathe recently.

Pushing the panties off her thighs, her hair fell over her shoulders, brushing against her breasts, like whispers of silk. When she'd pulled them off, she held them out to him by the side string.

He didn't take them. "Put them in my pants pocket."

She had to take a step closer to reach him. Her gaze dropped to follow her hand and snagged on the thick ridge behind his zipper. Totally ruined the perfect cut of his slacks.

And made her want to drop to her knees and release him so she could suck on him.

"Kate, put it in my pocket then kneel on the bench facing away from me."

A smart-ass comment leaped to the tip of her tongue but she found the strength to hold it back. Tonight, she'd give him what he wanted.

She did as he asked, using one hand to hold open the pocket and the other to slip the silk inside. She made sure she brushed against his erection, smiling when it jerked in response. Loving the way his jaw tightened and his eyes narrowed.

Testing Tyler's control was fast becoming her favorite pastime.

She took her time withdrawing her hand before staring back up at him.

Her pussy felt slick and puffy and he hadn't touched her yet.

Soon.

Finally, she turned toward the bench again.

And had the split-second urge to shake her head at the image she was about to present to him.

Submission.

Who would have thought she'd get off on this? But she was. Totally.

First one knee and then the other.

Bracing her hands on the top of the hump, she leaned forward. The leather was cool to the touch at first but she knew it would warm quickly.

Still, it was a shock, and her skin erupted in goose bumps as her stomach came into contact with it.

"Lean over it, Kate. And spread your legs a little. I'm going to cuff your ankles. Tight enough that you won't be able to move your legs." He paused and she knew he was about to ask for her permission. Luckily, he didn't. If he had, she wasn't sure she would have said yes.

She knew she could say no to anything, but she was determined to see this through. She *wanted* to see this through.

With the position of the bench . . . horse, he'd called it a horse—she couldn't see what he was doing. She heard him moving around behind her, opening drawers and closing them. The clink of chain.

Leaning on the horse, she tried to breathe normally, but that was an impossibility. She was so turned on, she wanted to squeeze her thighs together to relieve some of the ache.

When his fingers circled her ankle, she started, biting back a moan at the conflicting rush of emotions.

"Easy, sweetheart. I'm not going to hurt you. And if I do, you can bet you're going to like it."

Jesus, she might just have a heart attack before he fucked her.

Which now sounded like such a crude word for what they were engaged in. For her, it went beyond just the act.

And if she were being truthful, it had from the beginning.

Closing her eyes, she just breathed.

And simply enjoyed the feel of his fingers on her skin. He stroked his fingertips up her calf before returning to her ankle. Hooking one fur-lined cuff to her left ankle, he pulled her legs farther apart so he could bind the other.

She felt more of a sense of exposure now than she had tied to her bed. Probably because this wasn't his bedroom. And the fact that anyone could walk in at any moment heightened the sense that this was . . . wrong?

No, not wrong.

Bad. But in a good way.

She nearly choked on a gasp when he smacked her ass. Not hard. At least, not hard enough to hurt. Just enough to send bolts of blinding sensation straight to her pussy, followed by a heated caress.

"Do I need to bind your hands or will you be able to control yourself and hold on to the horse?"

Truthfully? She wasn't sure.

"Bind my hands."

His hand stilled on her ass and she held her breath, waiting for another smack.

Then she felt his breath against her ear. "Good choice. I think you'll like it. But if you want out at any time, you only need to ask, Kate. And this is the only time I'll say that."

She nodded, not sure she could form coherent sentences.

"Put your hands out in front of you."

She did as he said, heart pounding a mile a minute. She felt the insane urge to laugh at the situation, but she was so turned on, she almost felt like she was going to cry.

Get a grip.

She didn't want Tyler to think she couldn't handle this.

And really, what was there to handle? He'd told her she could call it quits at any time and he'd release her.

She didn't want to be released.

Drawing in a shuddering breath, she looked up as Tyler appeared in front of her. He held a length of thin silver chain with a large carabiner on one end and two black leather cuffs on the other.

With an ease that only came from long practice—and didn't that just make her totally wet—he wrapped the cuffs around her wrists then connected the carabiner to a loop below the opposite side of the bench.

The chain allowed for a bare minimum of movement as she tugged at it experimentally.

He ran his fingers along her jaw in a gentle caress before he disappeared behind her again.

Staring straight ahead, her gaze fixed on the large, glass-front cabinet on the far side of the room.

She couldn't help but wonder if he was going to use any of the toys she'd seen in there.

Then again, the man didn't need any help.

"Oh, my God."

Her entire body tensed as he put his mouth on her pussy without any warning.

Using his lips and tongue to caress her sensitive flesh, he held her in place with his hands on her hips. It grounded her as his tongue flicked against her clit, circling the nub with lazy precision. Each wet flick drove her insane until he drew back to swipe along her already slick lips.

He lapped at her, slow and steady, taking his time, when all she wanted was for him to let loose, to make her writhe.

Instead he built her up with a slow, steady pace that made her fizzy and left her shaken. Pressure built in her womb, tightening like a slow-winding winch.

His tongue rasped against her labia, against her clit, his hands sliding down to clench her thighs, kneading her tight muscles.

If only he'd—

Yes.

She groaned, unable to form words as he forced his stiffened tongue into her slit and fucked her with it.

It was enough to relieve some of the ache. To make her sheath grasp at it, try to draw him in farther.

He refused to cooperate, moving at his own steady pace and working her into a state of bliss.

She had no idea how long she hung on the sharp edge of desire, but when he finally pushed her over with a gentle bite on her clit, she cried out his name as she came so hard, she thought she might have pulled the cuffs free.

As her body shook with her climax, she drifted in heat and lethargy.

Until she felt him moving behind her.

Though she didn't think she'd be able to be aroused again so quickly, her libido stirred when she heard the sound of his zipper releasing.

Her teeth bit into her bottom lip as that sound echoed in the quiet room. Gulping in breaths of air, she waited to feel his thick shaft plunge between her lips and sink deep into her body.

Instead, she felt his hand, shockingly cool, cup her between her legs.

"You are so wet." His voice caressed her in concert with his hand. "I can't wait to slide inside you and fuck you until I can't hold on any longer."

Leaning against her, she felt the brush of his silk shirt against her back and the fine wool of his pants against her thighs.

She loved that he hadn't wanted to take the time to remove his clothes, that he couldn't wait that long to have her.

It felt decadent. Like they were stealing this moment out of time.

And Jesus, did it make her hot.

She pressed back, rubbing her ass against the soft material covering his thighs, but he grabbed her hips and held her still.

"You move at my discretion, Kate. And right now I want you to stay still."

But she didn't want to stay still. She wanted to move, to entice him into screwing her like she needed. But she nodded and forced herself to freeze.

At least, as much as she could as he continued to stroke her.

Sliding his fingers between her folds, he rubbed the hardened knot of her clit. He played with her, working her back into a state of heightened arousal that pushed her close to the edge of orgasm. Pushed her to the point that she needed to come, needed the release for her sanity.

In the next second, he had his fingers shoved inside her, stroking the walls of her channel, hitting tantalizing new places of sensation that made her want to writhe.

She couldn't keep still for long. And when she clenched around his fingers, he withdrew them.

And smacked her ass. The burn made her moan.

"I see you can't listen to orders."

He'd leaned in close, his lips almost at her ear. She felt surrounded by him and wanted to rub all over him like a cat. The fact that she couldn't made her want it all the more.

"Do you want me to leave you high and dry while I jerk off in front of you?" he continued. "You won't like that, trust me. But you're so primed right now, you might be able to come just from watching me."

"No. No, I'll stay still. Just fuck me."

She barely recognized her voice, much less the words coming out of her mouth. She never spoke like this to a man, had never wanted to.

Now, it seemed like the most natural thing in the world.

"Whatever you want, Kate."

His hands landed on her hips and she pulled up against the chains binding her wrists as his cock slipped between her legs.

She wanted to sob with relief as the head rubbed against her clit, providing more stimulation. But not enough.

Trembling with the need to move, she bit down on her bottom lip, a moan gathering in her chest.

"So beautiful. Such pale skin."

He ran one hand up her naked back until he curved his fingers around her shoulder and yanked her back. Her moan broke free as her ass flattened against his thighs and his cock scraped along her clit.

"Dark hair."

With his other hand, he gathered her hair together then let it slide through his fingers.

"Gorgeous ass."

His hand smoothed over one cheek.

"One of these days I want that ass. Will you let me, Kate?"

"Yes."

God, yes, though she'd never done it before. She wanted to. Wanted him to be her first.

"Not tonight. I don't think I could be gentle enough tonight. Because I am so fucking hot for you."

He drew back and, in a split second, he'd thrust forward, split her open, and sank so deep, she swore he couldn't go any farther.

They both stilled then, Kate trying to adjust to the overwhelming sensation of being filled and Tyler . . .

She assumed from his groan that he was soaking in the tight fit. *So tight.*

She was so aroused, her sheath so sensitive, he felt ten times thicker than normal. If he retreated, she thought he'd never get back in.

When he began to withdraw, the pleasure was so intense, she would have promised him anything just to continue.

Turns out she didn't need to.

He moved, slow at first. Each thrust forward found new points of pleasure. Each retreat made her long for the moment he returned.

His rhythm increased by tiny increments, almost too tiny to realize at first. It'd been almost like torture, denying her what she needed, but it built until she could barely breathe.

With her hands cuffed together, she couldn't move her arms. She realized she'd fallen forward over the hump and that was all that was holding her upright. She didn't have the strength to lift her chest away from the bench.

She felt like she was hanging over a great cavern. She only needed the slightest push to send her . . .

Tyler paused behind her, his cock swelling even more, and she came.

She fell into that cavern and the sensation of falling overwhelmed her. Overloaded her senses and everything went dark as the sharp contractions of her pussy milked his cock. Sucked him deeper and drew him over with her.

She heard him groan out her name, felt his hands tighten at her shoulder and hip just before she felt the jerk of his cock inside her as he shoved even farther inside and held.

She'd never felt this way in her life before.

And she was pretty sure she never would again.

* *

As Tyler came down from the best damn orgasm he'd ever had, he realized he still had a pretty good grip on Kate.

His cock had finally stopped pulsing inside her but he found it hard to release her.

At least he could loosen his grip a little before he left bruises.

Still breathing like a freight train, he looked at her shoulder and winced.

Too late. He saw the barest hint of black smudges.

Damn it.

He pulled out, breath hissing between his teeth as her sheath clenched around his cock, almost as if she refused to release him.

He liked the thought of that.

"Kate, are you okay?"

She made a sound somewhere between a sigh and a moan as he got rid of the condom and tucked himself back in his pants.

Reaching for her ankles, he released the restraints, rubbing at the slight red marks before moving around the horse to release her wrists. As he did, he studied her face. Her eyes were closed but her lips curved in a satisfied smile.

Which made him smile.

"Time for bed for you."

"I think I could sleep until tomorrow night." She opened her eyes and looked up at him. "Undisturbed."

With a yawn, she twisted around to sit on the bench, flexing her fingers and twisting her neck, as if she were stiff. Then she held out her hand. "Can I have my thong back now?"

No, he didn't want to give it back, but he dug it out of his pocket and handed it over. Leaning back, she slipped it up her legs then stood.

He should take it back so he could watch her do that again. He could've watched her all night.

But when he looked into her eyes, he saw how tired she was.

And he had to admit, he was too.

"Let me get you a robe."

After he had her bundled into a thick white hotel robe, he lifted her into his arms and carried her back to his apartment.

She didn't give him a hassle as he stripped her, laid her in his bed, then pulled the covers over her.

After he'd shed his own clothes and climbed in next to her, he put his arm around her, deeply satisfied when she pressed herself against his side, sighed, and almost immediately dropped off to sleep.

He felt like a caveman, wanting to beat his chest at his own prowess.

But the thought was tempered by the fact that tomorrow she'd go back to her apartment and he'd have to face all the crap going on here.

Without her.

It took him a while to drift off after that.

Twelve

❧

"No. I'm not going to be able to work those extra shifts, Joe. I told you, I've got some things going on that need to be taken care of."

Joe Parisi had that look on his face Monday morning. The one that usually made Kate grit her teeth until she caved in to what he wanted.

But not this time. Damn it, she wasn't an indentured servant and she had her own life.

She had a meeting with a client for another wedding dress on Wednesday. She also needed to get moving on a couple of orders from one of the burlesque-wear companies that contracted her to create some of their custom pieces.

"Katie, I'm in a bind here. I need you. And what's so important that you can't help me for a few extra hours?"

"It's called a life, Joe. You know what that means, right? A personal life."

He waved his hands as if waving away her words. "I know what a personal life is, *bambina*. I've been telling you to get one for ages. But not now when I'm swamped."

"Then you need to get some more help like I've been begging you to do for the past five months since Mona left."

The part-time seamstress had left after the birth of her second child. Joe had sent her off with a gift basket and a smile.

"Why do I need more help? I have you."

And that was the problem, wasn't it? She'd lead him to believe she was staying.

When that was now the farthest thing from her mind.

But he had to know, didn't he?

They fought like cats and dogs most of the time and, besides her father, he was the only person who could piss her off in under five seconds flat.

Their Italian tempers clashed, and he was a control-freak taskmaster who demanded her absolute best work every single second of every work day.

She also loved the guy like a second father.

But this was her life they were talking about. The life she wanted to build.

And she wasn't giving that up. Not for anyone.

"But you're not always going to have me. You know that, right?"

She swore if he said something stupid, she'd walk out the door and never look back. Holding her breath, she waited, watching his expression.

His eyes narrowed and he crossed his arms over his barrel chest. Joe only stood about five eight but he weighed at least one ninety. If they were casting for another *Godfather* movie, he'd fit right in with his bald head and Mediterranean features.

And his penchant for using bastardized Italian swear words when he was pissed off.

The only way you could tell he was really angry was when his ears went beet red. Then you learned to stay out of his way.

But his ears weren't red.

"So you're finally going to do something with that fancy college education your father paid so much money for?"

That was so not the response she'd been expecting that her mouth actually dropped open, though she couldn't think of one appropriate response.

Finally, she realized exactly what she needed to say. "Yes, I am."

Joe's eyes narrowed. "Oh yeah? So how're you gonna make a living? You got another job I don't know about?"

The doubt in his voice stiffened her backbone. "I've got several. You know I've been doing contract work for a couple years and it's starting to pick up. And I may be investing in a small boutique."

"Now, Katie, you know how the economy is. It's the worst time to be starting a new business. It's a huge risk—"

"But if I don't take any risks, I'm never going to get anywhere. I love to sew, but this is not what I envisioned myself doing for the rest of my life."

His eyebrows rose. "So you're too good for tailoring?"

Ooh, he made her furious, but she reeled it back, struggling for calm. "You know that's not what I mean. Stop trying to put words in my mouth."

He held his hands out in surrender. "I'm not. It's just that I don't want to see you fail. And it's a tough time to be out in the world on your own. You need to make sure the people you're going into business with have your back. Katie." He was the only person beside her parents that ever used that nickname and it made her a little misty-eyed. "You know I only want the best for you. Make sure you know what you're getting into before you make such a huge leap."

She was still thinking about his last words when she sat down to eat dinner with Jared and Annabelle that night.

"Is everything okay?" Annabelle asked. "You're kinda not all here, if you know what I mean."

She sighed, knowing exactly what Annabelle meant. "I'm fine. Just thinking about a conversation I had with Joe today."

"That's your boss, right?" Jared leaned back in his chair at Annabelle's dining room table, one arm lying across the back of her chair, his fingers playing with her hair.

They both looked so . . . content, Kate thought. They still had that new relationship glow, so confident in each other.

And here she'd brought all of her problems to dinner.

Not to mention the fact that every time she looked at Jared, she wanted to interrogate him about Tyler.

He'd driven her home Sunday afternoon but hadn't been able to stay. And she was supposed to have had dinner with her father, but he'd canceled at the last minute. Work, he'd said. She hadn't argued because she hadn't really wanted to sit across from him after the weekend she'd had with Tyler.

Her dad probably would've been able to tell what she'd been doing just by the look on her face. Then he would've given her the "I hope you're being careful" speech.

Thank God she hadn't had to listen to that. She might've actually broken down and told her dad exactly what she'd done all weekend with Tyler.

Who hadn't called since he'd left. He had so many responsibilities at Haven, and now this business with the hotel board of directors. She didn't want to dump her problems on him, as well.

But she was dying to talk to him.

Which is why she'd jumped at the chance to join Annabelle and Jared for dinner tonight when Annabelle had called earlier.

"Yeah, Joe's my boss. He's a pain in the ass most of the time but he's a decent guy. He treats me great, it's just . . ."

She sighed.

"Just what?" Jared asked.

"He's too uptight, too set in his ways. He doesn't understand that I have to take chances if I'm ever going to get anywhere with my career. I don't want to be a tailor all my life. I want to design. He thinks I'm crazy."

"He's also almost seventy years old." Annabelle set a huge bowl of pasta on the table. Luckily, they'd already opened the wine. "And when he started his business, he charged two dollars to hem a pair of pants and had to walk five miles uphill both ways in the snow to school."

When Jared aimed a smile at Annabelle, Kate felt like she was intruding. But oh my God, could the man smile.

No, it didn't do the same things to her that Tyler's much rarer smile did, but still. It would take a better woman than she was not to notice and appreciate it.

"You know that smile should come with a warning label, right? I mean, really, dude, dial it back. You've already sealed the deal."

If anything, his smile widened when he swung his attention back to her. "Nice to know I haven't lost my edge."

Then he winked and Kate shook her head at him, just before she tossed the wine cork at him.

"You're a menace."

"Hey, that's my boyfriend you're denigrating." Annabelle sank into her seat and started to eat the pasta Jared had dished onto her plate.

They already acted like a cute little old married couple, which should have made Kate want to say inappropriate things about how they'd become worse than Rita and Sam Shumacher.

The sixty-something husband and wife lived up the street above Rita's hair salon, and they still held hands and talked about how good their sex life was to anyone who would listen. Or didn't move fast enough.

But she couldn't, because she thought Rita and Sam were adorable. And because she wanted the same for herself.

"Sorry, but you know he is, Annabelle. I have no idea how you and Tyler are at all related, Jared."

"He inherited the stick up his ass from our dad. Unfortunately, the control issues . . ." He shared a look with Annabelle. "They come from our mom."

Kate grimaced. "I'm sorry. I know your mom's bipolar. Tyler told me. That had to be tough growing up."

"It was. Tyler dealt with it by internalizing everything and making sure he controlled as much of his life as possible. It's part of the reason we built Haven rather than going to work for our dad. We knew we wouldn't be able to have our own lives."

And now their dad was trying to force Tyler to take over the chairmanship of the board. And she'd been bitching because her boss was mean to her today.

With a sigh, she started twirling pasta around her fork. "Sorry for dumping this on you guys."

Annabelle reached over and smacked her arm. "Stop that. It's not like you didn't listen to me bitch before. That's what friends are for."

"And other things."

Jared's deliberately suggestive comment left both of them in stitches and, for the rest of dinner, she made a deliberate effort to pull herself out of her funk.

By the time she wandered back to her apartment, not long after they'd polished off a third bottle of wine, Kate lay in her bed, nearly asleep when her phone rang.

She thought about not answering it, but then it could be Tyler. Maybe he was sitting in her parking lot again.

That got her moving.

"Hello."

"Kate."

Yes. "Tyler. I'm so happy to hear your voice."

"Is everything okay?"

"Everything's fine."

She thought she heard him chuckle. "Yeah, it sure sounds that way. What were you drinking?"

"A few bottl—glasses of wine. What makes you think I was drinking?"

She definitely heard him laughing now. "No reason. Just a lucky guess. How was work?"

"Sucked. Are you in my parking lot again?"

"No, unfortunately I'm not. I had a sucky day here too."

"When will I see you again?" The words slipped out before she could check them. She didn't want to be the clingy type but alcohol loosened her tongue. And her inhibitions. "I wish you were naked and spread out on my bed so I could do whatever I wanted to you."

He paused before asking, "And what would you do?"

His voice had dropped to a low growl that made her go wet. As payback, she told him.

"I'd sit on your thighs and put my hands on your chest so you couldn't move. Then I'd bend down and bite your nipples. Not too hard. Just enough to let you know I was using my teeth. Then I'd lick them so they wouldn't hurt at all."

"So far, so good."

Did he sound a little out of breath? She smiled. "Oh, I've got lots more planned. Next, I'd pet you for a while because you have such a great chest. Firm and hard and—wait, they mean the same things. Never mind."

"No, please continue. You can call my chest any version of *hard* you want."

"Hey, are you making fun of me?"

She definitely heard amusement in his voice.

"Not at all. I'm enjoying you talking about my hard chest. Tell me more."

"I'm not sure you totally appreciate the effort I'm putting into this."

"Honey, if I were there, I'd show you how much I appreciate it."

She smiled, loving this side of him. Tyler had serious down to an art but his dry humor had a way of sneaking out when you weren't expecting it.

"Oh, yeah?" she said. "Tell me?"

"I'd kind of like you to finish what you were saying."

"About how I was stroking your chest?"

"Will you be stroking anything else?"

"Do you want me to?"

"I want you to stroke anything your heart desires, Kate."

"Then after your chest, I let my hands stroke down your stomach until I reach the waistband of your jeans. I'd open the button at the top and pull down the zipper, carefully because your dick's so hard, it's pushing against it."

She swore she heard him swallow over the phone. "Because I want you to suck me."

Yes, she wanted that too. "I push you until you're lying on your back. I have your pants and your underwear around your thighs and your cock is right at my mouth."

"Jesus, Kate—"

"I open my mouth and take in the tip, let my tongue swirl around it." She swore she heard him groan, and it made her even bolder. "I put my hand between your thighs and cup your balls. They're so tight and hot and I know you like me to play with them. Your cock's swelling inside my mouth so I take you deeper. You taste so good."

Her eyes had closed and, in her mind, she saw exactly what she was doing to him. One hand slipped between her own legs to finger her clit, rubbing, trying to ease the ache in her gut.

"I let my mouth slide down your cock until I can't take any more. My nose rubs against your stomach and I swallow—"

His groan made her breath catch until she couldn't continue.

"Kate, are you playing with yourself? Get yourself off. I want to hear you moan when you come."

"Then you have to—"

"I've got my hand wrapped around my cock. I'm ready to blow but I want you to come too. Rub your clit. Imagine it's my tongue and I'm licking you hard and fast, like you like it."

"Oh, my God. Tyler!"

Her body convulsed as she found the perfect rhythm, just as she heard Tyler groan on the other end of the phone.

For at least the next minute, all she did was lay there and listen to him breathe.

"I wish I was there to see you right now."

His rough tone sent another shock through her body, and her sex tightened in aftershocks.

"Me too." She paused. "Will I see you this weekend?"

"I want that. Can you come down?"

If she worked eighteen hours a day for the next three days and switched her meeting—

No, she couldn't switch that meeting Saturday morning. She and the potential client had had trouble finding a time to meet and that had been the only time they could agree on.

"I should be able to come down Saturday afternoon, if that's okay?"

He paused. "Is there a reason you can't come Friday?"

"I have a meeting Saturday morning with a new dress client and I really need to get caught up on some projects I've been contracted for."

She realized she was holding her breath, waiting for him to say he'd come up Friday night.

"Then Saturday it is. I've got a shitload of meetings this week and I'm meeting with the GoldenStar board Friday afternoon. I have no idea how long that's going to take."

Well, there went Friday night. "So you decided to take the chairmanship?"

"Not yet, no. This is just a preliminary meeting. There are a few board members I'm not sure I can work with. I need to get a better read on them."

"Then I'll look forward to seeing you Saturday."

"Kate . . . are you sure that's okay?"

No, it was too long to wait. "I'm positive. Can't wait to see you then."

"Alright. Sleep well, Kate."

"Good night, Tyler."

* *

"Buddy, you need to get laid. Why the hell don't you just knock off for the night and drive up to see Kate? I don't think she'd be upset to see you. And you could use the downtime. Especially before that meeting tomorrow. You're already twice as uptight as you nor-mally are."

Tyler gave Greg the finger but didn't spare a look. He'd been pouring over GoldenStar financial reports dating back ten years for at least the past two hours. Maybe more. He couldn't remember when he'd picked up the packet, knowing he'd been avoiding it since it'd arrived Monday.

Knowing he couldn't avoid it any longer.

"Seriously, Tyler. Take a fucking break."

He sighed, reaching for the cup of lukewarm coffee he'd been nursing for half an hour. "I can't. There's something about the numbers that isn't adding up, but I can't tell if I'm just not reading them right or there's something I'm missing."

"You don't tend to miss too much." Greg shifted forward as he sat across from Tyler's desk. "What's the problem?"

With a disgusted exhale, Tyler shoved the file across the desk and sat back to scrub at his eyes. "The problem is I feel like I have to do this. I feel like it's what my grandfather wanted. And, God damn it, I want the damn thing."

Greg's eyes widened. "I think that's the first time I've heard you say that. Why the sudden change of heart?"

"It's not a change of heart. I've always wanted the chair. I just . . . I didn't think my dad was going to retire this soon and I don't like feeling forced into it. Jesus, I sound like Jed, don't I?"

Greg smiled. "No, you sound like a guy who's got a shitload on his plate at the moment. Haven, the spa, a new girl. Now this."

A new girl. It sounded so juvenile.

And yet, it was true.

Kate was on his mind all the time, whether he was working or not. He'd taken to carrying his grandmother's ring, the one Kate had found at the flea market. He liked having it in his pocket, the weight of it comforting somehow.

But every time he thought about the ring, he thought about Kate and everything else became secondary.

He wanted her here. Wanted her to be waiting for him in his bed when he finished whatever the hell was left on his to-do list.

"I don't have time for her right now." It sounded cold, and he felt like a bastard saying it out loud, but it was the unvarnished truth. "I should stop stringing her along."

This was the absolute worst time for him to fall for a woman.

A new relationship required time. It required commitment and a willingness to compromise. Neither of them had those luxuries at the moment.

What they had was lust. And that wasn't enough on which to base a lasting relationship.

"So that's what you're doing? Stringing her along?" Greg snorted. "I think that's one sorry-ass excuse. At least admit it. You're afraid."

Tyler barely managed to control his grimace. Greg would see it as a sign that he was right.

"I'm not afraid of anything except raising her expectations and then not being able to meet them."

"And I think you're going to use all the rest of this shit as an excuse to not get close to her."

"Why the hell would I do that? I like her. Jesus, Greg, I really like her. She's smart and driven and— Why the *fuck* are you smirking at me?"

Greg shook his head, not losing the smirk. "Because you're an idiot if you let her get away. You're right about everything you just said, but you didn't add that she's willing to bend for you. Are you willing to work a little harder for her?"

"You think that's all I need to do? Work a little harder? If I work any harder, I'm going to end up in the psych ward because I won't have a brain left."

"And that's the underlying problem, right there, isn't it?" Greg shook his head. "How long are you going to let that fear rule you? You're not your mother."

No, he knew he wasn't bipolar. But he did have issues. "I know that, Greg. That's not what this is. There's just so much shit that requires my attention right now and I don't want to give her less of me than she deserves. I know I can't have everything—"

"Why not?" Greg shrugged. "My parents both had careers. My dad coached my little league team, and my mom volunteered at the school and the local theater where my sister and I acted. And they still love each other after all these years. You're getting too old to let opportunities pass you by, Tyler."

Something about Greg's tone made Tyler bite back a sharp response. Pushing aside his own shit for the moment, he looked at Greg. *Really* looked at him. Something was up. Something he'd missed because he'd been so damn preoccupied.

"What happened?"

Greg's expression didn't change. "I don't know what you mean."

"Yeah, you do. What's going on?"

Greg shifted his gaze out the window. "Let's just say I've had a crash course in missed opportunities recently."

They sat in silence for a few minutes as Tyler considered everything Greg had said. And hadn't said.

"Do you mind if I abandon you tonight? I feel like taking a ride."

Greg's wry smile finally made an appearance. "No problem. I'm sure I can find some way to amuse myself for a few hours."

Thirteen

❦

"I'm sorry to call you out so late, Sabrina. I totally appreciate your help and your willingness to come over."

Sabrina Rodriquez waved a hand as she took Kate's apartment by storm Thursday night. The five-foot-two part-time coffee shop worker had a personality that didn't need the stimulant of caffeine to keep her at a constant bubble.

"No problem, *chica*. It's not really that late and it's not like I had any plans. The men around here are dumb as stumps, I swear. Did I tell you about . . ."

Sabrina launched into a story about one of her many cousins, not needing Kate to do more than nod at the appropriate places as Kate had Sabrina get up on the stand in her workshop and stand there with her arms out while Kate got to work.

The twenty-two-year-old was taking classes toward an associate's degree in hotel-restaurant management and worked as the assistant manager of the catering service Talia used for most of her weddings. She also filled in at the coffee shop down the street.

Sabrina had been modeling for Kate for the past couple of months when one of the burlesque companies had asked her to make a costume for a performer who almost perfectly matched Sabrina's measurements of thirty-eight, twenty-two, thirty-two.

After Sabrina had stopped laughing, she'd said she'd be happy to model, as long as Kate supplied her with panties that didn't creep when she spent long hours on her feet.

Worthwhile trade, considering it only took Kate an hour or so to make the panties now that she had the pattern and Sabrina had to stand, sometimes for several hours and get stuck with pins.

Most people couldn't believe the two women were friends, mostly because no one could figure out how either got a word in edgewise. Kate admitted it could be a little nerve-wracking for anyone listening.

Tonight, Kate let Sabrina hold up most of the conversation. Apparently her younger cousin had stolen one of another cousin's boyfriends and that was making for some interesting family dynamics.

Sabrina's stories about her four brothers, three sisters, and nearly twenty cousins usually made Kate happy to be an only child. There were times, though, when she wished she had a clan to visit and drive her crazy.

Annabelle had added Jared to her admittedly small clan. Kate wondered if she'd ever be able to include Tyler in hers.

"Kate, you know I don't know a damn thing about sewing. But shouldn't the shiny side of the material be facing out?"

Kate sighed and removed the piece of satin she'd been about to pin into place wrong side out.

"I'm sorry. My brain's just not into this tonight, but I need to get this finished."

"You wanna tell me where exactly your brain is tonight? Maybe with that hunky guy you've been seeing?"

Oh no. "What hunky guy?"

Sabrina rolled her eyes. "Oh please. The coffee shop was buzzing the other morning about your new guy."

Kate grimaced. "Shit. What were they saying?"

"Only about how you'd picked up some awesomely hot, rich guy who might be named Bruce Wayne or Clark Kent because apparently he's superhero material."

Swallowing a groan, Kate gave up all pretense of trying to work, removed the costume, and waved Sabrina off the box. "I think I need a drink for this conversation. You want something?"

"I'll take an orange soda if you've got one." Sabrina hopped down, pulled on her jeans and T-shirt, and followed her to the kitchen. "So come on. Spill the beans. Who is he?"

"Well, I can tell you he's not Clark Kent." She pulled out a soda for Sabrina and grabbed a bottle of wine for herself. "His name's Tyler Golden and he's—"

"Holy shit! You're dating one of Pennsylvania's most eligible bachelors? Seriously? When—Where'd you meet him?"

"You know who Tyler is?"

Sabrina's expression was classic exasperation. "Hell, yes. We studied the GoldenStar in my business class. My professor is a major fan."

"And you probably got an A in that class, didn't you?"

"Of course."

Not a surprise. Sabrina had an incredible work ethic, probably because every cent she earned from modeling for Kate and working for Tracy's Catering went toward paying for her education. She and her mom had been scrimping and saving pennies for years to send Sabrina, the oldest of eight, to college. She'd be the first in her family to attain a college degree. Hell, she'd been the first in her immediate family to get a high school diploma.

And, if Sabrina had her way, she'd be the first member of her family to own her own business.

When Kate didn't respond right away, Sabrina prompted, "So, when did you meet him?"

"At a New Year's Eve party, but we didn't start dating until after Arnie and I broke up."

Sabrina brushed that last hurried statement off with a wave of her hand. "No offense, Kate, but you and Arnie . . . That just wasn't meant to be."

She grimaced. "Did everyone think that way but just didn't tell me?"

Sabrina's raised eyebrows kept her grimace in place. "Would you have listened?"

"Alright, stupid question. Of course I wouldn't have."

"You came to the right decision in the end. Don't sweat it now, sweetie."

Kate hesitated before voicing the question she'd been dying to ask someone. "Have you seen Arnie lately?"

"Oh yeah." Sabrina brushed off her concern. "He seems fine. You know Arnie. Nothing seems to rattle the guy."

Guess she wasn't that unforgettable, which was a shitty thing to think considering she'd broken up with him.

"Damn, there goes my mouth again." It was Sabrina's turn to grimace. "I'm sorry, Kate. That doesn't mean he—"

"No, no. Stop. I'm being foolish. It's been weeks. I'm glad he's moved on."

"So tell me more about this new relationship. What's Tyler like?"

Kate smiled and tingled just thinking about him. Something she'd never done with Arnie. And there was that guilt again. "He's smart and handsome and sexy and—"

The knock on her door made them start like teenagers caught talking about sex by their parents, which made them burst out laughing.

"Hold that thought." Kate headed for the door and turned the knob. "I'll be— Tyler!"

She had a bare moment to process the fact that he was there before he reached for her, one hand around her neck, the other on her hip, pulling her tight against him. His lips landed on hers and, in the next second, he was kissing the hell out of her.

After a brief moment of shock, she returned it, wrapping her arms around his neck and opening her mouth so he could slide his tongue against hers.

He felt so damn good and she'd missed him, so much more than she'd ever admit.

She forgot all about Sabrina, all about everything but the feel of him against her and how she responded.

Apparently, he felt damn happy to see her, if the ridge in his jeans was anything to go by.

He hadn't even made it in the door yet and, without breaking the kiss, she tugged him through and closed it behind her.

Just before she could manage to climb him like a tree and embarrass the hell out of him, her, and Sabrina, she pulled away.

At least, as far as he'd let her get, which wasn't far at all.

"Tyler—"

"I'm sorry for not calling first."

His low tone made her body tighten in interesting places. "I'm glad you're here. I'd like you to meet someone."

His gaze immediately searched the room, spotting Sabrina.

He grimaced for a split second before wiping it away. "I'm sorry. I didn't mean to inter—"

"No, it's okay. Really. Come say hello."

Sabrina couldn't quite hide her huge grin, and she jumped up from her chair to shake Tyler's hand. "Hi. I'm Sabrina Rodriguez."

"Tyler Golden. Nice to meet you."

Kate put her arm around the girl and hugged her. "Sabrina models for me, but she's a college student too and works for a caterer. She's getting a degree in hotel-restaurant management, as a matter of fact."

Tyler's smile made Sabrina's expression go slack. Jared had the reputation for being a lady-killer, but Tyler had just as much charm to spare.

"So which half of that major are you more interested in?" he asked.

Sabrina's bubbly personality leaped at the question. "Oh, definitely the hotel. I just find there's more to keep you busy with hotels."

"Yeah, they can be a definite challenge."

And there was definite stress in his voice. Kate looked up to search his expression. Nothing showed on his face, but his eyes looked exhausted.

"I don't know if Kate told you, but my brother and I are opening a spa retreat locally and—"

"Yes! I know. It sounds amazing." Sabrina's enthusiastic response made Tyler smile, and Kate's breath caught.

Wow. She'd never realized how easy it was to fall in love.

Guess it really did just take the right guy.

As Sabrina gushed about how excited she was about the spa and the economic opportunities it would bring to the area, Tyler encouraged her to give his human resources manager a call about a job.

And Kate dealt with the terrifying-electrifying sensation of knowing she could be totally destroyed by emotion.

* *

Tyler liked Sabrina. He really did.

She was bright, bubbly, and had absolutely no artifice. And no filter. Whatever she was thinking came straight out of her mouth.

But right now, he wished she'd leave. As soon as possible.

He wanted Kate to himself.

It made his chest tight to think how easily he'd fallen for her. It hadn't taken any effort at all.

Mia had required effort. And he felt like shit admitting that, even if it was only to himself.

But he refused to wallow in it. Mia was gone.

Kate was . . . his.

And he planned to prove it tonight. If he didn't pass out first.

He hadn't realized how god-awful tired he felt. He'd only slept about three or four hours a night this past week and it was catching up to him. Which sucked because he'd had big plans for tonight.

"Hey, Sabrina, do you mind if we finish this tomorrow?" Kate cut back into the conversation as Sabrina paused to take a breath.

The other girl didn't seem at all put off by Kate's suggestion. "No, of course not."

And if her grin was anything to go by, Sabrina knew exactly why he and Kate wanted to be alone.

But he couldn't let her leave without adding, "I was serious about you applying for a job, Sabrina. Can I let the HR guy know you'll be in contact?"

"That would be awesome! Thank you so much." With a huge grin and a wave, Sabrina flew out the door, leaving Tyler and Kate staring at each other across the room.

"She's a bundle of energy," Kate said to fill the void that opened between them. "You won't be sorry if you hire her. She's incredibly loyal and she takes whatever she's doing as serious as a heart attack and—"

Tyler's mouth descended, cutting off whatever she'd been planning to say and wiping out everything but the taste of him and the feel of him pressing against her body.

His mouth moved over hers without the typical sense of urgency she usually felt from him. This felt more like comfort, like he needed to kiss her more than he wanted to devour her.

So, instead of throwing herself at him like she normally did, she wrapped herself around him, seeking to give him what he needed.

His arms tightened, and the kiss took on a deeper sense of intimacy. His hands spread across her back as his tongue slipped between her lips to tangle around hers.

She wished their clothes would melt away so they could be skin on skin.

But she swore she could taste the fatigue in his kiss. Not that he wasn't giving it his all. Just that he didn't have his all to give.

She pulled away, but he wouldn't let her go far. "Tyler, you're exhausted. Have you slept at all this week?"

His lips twisted until he was almost smiling. "If you're trying to get me into your bed, I've gotta say I wouldn't turn you down."

She wanted to ask him what he was doing here but Tyler didn't look like he needed an interrogation. He looked like he needed someone to take care of him. And she wanted to. So badly it was almost a little scary.

Was this why her mom had given up her dream of traveling? Had she loved Kate's dad so much that she'd been willing to toss over everything else she'd ever wanted?

Refusing to dwell on those thoughts now, she smiled and took his hand to pull him toward her bedroom. He let her.

When she had him next to her bed, she began undressing him. She started with the shirt, unbuttoning it with no hint of a tease. She had to bite her tongue so she didn't lean forward and bite his broad chest as it came into view but she restrained herself and let his shirt fall to the floor.

His pants proved a tougher challenge to her composure. She wanted to linger as she pushed the button through the hole and unzipped the zipper. But she forced herself to rein in her desire to shove her hands down the front of his black boxer briefs and cup the impressive erection that made her mouth water.

He toed off his oh-so-formal black wingtips before she told him to, and she had to smile when he stepped out of his pants to stand before her in only his boxers and socks.

"I think I might like this look on you." She looked up at him with a deliberately sexy gleam in her eye and watched him return her smile.

"And I think you're wearing way too many clothes."

"Ah, but you need some sleep."

"I didn't come here to sleep."

No, he'd come here to have sex with her. Although having sex with him had become so much more than that for her.

"I know that, Tyler. Humor me. Lie down for a little while. I can see how tired you are."

"Only if you lie with me."

"I plan to."

"Naked."

She heard the command in his voice but refused to give in to it. "If we're both naked, you know what's going to happen." His smile made her thighs clench, but she wasn't going to be deterred just yet. "Just lie down. I'm not going anywhere."

His gaze searched hers for several seconds before he nodded and moved to her bed. When he lay on his back with his arms crossed under his head, watching her, she had the almost undeniable urge to do a striptease for him. But then she'd ruin her own good intentions because she wouldn't be able to justify riling him up then not coming through.

And she'd be just as turned on.

Instead, she pulled her sweatshirt over her head and shoved her yoga pants to the floor seconds before crawling into bed next to him in her panties and camisole.

She pressed against his side, his body fitting against hers like they belonged together.

If they were going to continue this relationship, she really needed to think about getting a bigger bed.

Beneath her cheek, she felt his chest rise and fall on a sigh and his body relaxed almost instantly. She swore he was asleep in seconds, although his arms never lost their grip on her.

She didn't mind. She didn't plan on going anywhere.

* *

Tyler came awake with a start.

He knew exactly where he was. And where Kate's mouth was.

On his cock.

He groaned, his hands finding her head and sinking into the silky strands trailing along his thighs. "Jesus, Kate."

One of her hands stroked between his thighs, teasing the sensitive skin before running her nails along his balls. Her lips ringed his cockhead, the tip of her tongue swirling around it like it was a lollipop she couldn't get enough of.

After a long, deep suck, she let him slip from her mouth to run her lips down his length.

His head kicked back into the pillow, his hands tightening in her hair. He couldn't let her go, couldn't loosen his grip, and she didn't seem to mind at all.

God, he wanted to be back in her mouth.

His eyes opened, but the room was totally dark. He couldn't make out anything.

He could only feel.

Her teeth nipping at the base of his cock. One hand gripping his thigh, the other wrapped around his balls, massaging them.

He tried not to move as her lips slid back up his shaft just before she sucked him deep. The head nudged at the back of her throat and she swallowed, her throat tightening around him, encouraging him to come.

Not yet. Hell, no. He wanted so much more.

But Kate seemed determined to break his control. Her lips and mouth worked to rile him to a point that he had to give in.

It became a battle of wills. One he was determined to win.

On her next slide up his shaft, he was ready for her. He pulled her hair just hard enough to keep her from descending once again. She tugged, but he held on.

"Are you feeling more rested?"

Her tone held a note of teasing that made him want to smile.

"I think you're going to be surprised how much energy I have now, sweetheart. But first . . ."

He sat up without warning, eliciting a yelp from Kate. Before she could get oriented, he had her splayed over his lap.

He was going to take her at her word and not ask for permission this time. If they were going to continue this relationship then she truly needed to know what she'd be getting with him. He needed to know she could handle everything about him before he let himself move forward and she decided she couldn't take certain aspects of his personality.

And Saturday night, maybe . . .

Well, he'd worry about that later.

Right now, he had her right where he wanted her.

He ran his hand from her waist to her thigh, stroking her soft skin, making her squirm.

Right before he smacked her ass with a stinging slap.

He expected another yelp. Instead, she moaned.

"Tyler. What—"

He smacked her again, the slight jolt traveling up his arm and straight to his cock.

Already stiff as a board, it ached to sink deep in her pussy.

And he couldn't wait any longer.

Twisting her around again, he set her on her knees on the bed then got behind her and pushed on her back until her chest lay on the bed with her ass raised high.

She started when he put one hand on her hip but didn't move. He felt her tremble, but she didn't tell him to stop. Or shy away from him.

She waited, breathing so hard he could hear her.

Instead of putting his knees between hers, he put one on the outside then put his bent leg on the side.

Leverage. It was all about leverage.

He dipped his fingers between her legs, making sure she was wet enough to take him, and found her slick and hot. He fucked her with his fingers for several seconds, stroking her sex high inside, making her writhe and clench around him.

When she moaned out his name a second time, he couldn't wait any longer.

He grabbed his cock in one hand—

And realized he didn't have a condom.

"Kate. I need—"

With a groan, she reached for the bedside table, opened the drawer, and fumbled around for a few minutes before practically throwing a little foil square at him.

They were exchanging medical info as soon as possible. He was growing to hate condoms.

Once he had it in place, he guided his cock to her entrance and slammed home in one, smooth motion.

God damn, she was so fucking tight like this. His cock pulsed a warning and he froze, not wanting to move and set off his orgasm.

But Kate couldn't stay still. She pressed back against him.

So he spanked her again. The way she clenched around him made him bite back another groan.

Bending over her, he let his cheek rest against her back, felt the wild pattern of her breathing.

"Move, God damn it."

Her demand made him want to spank her again, so he did. Twice.

Then he fucked her. Hard and fast and with everything he had. And she let him.

He realized his eyes had grown accustomed to the darkness and he could see her hands clenched in the sheets, holding on as she pressed her ass against him with his every thrust.

His rhythm increased, dragging her along with him, their mating a primitive force that unleashed his usually suppressed wildness.

He fucked her with brute force until he felt her tighten around him, her moan signaling her release. Seconds later, he came so hard, he swore he saw stars behind his eyelids.

With a groan, he took them both to their sides, his cock still deep in her body, her pussy still clenching around him.

She was breathing so fast, he was almost worried she was hyperventilating until she finally began to calm down.

He had his arms wrapped so tight around her, he had to make a conscious effort to loosen them. Which she didn't seem to like, because her fingernails dug into his forearms, stopping him.

"I want you to come back to Haven with me tomorrow," he said. "Call in sick. I've got a meeting I must attend and then I want you to join me at the Salon."

He felt her breathing hitch as she shook her head. "I can't call in sick, and I have a meeting I can't reschedule Saturday morning. But I'll be there as early as I can Saturday."

It was on the tip of his tongue to demand she drop everything for him but he knew that'd be a major mistake.

Still, the frustration wanted to eat away at him.

"Is there something special going on at the Salon?"

She sounded curious but tentative and he knew if he said yes, he wanted to fuck her while another man watched, she'd be shocked.

He wanted her to agree to it. *Needed* her to agree to it until it was a gnawing ache in his gut.

And he wanted her to want it as much as he did.

So just tell her what you want.

She'd been game for everything else he'd asked her to do. Why would this be different?

Because he'd be bringing another man into the mix. And he was pretty damn sure she'd never done anything like that before.

For all of Mia's instinctual reserve, the voyeuristic aspect of their sexual relationship had excited her. She'd become a different person while having sex with him in front of another man. Almost as if she had permission to be someone different.

But, as he had reminded himself many times before, Kate wasn't Mia.

"No. Only Greg will be there to watch."

She lay still for several seconds before turning in his arms to look at him. She stared at him for several seconds, her cheeks flushing a bright pink. "Are you expecting me to have sex with him?"

Her voice sounded steady and she continued to hold his gaze. He couldn't tell if she was angry, shocked, appalled . . .

Or turned on.

"I don't expect you to. Do you *want* to have sex with Greg?"

It wouldn't be the first time he and Greg shared a woman, though Greg had never had sex with Mia. But with Kate . . .

After almost a half-minute silence, Kate finally said, "I'm not sure."

She hadn't said no, but it wasn't a definite yes either. Would this be the point at which she said stop?

She took a deep breath. "I can be there around eight, depending on traffic into the city."

Yes. Instead of grunting out his triumph, he kissed her. Hard. Probably harder than he should have. But she didn't push him away. She let him push up onto his elbows and loom over her.

His cock began to rouse again, brushing against her thigh. Bending her knee, she used that thigh to rub her soft skin against his, winding him up again.

Her tongue slid into his mouth, playing and teasing. Drowning out the tiny seed of doubt that he was pushing her too far, too fast.

Fourteen

✦

"So I'm going to Haven again Saturday."

Kate and Annabelle sat in a quiet corner in the antiques shop around noon on Friday. Kate had needed to talk and Annabelle had been tied up with customers, so Kate had brought lunch to her.

The customers had finally left, purchases loaded into the back of their van, a few minutes ago.

Kate had so far been able to keep from blurting out the fact that Tyler wanted her to have sex with him while another man watched—and possibly joined in—but she knew she wouldn't be able to for long.

"And?" Annabelle raised a brow at her. "What does Tyler have planned?"

Kate blushed. She couldn't help it. But not all of it was embarrassment. A lot of it was heat.

She wasn't a prude. And she wasn't worried about what Annabelle would think.

Annabelle had told her about her experiences at the Salon and the few times she'd spent with Jared and his friend, Dane.

Sure, she'd been shocked, at first. But her shock had quickly turned to curiosity.

And wonder. What would she do if she found herself in the same situation?

"He wants us to make use of the Salon."

Annabelle's eyes widened as she put her sandwich down without taking a bite. "Oh really. And what use does he want to make of the Salon?"

"He wants to have sex with me in front of another man."

Annabelle didn't look surprised. Only curious. "And what did you say?"

"I said yes."

Annabelle nodded, as if she'd expected her to. "And are you sure it's something you want to do?"

"I wouldn't have said yes if it wasn't."

"*Are* you sure, Kate?"

It was on the tip of her tongue to say yes immediately but she took a bite of her sandwich before she did. And thought, really thought, about her answer. Annabelle didn't push her to respond and they sat in silence for several seconds.

"Can I ask you a really personal question?"

Annabelle wrinkled her nose at her. "Of course you can. You know that. Anything you want to know."

"Do you think I'm rushing into a relationship with Tyler too soon after breaking up with Arnie?"

Annabelle began to shake her head even before she'd finished asking her question. "No. Because you didn't really love Arnie. You know that."

"I know that I strung along a nice guy I knew I didn't love for years before I came to my senses."

Scowling, Annabelle waved her sandwich at her. "Now you're just being too hard on yourself. I know you cared for Arnie. But I also know you think you're at fault for everything that was wrong with your relationship. But you're not. Do you think Arnie didn't know you didn't love him the same way he loved you? And do you really think if he loved you more than life itself, he wouldn't have fought harder to keep you?"

Kate's mouth dropped open for a second before she snapped it shut. She'd never looked at it like that before.

"Seriously, Kate, the only problem you're going to have is getting addicted to how much fun you can have at the Salon."

"So wanting to have sex in front of another man doesn't make me a pervert?"

Annabelle rolled her eyes. "If it does, then welcome to the club. I'm going to be a charter member soon."

"So Jared . . . and Dane . . ."

Annabelle's smile told a story of its own. "Do you want details? I've actually been dying to talk to you about everything but you've been so preoccupied, I didn't want to burden you. Or make you think I'm sex-crazed."

Kate sighed in relief. "God, it's so good to know I have someone to talk to about this. Someone I trust."

"I would've brought up the subject sooner but you've had so much going on and I had so much going on and . . ." Annabelle grimaced. "Alright, maybe I was a little afraid you'd think I'd gone off the deep end. I mean, sure, my parents were in a three-way relationship. But, oh my *God*, Kate. The sex is . . . amazing. And I love Jared more than I thought I'd ever love anyone. And I can't imagine ever losing him. But when Dane joins us . . . Or we're at one of the Salon's game nights . . . I've never felt anything like it in my life. But it's not just the sex. I can't imagine sharing the rest of my life with anyone other than Jared. We complement each other. Do you know what I mean?"

Sighing, Kate nodded. Yes, she knew exactly what Annabelle meant. "So I shouldn't be so uptight about Saturday?"

"Oh, no. That's not what I'm saying. If you don't feel comfortable doing something, you shouldn't do it."

And that totally wasn't the problem. "But it doesn't make me a slut to want it?"

"Stop that right now." Annabelle's tone brooked no defiance, and Kate's lips twisted in a wry smile. "Stop calling yourself names like that. Enjoying sex isn't anything to be ashamed of. And just because we're enjoying it with more people than our boyfriends doesn't make us sluts."

"You sound like you've had this conversation with yourself a few times."

"I have." Annabelle nodded, her gaze dead serious. "And I refuse to let other people label me. And what your dad doesn't know won't hurt him."

Kate shuddered. "I can't even let myself think about what my dad would say if he ever found out."

"And he never has to. Your dad isn't entitled to run your life. You're an adult. You've been doing pretty damn well for yourself, if you ask me. You've finally taken back your life after being off course for a while."

Off course. That definitely sounded better than *screwed up.*

And left her feeling much better about Saturday night.

She hoped the feeling stayed with her.

* *

"The stipulations left behind by your grandfather are pretty clear, Tyler. If a Golden heir is not sitting in the chairman's seat on the board then another stockholder can purchase a majority share of the company."

Tyler's jaw felt ready to crack as he listened to the GoldenStar board's legal counsel explain exactly how screwed he was.

And it all boiled down to this—if he didn't step up and into the chairman seat's his father wanted to vacate, Mark Vasser's company would eat it up and spit out the parts.

When the lawyer finally stopped droning on, Tyler let it all filter through. The information wasn't anything he hadn't known. He'd studied the contracts and legal provisions of the GoldenStar chain as part of his master's thesis.

He'd never suspected his father would want to step down any time soon. The man was only in his fifties.

"Wes, could you give us the room? My son and I need to discuss a few things."

His father's voice drew his attention back to the present. And the weight bearing down on his chest.

He barely noticed the door closing behind the lawyer, more focused on not revealing any of the turmoil in his head.

His father was a master at playing on those feelings.

"So." His dad sat in the chair opposite him at the table and Tyler forced himself to meet Glen's eyes. "Kind of a shock, wasn't it?"

Tyler just waited, knowing his dad was working up to something. He had to be.

There was no way he wasn't orchestrating some deal behind the scenes, some way to either bring Tyler to heel or to bring Haven into the GoldenStar line.

Something—

"Your mother and I are planning to take a trip." The non sequitur practically made Tyler's head spin. It wasn't at all what he'd been expecting, and it threw him off balance. Which is probably exactly what his father had intended.

So he waited for his dad to continue. Waited for the other shoe to drop.

"It's been a long time since we traveled together," his dad continued. "For years, she wanted nothing to do with me. I foolishly thought other women would fill the void. And I suppose they did. For a while."

Tyler blinked, unable to believe his dad wanted to talk about being unfaithful to his wife. To Tyler's mother.

"But I never stopped loving your mother, not even after she told me she'd never be able to give me what I wanted and I should find someone else to fulfill my needs after she'd had you and your brother."

"She was sick." The words came out almost in a growl, surprising him with their vehemence.

Jed had always been the one who hated their dad, who'd wanted nothing to do with the man. Tyler . . .

Well, maybe he had some latent hostility. He thought he'd understood. His parents' marriage had always been a sham. The joining of two old Philadelphia families. He'd never understood why his grandparents, who he'd always idolized, had thought the wedding was a good idea.

"Yes, I knew that," Glen continued, watching him with a clear gaze. "I just didn't know how severe or what was wrong with her. And I didn't care at the time. But funny things can happen when you're married as long as your mother and I have been. Love's a strange thing. I told your brother this a few months ago. He gave me the same look you are."

Still trying to get a grip on the conversation, Tyler shook his head. "Is there a point to all of this?"

"Your mom and I thought we'd take a few months, travel, maybe take a few cruises. We've both traveled, but never together. And we can't do that if I'm tied to the company."

It sounded so rational, so . . . not manipulative that Tyler knew there had to be a catch. An ulterior motive.

"Why now?"

His dad smiled, though it didn't hold much amusement. "Because neither of us is getting any younger. And none of us know how long we'll have."

A cold chill ran up Tyler's back. "Is something wrong with Mom?"

"No. Nothing beyond the issues she's been dealing with for years."

Tyler was fast losing his control on his temper. "Jesus, Dad, then forgive me if I find your timing a little suspect. Jed and I are finally expanding, something we've been waiting to do for years. And now you drop this on us?"

No longer able to sit still, Tyler pushed off the chair and began to pace. His dad just sat there, watching him.

"How the hell do you expect me to run both companies without giving up my life?"

"Good question, isn't it? And if I'm being totally honest with you, the GoldenStar chain is more than a forty-hour-a-week commitment. At first, it'll be more like fifty or sixty. So where does that leave Haven and your new venture?"

Tyler stopped pacing to stare at his dad. "You want to sell, don't you? You want to get rid of the chain?"

"Son, I'm stepping down no matter what. I know now there's more to life than making money. The only question is, do you?"

* *

"Hello, sweetheart. I haven't seen you for days! You're always so busy. You work too hard."

Tyler leaned down to kiss Beatrice Golden's cheek late Friday afternoon, not bothering to hide his twinge of regret. "I'm sorry I haven't been by to see you lately, Nana. I've got a lot going on right now and—"

"Now, now, that wasn't a criticism." She waved aside his apology with one graceful hand. "I know you've got responsibilities. I'm just so glad to see you now. Would you like a drink?"

Yeah, he would, but not the iced tea or soda he knew she meant. "Sure. How about a Coke?"

Nana raised an eyebrow at him as she moved to the bar along the wall. "And maybe a little rum to go with it? You look like you could use it."

With a sigh, he sank into a chair facing the wall of windows. From here, he could see the city spread out before him. Including the flagship GoldenStar hotel blocks away.

"Nana, did Granddad ever consider selling the chain?"

When his grandmother didn't answer right away, he turned to find her smiling at him. "You talked to your dad, I assume."

Shock had his eyes widening. "You know what's going on?"

"Of course." She finished pouring a healthy amount of rum into his glass then waved the soda bottle over it until the liquid became a slightly darker color. "He can't sell without my okay. I thought you knew that."

Yeah, he did. "I guess I just never considered that you'd go along with a sale."

Handing him the glass, Beatrice sat on the couch opposite him then sipped her own drink. "The hotel was your grandfather's baby, not mine. He enjoyed building things from the ground up and, after the first hotel was finished, well . . . He just kept going. Your dad . . . He wasn't a builder. He only wanted to maintain. Actually, what he really wanted to do was design."

"Design what?"

"Cars."

Tyler barked out a laugh. "Seriously? Dad wanted to design cars?"

"Oh, yes. You know how much he loves to collect them. Has an entire garage filled with them. And for most of his teenage years, all he did was design them."

Tyler felt like he'd been struck with a two-by-four. His father had wanted to design cars. He'd never thought of his father wanting to do anything other than run the hotels. And he'd made it seem so effortless. Almost as if he didn't care.

"But your grandfather wanted your dad to take over the business. By that time, your parents had married and had you. And life with your mom was difficult." Beatrice grimaced. "If we'd only known why back then, we might have been able to get her some help, but her parents had covered up her problems for so many years, it was second nature by then."

As it had been for him and Jed growing up. They'd become experts at evading questions about their mom. They'd give just enough information to satisfy teachers who asked where they'd been for days on end when she'd pull them out of school to fly to Europe at a moment's notice because she felt the need to escape.

"So Dad took over the business because Granddad forced it on him. And now he's doing the same to me."

"Are you positive about that?"

"Well, he told me that if Jed or I don't take over the chairman's seat on the board, he's going to sell. That kind of feels like he's forcing the issue to me."

"And do you want the job?"

"It's more complicated than that, Nana. You know that."

"Is it?"

Beatrice's seemingly simple question made the roiling thoughts in his head slow. She definitely had something she wanted him to hear but obviously wanted him to come to it on his own.

"Are you trying to tell me there's an easy answer to all of this? Because if there is, I haven't come up with it."

"Then maybe you're overthinking the problem."

His gaze sharpened on his grandmother's amused blue eyes as an idea occurred to him. "Thanks for the drink, Nana, but I have to go. I have a little research to do before tomorrow."

He rose, kissed her cheek again, and headed for the door, still carrying his drink. He had a feeling he'd need it.

"Something special going on tomorrow?" his grandmother asked. "Or should I say, someone special?"

Hand on the doorknob, he turned, hiding a smile at the knowing tone of her voice. "You could say that."

"Why don't you bring Kate for brunch with me Sunday morning? Not too early, of course. I'd love to see her again, get to know her a little better. After all, she did find my ring."

And Tyler knew exactly where his grandmother was going with this. "Nana—"

"No, no. Don't say anything. Off you go. You have work to do. And I . . . Well, I think I'll go shopping. One can never have too many purses."

* *

"Kate, hi. This is Dinah Malinowski. I wonder if you have a few minutes to talk."

It took a second for the name to register when Kate answered her phone Friday afternoon, but her heart had already begun to pound.

Setting aside the dress she was taking in, she stood and headed for the bathroom. "Prof—Dinah, how are you?"

The laughter in her ear made her smile as Kate shut herself in the bathroom. "I'm fine. Especially since I hope we'll be working together. You're talking to the new costume designer of the off-Broadway Downstairs Playhouse, and I've got the perfect job for you."

Kate's mouth opened but all that emerged was "Oh, my God."

After Dinah finished laughing, she started to talk about the theater and the job while Kate's head spun.

"I know it's a lot to take in immediately, but I'd like you to come up to the city so you can get a feel for the job and make a decision. Would sometime next week be okay?"

It would take some finagling with Joe but . . . "Of course. I should be able to carve out some time in the middle of next week. Dinah, I can't thank you enough."

"Oh, don't thank me yet. You might not want the job after you see what it entails. But after we talked last week, I knew you were the right person for this spot."

Kate spent the rest of the day in a fog. Luckily, she didn't screw up anyone's clothing, but Joe had that look in his eye. The one that said he knew something was up.

Between Joe's constant attention and the fact that she couldn't wait to see Tyler tomorrow, the day couldn't pass fast enough.

Of course, tomorrow she'd also be seeing Greg. And he'd be seeing a hell of a lot of her.

Which made her nervous. And horny.

God, was she horny.

And wet.

Damn it, she needed to stop letting her mind go there.

She forced herself to work Friday night until she couldn't keep her eyes open and paid for it Saturday morning when she had to get up at seven to be at her nine o'clock meeting with a potential client, who wasn't just a potential two hours later. Kate had a down payment check in her hand and a rough sketch of an idea to get started.

By the time she got home and decided on what to wear and what to pack, it was close to one. At this rate, she wouldn't get to Haven until four.

By that time, she might spontaneously combust.

It was after five when she parked in the garage, and her agitation level had spiked somewhere on the Schuylkill Expressway between the bumper-to-bumper traffic and the three accidents.

Combine that with high-octane lust, and she was a needy mass of nerves when she finally knocked on the door to his apartment.

She waited impatiently for him to open the door and, when he did, she nearly melted into a pile of goo at his feet.

He wore a pair of black slacks that looked custom made and a white button-down shirt that should've screamed conservative but made her want to rip the buttons off, one by one. With her teeth.

Her first clue that he was distracted came from the quick kiss he gave her before waving her through the door. The next was when he told her he needed time to finish what he was doing.

"Make yourself at home. This won't take me more than a few minutes, I swear."

When he'd disappeared into his office, she took her overnighter to the bedroom. And started to undress.

She'd brought new lingerie. Something she'd designed specifically for him, although she hadn't known it at the time. She'd designed it right after they'd met, when she'd still been engaged to Arnie but had known it wasn't going to work out between them.

She'd gotten the idea from one of Annabelle's paintings, and she'd thought it would fit tonight's mood perfectly.

And fit her mood, as well.

She was just pulling on the matching satin chemise when she heard motion behind her.

"Shit, I'm sorry, Kate. I was looking for Tyler."

Greg.

She froze for a second before making sure the chemise was straight. Then she turned to face the man who was going to watch while she and Tyler made love tonight.

Instead of embarrassment painting her cheeks red, she felt excitement.

But if he'd been leering at her, she would have stomped across the room and slapped his face. Which was stupid, all things considered.

God, it all should've made her crazy. Instead, she wanted this man to get so hot and bothered while she and Tyler made love that he had to join them. Had to have her.

But he wasn't even looking at her.

In fact, he'd turned his back to her, though he didn't move out of the doorway.

"When did you get here?" he asked, his tone steady. As if he didn't know or care what was going to happen later.

And maybe he didn't. Maybe this was just another night to him. Maybe—

She shook her head and took a deep breath. "Just a few minutes ago. Traffic was worse than I expected. You can turn around now. I pretty much covered everything vital."

When he turned, his gaze met hers and his grin . . . God, the man had a smile that made his broad features light up.

"Honey, I wouldn't consider your legs nonvital. They're damn near pretty enough on their own to make me throw myself at your feet. And at my age, that's saying something."

Torn between so many conflicting emotions, she fell back on the tried and true: sarcasm.

Crossing her arms under her breasts, she raised an eyebrow at him. "Please, you're what . . . thirty-five? That's not old in my book. And you, Mr. Bigshot Hollywood Producer, are you trying to tell me your casting couch is ever empty?"

Mimicking her by crossing his arms, and drawing her attention to his broad chest, Greg leaned one shoulder against the doorjamb, that grin getting more wicked by the second.

And making it harder for her to breathe.

"I'm thirty-six. And would you like to test my casting couch?"

God, did she? What—

Tyler appeared in the doorway next to Greg, entering the room and stealing all the air. At this rate, she'd be dizzy in seconds.

"Ignore him, Kate. Greg pretends to be an ass but it's usually an act."

As her gaze met Tyler's, she realized his laser-sharp focus had returned. And landed squarely on her.

As if he'd shut out every other distraction and she was the only thing in his life worth having at the moment.

It literally took her breath away to have him stare at her like that. Only when her lungs began to ache did she draw in air.

Tyler's half grin had a definite edge to it as he stopped in front of her, blocking out everything but him.

"I see you took my advice and made yourself comfortable." He reached out and let his fingers play over the wide strips of black lace that held up the bodice. She'd used the lace as decoration around the top of the chemise, at the hem and up the side split. "I think I recognize this."

She'd wondered if he would. It was the same lace he'd used to tie her to her bed.

That dull flush of color spread across his cheekbones and she knew if she looked down, his erection would be tenting the front of his pants.

"It's a new design." She took a step back and did a slow turn. "I got the idea from one of Annabelle's paintings."

"It does look Victorian, but it also reminds me of something from the twenties. I like it."

"I'm glad."

"And it looks easy to get off."

That made her blush. She had no idea why, considering she'd been thinking about stripping in front of his friend.

"Are you having second thoughts?"

He pitched the question in a low voice, low enough that Greg wouldn't hear.

Although, looking over Tyler's shoulder, she saw Greg watching them intently, his smile gone.

Her thighs clenched and an ache started in her gut. Now was the time to back out, if she had any doubts at all.

Her gaze reconnected with Tyler's. "No. I'm not."

She spoke loudly enough that Greg could hear her. Though she didn't see his response, she did see Tyler's. And the scorching intensity in his gaze was enough to make her sex tighten and moisten.

And when he bent down to kiss her, she almost wasn't prepared for the sensation of drowning. She felt like she was going under and she'd be damned if she cared to resurface.

He tasted hot, felt hot, and made her want to melt beneath him. Her hands rose to cling to his shoulders, her body doing a full press against his. In her bare feet, she barely came up to his chin, so she rose onto her toes to get a better angle at his mouth.

Before she realized it, he'd wrapped one arm around her waist and lifted her off her feet. She floated, weightless, even though she ached with a lust so hot, it felt like molten lead rushing through her veins.

She wasn't ready to release him when he broke away and set her on her feet. She curved one hand around his neck so she could take one more kiss before drawing away.

The flush on his cheeks had deepened and his eyes glinted with promise.

"Did you eat yet?"

She shook her head. "I'm not really all that hungry."

"Humor me. I haven't eaten all day. I'm going to order some steaks up to the Salon. Okay?"

"Okay."

Nodding, he turned to Greg. "You?"

"Yeah, I could eat."

And again, that sarcastic little devil that hid in her brain and only emerged in intense sexual situations popped its head out again. "I guess you need to keep your strength up, being almost forty and all."

There was that smile again.

Had something happened to her to make her sex-crazy? She never had been before. Sex with Arnie had been nice. Sweet. Comforting.

She'd never once considered inviting another man into their bed. Arnie would have been scandalized. And hurt.

Tyler *wanted* to share her with Greg. Almost as if he were showing off a favorite toy.

Was that why?

Was she merely a possession he could show off, like one of Annabelle's prized paintings or—

"Kate, are you okay?"

And then he spoke to her in that tone of voice, as if she were the most important thing in his world, and she knew that wasn't it for him.

"Yeah, I'm fine. Why don't you order some food, and maybe we can have a drink. I have an urge to curl up in front of that fireplace in the Salon."

Fifteen

※

The food tray had been returned to the kitchen via the old-fashioned dumbwaiter when Kate crooked her finger at Tyler and summoned him to her as she lay on the chaise by the fireplace.

She practically glowed in the warm light coming from the blaze and the few lights he'd lit around the room.

For the past hour, he'd been watching her, couldn't take his eyes off her. She and Greg had kept the conversation flowing through the meal of steaks and baked potatoes. The chef had also sent up a cheesecake because he knew Tyler had a sweet tooth, but no one had touched it yet.

The three of them had polished off a bottle of wine while they ate, and only seconds ago, Tyler'd handed Kate a glass of champagne before giving Greg a seven and seven.

He'd wondered if she'd be nervous, but the look on her face as he crossed the floor didn't seem like nerves.

She looked like sex incarnate, lying on the chaise in that black satin slip, watching him as he crossed the room to her.

Greg sat on the wing chair at the far end of the seating group. He knew from experience that position would give him the best viewing angle—far enough away that he wouldn't interfere yet close enough to see everything.

Kate hadn't asked him to come closer so she must have figured out why he'd sat there.

And it hadn't seemed to upset her.

In fact, her excitement seemed to grow by the minute.

"Kate . . ."

She held up one finger. "You're not going to ask the forbidden question, are you? Because if you do, I'm walking out."

"Whatever the hell the forbidden question is, don't ask it, man."

Greg's amused tone barely made a dent in the sexual tension that filled the air between the three of them. It'd been building all through dinner but none of them had let the tone get too serious. Now . . .

Tyler hadn't been about to ask her anything. He'd been going to give her an excuse to leave, an out if she had any second thoughts.

But now . . . Now he was going to take her at her word.

Because he'd had more than enough foreplay. Watching her talk was foreplay. Watching her sip wine was foreplay, for Christ's sake, especially when her tongue slid out to lick her lips.

"No more questions," he said. "Take a sip of your champagne then set the glass on the table."

"Only one sip?"

It took her a few seconds to comply, her gaze on squarely on his. He saw no hesitation, only a sexual heat that threatened to blow apart his tenuous control.

"You can have more later."

Then again, he was fucking sick of reining himself in.

With Kate, maybe he'd found a complete match.

Putting one knee on the cushion next to her, he bent over her, fusing their lips together. He didn't hold anything back, forcing her lips open so he could plunder her mouth with his tongue.

One hand reached for her breast while the other went for her thigh. He felt her draw in a deep breath as he fucked her mouth with his tongue, felt her stiffen beneath him, as if in shock.

But he wasn't about to let her seize up now.

He wanted her burning and writhing beneath him, wanted her to be so wet with wanting him that her thighs got slick with it. He wanted to coat his cock in her wetness and then . . .

Then he wanted to fuck her ass. Just the thought of taking her in a way he was pretty sure no one else ever had made his balls tighten.

Running his hand up her thigh, he absorbed the sensation of her skin against his, the heat that sank into his blood and pushed him closer and closer to the edge of insanity.

Her hands clasped his shoulders but quickly moved up to sink into his hair, tugging at the too-long strands. He really needed a haircut but he'd been putting it off. There just hadn't been time. And if he had, well, then, Kate couldn't run her fingers through it and tug on it.

He loved the feel of her hands in his hair, mostly because he realized she liked it.

And he wanted to give her whatever she wanted.

That meant making her come until she didn't have the energy to move.

Behind him, he heard Greg shift in his seat. Kate must have heard him as well, because her eyes opened and she stared up into his. Again, he saw no hesitation, no shyness. Only heat.

"So how is this going to work?"

Her voice was pitched low but he didn't think she was trying to keep Greg from hearing. Just that she was hyperaroused.

Shifting around so he could sit on the chaise next to her, he wove one hand into her hair, smooth and silky between his fingers. God, he wanted to rub it all over his body. Against his chest, his thighs. Wrap it around his cock.

His cock throbbed at the thought, pressing against the zipper of his pants.

"How do you want it to work?"

She got that look on her face, the one that said he was testing her patience. He was coming to love that look.

"Considering this is my first time having sex with two men, I'm not quite sure."

His gaze narrowed on hers. "The deal was for Greg to watch. Are you saying you want Greg to join us?"

Her gaze flicked toward Greg for a brief second. "Are *you* saying you don't have a problem with Greg touching me?"

"No, I wouldn't. Do you want to know why?"

"Because you're not possessive?"

"I'd break any other man's hand if they tried to touch you. Greg is the only man I would trust in this room with you and me."

"Why?"

"Why do you trust Annabelle?"

She blinked up at him. "Because she's my best friend. But I've never had the urge to share a man with her."

"But she's the only person you would ever consider talking to about this. Because she's the one person you know who would understand why you did it."

She nodded, her gaze clearing. "Yes. I understand." She paused, her expression softening, the corners of her lips tilting up at the slightest angle. "Will you kiss me now?"

Didn't she already know there was nothing he'd rather do more?

He leaned down and sealed their mouths together. He'd kept a tight lid on his lust for the past hour, not wanting to overwhelm her. But now, he released his control and let every last bit of passion bleed out onto her.

She opened to him immediately, their tongues tangling. He savored her taste, drinking in her passion, letting it stoke the building heat in his blood. It energized him, electrified him.

Made him want to rush to take her.

No. This was going to be slow. He was taking his own sweet time and drowning himself in her. Drowning her. Showing her how it could be between them. If she stayed with him.

How good it could be.

And what pleasure he could offer her.

In his peripheral vision, he saw Greg sink deeper into the chair, his glass in one hand. He looked deceptively lazy but Tyler knew him well enough to know he missed nothing.

Not the way Tyler's breathing increased as they kissed, the need for air becoming more critical as he refused to give up her mouth.

Or the way her hands slid up and down his arms. Soft at first, as if he were fragile, then with more pressure until she couldn't seem to get enough of touching him.

The contact revved his heartbeat until he thought it would pound out of his chest.

He couldn't have cared less.

Her lips moved under his with a sinuous grace, drawing him deeper into the world they were creating between them.

That world shrank to encompass only the three of them, with Kate as the bright star in the center.

He soaked in her heat, one hand wrapped around her hair, the other wrapped around her throat. Her pulse beat strong beneath his thumb, and he stroked her fine skin until he felt goose bumps rise.

Shifting beneath him, she sighed into his mouth, encouraging him to take more.

His tongue sank deeper, became more forceful. And instead of letting him set the pace, she answered it. Her tongue stroked along his, refused to let him dominate her.

For now, he let her, knowing soon enough he'd be totally in charge. And that she would love it.

He stroked up her arm again, letting his knuckles brush against the curve of her breast. She breathed a moan into his mouth and shifted until her breast pressed more fully against the back of his hand.

Pulling back, he gazed down, seeing her taut nipple poking into the black satin.

"You have beautiful breasts."

Out of the corner of his eye, he saw her roll her eyes. "They're small."

"They're fucking perfect. I want to rub my cock against them."

She swallowed hard and took in a shuddering breath. "You have a dirty mouth. I never thought I'd like that about a man. I guess it just depends on the man."

That's right. He was her man.

To prove it to her, he cupped one breast, molding it with his palm. She arched her back, pressing more of herself against him.

"What do you want, Kate?"

"I want your mouth on my breast."

"Isn't my hand enough?"

"No. I need more. Give me more."

He grinned as she clutched at his shoulders, demand in her voice. "I'll give you what you want, Kate. I'll give you everything and more. Trust me."

Again, that eye roll. "I trust you more than I've trusted any other man I've let in my bed."

He wanted to pump his fist in the air, barely restrained himself from leaning down and biting her neck, marking her so everyone knew she was taken.

His emotions for her ranged from primal to absolute Neanderthal and he wasn't sure if he liked it. He only knew he wanted her to be screaming his name very soon.

Leaning close, he whispered in her ear, pitching his voice low enough that Greg couldn't hear. What he had to say was for her ears only. "And I never thought I'd fall this hard for another woman in my life."

When he drew away, the look in her eyes had softened to something very close to sweet.

And while he appreciated it, right now he wanted her to burn.

There'd be more than enough time later to tell her he loved her. When they were alone.

Tightening his hand on her breast for a few seconds, he pulled down the bodice until he could see her nipples peeking out.

He bent to put his lips around one hard tip, pulled hard on her pebbled flesh. Sucking her into his mouth and drawing on her until he swore he couldn't get any more in his mouth. Then he drew back until he could lap at her with his tongue. Her skin tasted of heat and salt and smelled like vanilla. Sweet.

He wanted to bite so he gave into the desire, his teeth sinking into her flesh. Her gasp didn't hold any pain and her fingers clenched in his hair as if afraid he might try to leave.

No way was he leaving. Not when this was exactly where he wanted to be.

Without moving his mouth, his tongue distracting them both in wicked ways, he repositioned himself on the chaise. Now he kneeled between her thighs, her legs spread on either side of his.

Her slip had risen up her thighs to allow her legs to part but still managed to cover the most interesting areas.

Even so, he swore he felt the heat emanating from her core against his knees.

And he knew he smelled the scent of her arousal. It made him want to desert her breast for other, softer parts of her body.

Soon enough.

Lowering his other hand to her neglected breast, he cupped that one, rubbing the nipple between his thumb and forefinger. Again, she squirmed. Her back arched, grinding his mouth even harder against her breast.

That little hint of pain made her moan and he tweaked her nipple with his fingers until she did it again.

He would never hurt her, but he knew the threshold between pain and pleasure was a thin one. It was all in the execution. And the level of trust.

Biting down a fraction of a second longer, he let that pain settle in before he soothed it with his tongue.

She cried out when he released her and tried to hold his head to her breast. Looking up at her, he saw her eyes were closed, the lids scrunched tight. Absorbing the sensations.

Okay for now. Mindlessness would come later. For both of them.

Lowering his mouth back to her body, he kissed his way across her chest, sucking on her skin and leaving tiny marks. The bite he left on the plump curve of her other breast showed as a bright red mark.

His.

Instead of pulling her nipple into his mouth this time, he circled it with his tongue, flicking the tip before using his teeth on the opposite side.

Her entire body shook when he released her, her chest rising and falling and making her breasts quiver.

Turning his head, he brushed his beard-shadowed cheek against one nipple and elicited another moan from her.

He loved the sounds she made. They sank deep into his psyche and stroked parts of himself he'd thought frozen into oblivion.

Lifting his head, he claimed her mouth again, whipping his tongue against hers, fucking her with it.

When she caught it between her teeth and sucked hard on him, he had to fight back the orgasm threatening to explode from his cock.

He didn't realize she'd started to unbutton his shirt until it gaped open. His nipples stood at attention as the room's cooler air brushed against them. When she'd done away with the rest of the buttons, her hands spread the fabric wide and she just stared up at him for several seconds.

"I love your body." Her words held a power that whipped against him like a lash. "So strong, so masculine. So touchable."

"Then go ahead and touch me. I'm all yours."

"Take the shirt off for me. I want full access."

He swallowed hard as he did what she wanted, knowing the time was coming when he'd be the ones making the demands. And his demands would require so much more of her than she asked from him.

Shrugging his shoulders, he dropped his arms to his sides and let the shirt fall to his wrists before he dropped it to the floor at his side. Her hands had already returned and settled on his pecs. She stroked him with delicate fingers, barely touching his skin. The hair on his chest felt as if he'd been electrified. It stood on end, adding to his sensitivity.

His eyes narrowed to slits as he absorbed her touch. He forced them to stay open because he wanted to watch her, see her reaction.

It was worth the effort. She looked mesmerized, fascinated. Her fingers swirled through the hair to his nipples, which she pinched and pulled.

Not nearly enough. "Harder, Kate. Use your nails."

She immediately complied, sinking her nails into his nipples and sending waves of sharp shock straight to his groin.

His breath hissed between his teeth only seconds later when she soothed that pain by stroking her fingertips over the nail marks.

"Lick them," he growled.

"I can do that."

Sliding one hand behind her back, he lifted her to him, cradling her head and bringing her mouth where he wanted her to be.

He felt the wet swipe of her tongue across one nipple then the other, her hands curving around his ribs then stroking down to his hips. Her teeth nipped at him a second later, biting each nipple in turn.

God, yes. Even harder.

As if she'd read his mind, she sucked on one tip before mimicking his earlier action and biting the muscle of his pec.

His entire body jerked in reaction and a growl rumbled in his chest. He felt her shiver, hands clenching around his biceps.

After several long seconds, she began to work her way up his body, placing kisses along his collarbone and neck. Her warm lips left a trail of zinging sensation that threatened his control. When she nipped at his earlobe, he groaned as his body absorbed the pleasure.

He had the almost overpowering urge to strip her naked and fuck her until they couldn't move. And then he'd flip her onto her stomach and start all over again.

He felt almost out of control and, for once, that might not be a bad thing. She wanted him to loosen his reins, trust her to know what she wanted and to tell him if he did something she didn't like.

She wanted him to trust her to know how far to go, to stop him if she felt uncomfortable.

He was about to take her at her word.

* *

Kate felt the exact moment Tyler's mood shifted.

Until that point, he'd been almost . . . restrained. That's the only way she could describe the feeling she got from him. As if he'd leashed all that dominance she knew he held inside but now he'd snapped the chains.

For her.

She wanted to grin with victory but she could only stare at him as he settled her back on the chaise and rose above her.

Out of the corner of her eye, she saw Greg, felt his presence, but it wasn't enough to pull her attention from Tyler.

His dark gaze focused with laser precision on her, almost feral in its intensity. She had a brief moment to savor the thought that she brought this out of him before he put his hands on her thighs.

He didn't rush, but he didn't make any attempt to tease as he worked the hem of the chemise up her body.

The satin slid against her skin as his eyes followed the material's progress.

As it cleared her hips, her black lace panties came into view.

His breathing changed, became harsher, as he realized they were split down the center, allowing him access to her sex while she kept them on.

His gaze lingered at her mound as he pushed the satin up her body, causing her to shift restlessly. She wanted him to pet her there, ease a little of the building pressure.

Instead, his hands continued up her torso to her breasts. The black lace bra lifted her breasts, pushing them into slightly fuller mounds, but the half cups revealed more than they concealed. Her nipples were fully exposed and so tight they actually hurt when he dragged the satin across them.

She couldn't completely control her moan, and the corners of his mouth twisted in masculine triumph.

Her sex clenched and moisture slicked her lips, dampening the panties. Tyler's nostrils flared as he sucked in a deep breath, drawing in her scent.

Her tongue emerged to lick at her lips even as her mouth went dry as she thought about him licking up that moisture.

"Lift your arms."

He'd gotten the chemise to just above her breasts and she did as he demanded without hesitation.

The world went black for a second as he pulled the chemise over her head. Then Tyler reappeared. He sat back on his heels, rubbing the satin between his fingers for several seconds. She knew what those fingers felt like on her nipples and, unbelievably, they hardened even more.

In the next second, Tyler tossed the material to the side. Toward Greg. She turned to see him catch the chemise with one hand, as if it were a fly ball at a game.

In contrast to Tyler's, Greg's expression wasn't as dark, though it held the same intensity. His mouth curved in such a sensuous motion that her breath got caught in her chest.

Then Tyler shifted above her, drawing her attention like a moth to the light. She'd gladly burn in his arms.

Please God, she wanted to burn, wanted to feel that amazing sensation of free-falling again, knowing Tyler would be there to catch her. And take her back up again until she was barely conscious.

How had she ever thought sex had been good before?

That one was easy. She really hadn't.

"Kate." Tyler's voice held an edge that commanded her attention. "I want your eyes on me until I tell you otherwise."

She'd never thought she'd want to rub herself against a man and purr. Damn, she wished she could right now. She settled for a quick nod.

"I'm going to have you make a set of this in every imaginable color." His words almost didn't make sense in her sex-focused brain until he ran a finger down one of her bra straps. "I predict these will be huge sellers in your boutique."

She swallowed, tried to think of something intelligent to say and gave up when his fingers surrounded one nipple and pinched.

Her lips parted as she drew in air just before her teeth sank into her bottom lip and held there. Her sex ached to be filled, clenching around nothing, and her thighs tried to close.

But his knees held her open, displaying the slick, swollen lips of her pussy pushing through the slit in her panties.

"I like the detail here." His fingers traced the satin trim on the cups just below her nipples. "How the bra forces your breasts out and up. Perfect to get my mouth on."

He bent forward and did just that, sucking and licking at her nipples as if he had all the time in the world. She reached for him, but he grabbed her wrists then used one hand to hold them above her head. The position, combined with the curve of the chaise beneath her, made her shoulders ache.

She arched even more, intensifying the burn and competing with the feel of his mouth sucking at her breasts.

She'd have marks there tomorrow. Hopefully she'd have matching ones lower on her body, as well.

Twisting against his hold, though she didn't really want him to let go, she managed to rub her sex against his knee, providing some much needed friction.

But as soon as he realized what she was doing, he moved.

"Not yet, sweetheart. Not until I'm ready to shove my cock inside that tight pussy."

She should be used to him using that language with her, but it still managed to make her stomach hollow with pleasure every time.

Tyler bent forward again, but this time his lips sucked one lobe into his mouth before he breathed into her ear. "After that, I'm going to take your ass."

Yes. She'd known that would be part of tonight and was prepared to say yes. Wanted to say yes.

"And maybe I'll finally let you come when Greg has his cock shoved inside you at the same time."

A sharp orgasm lit through her, short and fierce. Her eyes closed as her body bowed with the fiery burn that lasted only seconds.

And only made her hungrier for him.

She bit back a whimper, though the slight sound that escaped didn't embarrass her as much as she thought it would.

"Don't," Tyler said. "Don't hold back. I want to hear you, Kate. I love hearing your response."

She opened her eyes and found him sitting back on his heels, hands on his thighs, gaze on hers.

"Now, I want you to sit up and undo my pants."

"With my teeth?"

Greg's bark of laughter made her smile but it was Tyler's full-out grin that caused her stomach to twist in knots. She still had no idea how he managed it. Why just a twist of his lips could cause her entire being to go up in flames.

"Honey, if you can do it with your teeth, go right ahead."

She cocked her head to the side, as if she needed to consider it, when really, she was up for anything with this man. Didn't he know that yet?

"Switch."

He understood what she wanted without her having to explain.

He rose onto his knees before he stood then reached out to grab her around the waist and set her on her knees on the flat end of the chaise. She put her hands on his waist before he could sit, drawing him close and pressing her mouth to his flat abdomen.

She felt his muscles bunch and flex against her lips and opened them just enough to nip at the skin. He groaned and his hands went to her head, holding her close but not tight.

Leaving her room to play.

His skin radiated heat as she pressed kisses from one side of his stomach to the next, just above the waistband of his pants. The bulge behind the zipper made the button too tight to release with only her teeth so she took care of that with her fingers. She took her own sweet time, bumping against the fat head of his cock every chance she got.

When the button gave way, she heard him curse beneath his breath, his hands winding in her hair. Then she did use her teeth.

The zipper tab was just long enough for her to grip between her front teeth and tug it down. His breathing sounded labored and only got more so when she turned her head to brush her cheek against his cock, nearly bursting out of his boxer briefs.

"Take them down and suck me, Kate."

"My pleasure."

And it certainly would be.

Making certain she didn't hurt him as she tugged his pants and briefs down his powerful thighs, she watched as he kicked off his shoes and the rest of his clothes, along with the last vestiges of her propriety. It had no place here.

Only pleasure.

She leaned forward and took him straight to her throat, the thick shaft spreading her lips until the corners burned. Her saliva coated him, making it easier for her to give him a blow job he'd always remember.

She held nothing back, allowed no hesitation or notion of how she should act come between her and him and what she wanted to do.

Her hands curved around his hips then clutched at his ass, kneading the tight muscles as he groaned and began to fuck her mouth with short thrusts.

She let him use her mouth, flattening her tongue along the underside to provide a little bit of friction. He nearly pulled out on each third thrust, until only the tip still remained in her mouth before he tunneled back in.

From this angle, she couldn't look up into his face but she could hear his gasping breaths.

And she could hear Greg's, as well.

On Tyler's next retreat, she let him slip completely out of her mouth so she could tilt her head back to look up at him. He had his eyes closed tight, his face all sharp angles and shadows.

Looking back down, she licked at the slit in his cock then drew the tip of her tongue down the front of his cock to his balls.

Reaching between his legs, she cupped him before circling her fingers around the base and tugging. She'd never imagined all those romance novels she'd devoured in college would come in handy.

"Christ, Kate. Suck me, baby. Just a little more."

Of course she would. Gladly.

She dipped her head and swallowed him again, sucking on him until her cheeks hollowed. His cock jerked against her tongue and she tasted pre cum.

Just as she felt Greg's hand slide down her back.

She moaned, her body thrown into shock. Tyler's hands went to her shoulders to hold her steady as she shook, her mouth still wrapped around his cock.

While Greg's hands began a slow, steady exploration of her body.

As she adjusted to the fact that two men had their hands on her, Tyler took over their rhythm.

So many competing sensations bombarded her, her brain short-circuited trying to keep track of what each man was doing to her.

Tyler's hands gripped her shoulder and cupped a breast, while Greg's hands smoothed down her back to her ass.

His hands were bigger than Tyler's, and rougher. He didn't treat her roughly but he had a distinctly different way of caressing her.

Tyler touched her as if he wanted to memorize every inch of her. Greg . . . Greg touched her as if he wanted to fuck her.

God, could she actually pass out from the lust beating through her veins?

"Breathe, Kate. Through your nose. Your mouth is fucking heaven. I'm not ready to give it up yet."

Tyler's voice calmed her even as Greg's confident hands continued to discover her body.

Her attention splintered. Tyler continued with slow, steady strokes in her mouth, rubbing over her tongue and lips. Greg stroked her back, as if to gentle her. Getting her used to his touch.

She didn't think that'd be possible. The reality of what they were engaged in was so much more intense than she'd ever thought possible. She wanted to drown in it. Wallow in it.

Let it take her out of her head.

Because she heard the murmurs, the doubts. She'd had no trouble keeping them at bay until Greg had touched her.

And even though she loved what they were doing to her, she couldn't shake the feeling that she shouldn't be allowing this.

"Kate."

Tyler's voice made her pull back, his cock sliding from her mouth so she could look up at him. Behind her, Greg stilled, though he didn't release her, his hands holding steady on her hips.

"Kate. Do you want to stop?"

How had he read her mind so easily? How had she betrayed her thoughts?

"I won't force you to do anything you don't want to do," he continued when she stayed silent. "You want to stop, all you have to do is say the word and that's it."

Except she didn't want to stop. She wanted this. So why was she faltering?

Her attack of nerves seemed pretty damn ridiculous when she was mostly naked and staring directly at Tyler's straining erection only inches from her mouth.

She knew it was Greg's presence, knew her upbringing hadn't prepared her for anything like the situation she found herself in now.

But she didn't want him to leave. She wanted this. Wanted Tyler. Wanted Greg to be here with them.

Damn it, she wasn't going to let her insecurities get in the way of what she wanted. Not now.

"I want this."

The corners of his mouth lifted and he stroked his fingers along her chin. "So do I. But we don't want you to regret this. Not any of it."

"Do you want me to leave?" Greg's voice made her start. "I'm not going to lie and tell you I don't want to stay. I do." He stroked one hand up her back, making her shiver in response. "You're beautiful and sexy as hell, and we will make this night amazing for you. But if you're in the least uncomfortable, I'll go. No hard feelings."

Over her shoulder, she saw Greg watching her, no hint of recrimination on his face. If she said no, he'd walk out.

"Stay."

Greg smiled, lazy and satisfied. Like a predator who'd just spotted easy prey. "You won't regret this."

His hands began to move again, one up her torso, the other down the back of her thigh, returning her to the most amazing sensual experience.

Her eyes wanted to shut but Tyler gripped her chin. "Turn around."

She nodded, not trusting herself to speak, then took a deep breath as she maneuvered until she was facing the opposite direction. Staring at Greg.

He caught her gaze but stayed silent as she knelt there, so turned on she couldn't think, much less breathe.

Behind her, Tyler leaned into her, his chest to her back, his cock nestled into the crease of her ass. She blinked, feeling a moan begin to build in her chest. When his teeth nipped at her earlobe, she shook.

"I'm going to take you just like this," he said. "And Greg is going to suck on your nipples and play with your clit until you come so hard, you won't know where you are."

Her moan escaped, a deep, guttural sound that made Greg

smile as he reached out to pluck at a nipple. "I think she likes when you talk dirty. Don't you, Kate?"

She wanted to answer but couldn't find the words because Tyler had shifted, one hand positioning his cock between her legs.

He didn't enter her yet, just rubbed his shaft between her legs, against her labia. Already overstimulated, her sex clenched and unclenched around nothing. She wriggled, trying to get him to pierce her and fill that aching void.

Tyler grabbed her hips to hold her steady as he increased his pace.

"So wet. Think how good it will feel when I get inside. Not yet, though. The anticipation is half the fun, isn't it?"

Greg chose that moment to use both hands to pinch at her nipples as he molded his palms to her breasts.

Her mouth parted but no sound emerged. She was too caught up in the sensations rioting through her.

"Take Greg's clothes off now, Kate." Tyler's voice held an edge that hadn't been there before. "When you're done, then I'll fuck you."

Without thought, she reached for the hem of Greg's long-sleeved T-shirt, pushing her hands beneath to touch his skin.

Her fingers played over his abdomen, ridged with muscle. She hadn't expected him to be so cut. It made her want to see more.

Greg released her breasts so she could shove his shirt up, pausing for a moment to catch her breath when the head of Tyler's cock hit her clit. But he stopped moving when she froze.

So she continued to pull Greg's shirt over his head, and Tyler began to stroke her again.

She was starting to learn the rules and found she really liked this game.

When she had the T-shirt high on his chest, Greg reached behind him and yanked it over his head.

She hadn't expected the tattoos. An intricate design covered the right half of his torso, so colorful she couldn't quite make out the design.

Behind her, Tyler stilled his thrusts, his cock poised at the entrance to her body as his hand slid around to her front to lie over her mound.

"What is it?" she asked.

Greg reached for her, weaving his fingers into her hair and pushing it over her shoulder. "It's a dragon. My first directing job was a fantasy. A dragon, a virgin, and a hero. But it turned out the dragon was the good guy and the hero was the villain, and the virgin saved the dragon in the end."

She smiled at the wry tone of his voice and pleased smile that seemed to contradict it. "*The Virgin and the Terror.*"

His expression was equal parts shock and almost childlike glee. "You've seen it?"

"I have a thing for cult movies. I always wanted the dragon to shape-shift into a gorgeous guy so they could have mind-blowing sex. Turn around."

As Greg moved to show her his back, Tyler bent closer, brushing aside her hair so he could put his mouth on the sensitive skin of her nape.

She shivered, her fingers clutching at Greg's waist as her vision dimmed. But she forced her eyes open. She needed to show she wasn't the timid, quivering idiot she'd been only seconds ago.

"This is stunning."

The tattoo had been done by a master and covered his entire back along with his right side.

"Thanks. Took fucking forever to finish, but I was still young enough to think lying on a tattoo table for hours on end while getting shit-faced was fun."

"Now he's old enough to know that this is a hell of a lot more fun," Tyler's voice whispered against her skin, and the lust roared back with a vengeance.

Her eyes closed, shutting out the brilliant colors as Tyler began to move again. Slow enough to be considered torture.

When Greg's lips covered hers, she was ready for him. Ready for the shock of the different. The forbidden.

Ready for it to burn her to the core.

Sixteen

❦

Tyler knew surrender when he saw it.

It was in the fall of Kate's hair down her back as she lifted her face to Greg's. In the arm she curved around her back to reach for him.

When she flattened her hand on his ass and pulled him tighter against her, he knew he didn't have to wait any longer.

The tight fit of her thighs around his cock felt great, but he'd feel even better when he pushed inside her. She was so wet, so hot.

Mine.

He retreated one more time, her thighs clenching around him as if to hold him there, squeezing the tip of his cock.

When he pulled free with a groan, he took a moment to watch her kiss Greg.

She was lost in the sensuality of the moment and he knew exactly how that felt. Like he was coming apart from the inside out. Like the heat roaring through his blood would make him explode.

When he did, he wanted to be buried inside her.

Moving his hands to her thighs, he gripped the sleek muscles just below her ass and spread her legs to make a place for himself between them. She gripped him tighter, her nails digging into the skin. The slight burn made him grin and bend forward to press his lips to her shoulder.

He felt a shudder move through her body and couldn't resist the temptation to bite her. Just hard enough to leave a slight red mark.

And make her moan.

Pulling away from Greg, she tried to turn, but Tyler held her in place.

"Lean forward, sweetheart." His voice sounded rough, almost gritty. "Don't worry. Greg won't let you fall."

When she didn't move right away, he put a hand in the center of her back and guided her down. Greg had already moved to accommodate the shift in position, putting his cock in reach of her mouth. Tyler didn't know if she realized that Greg wouldn't take advantage.

Despite his Hollywood playboy reputation, Greg had an old-fashioned sense of honor that Tyler had only ever seen surface in the bedroom.

Greg wouldn't even hint at having Kate suck him off unless she made the first move.

Tyler had no such compunction.

With the head of his cock lodged at the slick entrance to her body, he stopped and pressed his lips to her ear. "Go ahead. Suck him, Kate. You know you want to, and I want to watch you. I know there's nothing as good as being in your mouth and I know you enjoy it. And that's all this is about tonight. Pleasure."

She didn't respond immediately but he knew she was thinking about what he'd said. And what he hadn't. That nothing she did here would affect the way he felt about her.

And he knew it wouldn't be long before he made his feelings clear on that point.

But now wasn't the time.

"Go on. Take what you want. No fear. No reservations."

"Will you give me what I want?"

His cock bucked at the husky tone of her voice, and he saw Greg's hands tighten on her shoulders.

"Absolutely."

"Then fuck me, Tyler. Now."

He pulled her back with a jerk, impaling her on his sheathed cock in one smooth glide.

The guttural sound she emitted made his balls tighten in a breath-stealing rush.

And when she clamped around him with the tight grip of a fist, he had to stop and hold back on his immediate need to thrust.

If he did, he'd come in seconds. He'd lose himself in her and deprive her of the feeling of being fucked while she pleasured another man.

Her body stiffened as he sank deep, but only for a second. Then she wriggled her ass against him as she craned her head forward and took Greg into her mouth.

He heard Greg's indrawn breath and the sharp profanity that followed, and forced himself not to move so he could absorb the feel of her and watch her explore her own sexuality.

She moved tentatively at first, as if she was afraid to hurt Greg. But as she became more confident, gave into the sensuality she held too close inside sometimes, he couldn't hold back anymore.

He started to move. Slowly. Excruciatingly slowly, because what he really wanted to do was rush. Pound against her and pour himself into her.

Selfish. Can't be selfish.

But it was so hard when he saw the picture she made. Her skin glowed in the low light, contrasting with the darkness of his thighs pressed against her ass. The silky mass of her hair slid against her slim back and fell over her shoulders. He didn't know how Greg resisted rubbing that hair against his stomach.

From this angle, he could see only the side of her face, the way her cheeks hollowed as she sucked Greg's cock.

Greg's eyes were closed, his expression tight with lust. From the looks of him, he wouldn't last long.

Tyler knew he wouldn't. Kate had that effect on him.

His pace increased without conscious thought, his hips driving him deeper on each forward thrust.

She clenched more tightly around him with each thrust, taking Greg deeper each time she moved on him.

Tyler knew how that mouth felt around his dick, the way she licked and sucked as if she was enjoying some amazing treat. Knew the control Greg was exerting not to hold her steady and take over.

A soul-deep urge to give her anything and everything she wanted made him work his straining erection even deeper inside her. He heard her breath hitch when he hit a certain spot inside and he made sure he scraped the head of his cock there every chance he got.

He knew when she reached her breaking point. With a gasp, she pulled away from Greg, both hands reaching behind her to grab at him.

Greg didn't let her fall, even though he had to be aching for release. He held her up as she moaned out Tyler's name and clamped around his cock.

The intensity of his orgasm blinded him as she came in waves of rippling pleasure that dragged him down with her.

* *

After several moments where the only sound was heavy breathing, Kate felt Tyler pull out.

Her oversensitized body protested by clenching around him, which set off another wave of pleasure.

When Tyler wrapped his arms around her and took them both down to the chaise, she found herself trying to catch her breath and fight out of the lethargy that wanted to steal all rational thought.

"Next time," Tyler's voice rasped in her ear, "I'm taking your ass while Greg fucks you."

Oh, my God.

Her body responded to the roughness in his tone with a renewed burst of lust, so fiery in its intensity she felt scorched.

"Tyler—"

"Don't say you haven't thought about it."

With Tyler wrapped around her back, she could only stare forward. Straight at Greg, who'd retreated back to his chair.

He'd hiked up his pants but hadn't replaced his shirt. His head rested against the back cushion, his gaze on hers.

He didn't look ruffled at all, while she felt . . . on fire.

Until she noticed the still-rapid rise and fall of his chest. And the glitter of his eyes.

He didn't come.

Was that her fault? Had she not done something right?

Or was he simply biding his time?

She hoped to hell it was the latter explanation. Because she so much wanted to experience everything Tyler wanted to give her.

Including, apparently, Greg.

"Kate, are you okay?"

She didn't scold him for asking the question. Not this time.

"I'm fine." She reached around to pet his thigh, rough against the back of hers. "Well," she smiled, "maybe not fine. But there's definitely nothing wrong. Except . . ."

His hand flattened against her stomach. "What?"

"Greg didn't come."

A part of her couldn't believe she'd said those words.

Another part was thrilled she had.

Tyler's lips found the sensitive spot on her neck right behind her ear and bit her before he soothed it with his lips. She was pretty sure he was smiling.

"Greg's got control issues."

Tyler's dry tone made her smile, which in turn made Greg's lips curve in a sensual grin.

Her chest tightened. Hard to believe she'd only met the man a few days ago. Even harder to believe she'd had his cock in her mouth only minutes ago.

Heat drenched her at the thought, but she refused to feel guilty. Absolutely refused to let anyone else's idea of morality affect her own.

"How do I break through that control?"

Greg's grin receded but his eyes burned as he radiated lust.

Her body tightened and moistened as her heart began to speed again.

At the rate she was going, she'd have a heart attack.

But, oh, God, it'd be worth it.

"Show him genuine affection."

Tyler pitched his voice too low for Greg to hear, as if what he was telling her was a secret. And maybe it was.

The answer sounded almost too simple. Too easy.

And yet . . . Why should it be?

She couldn't imagine how many people wanted something from Greg at any given moment. The man held an inordinate amount of power in a business that thrived on it. Every woman he met probably had an ulterior motive.

Which made her realize why this situation worked for him. Because he knew she had no interest in him other than as a sexual partner.

Except that she truly liked him . . . as much as she knew him.

She knew he had a dry wit, an awesome body, and a gentle nature he hid completely.

And he was one of Tyler's best friends, and she trusted Tyler implicitly.

Holding Greg's gaze, she propped herself up on one elbow and crooked her finger at Greg.

He didn't respond right away but he did smile, those green eyes narrowing down to slits.

When he finally stood and walked over, she held up that one finger again and had him stop several inches away.

Though his pants hung open, she couldn't see anything interesting.

"Lose the pants."

Her voice sounded seductive, sexy. She liked it. Apparently Greg did too, if his expression was anything to go by.

After a brief hesitation, he shoved his pants down until they pooled around his ankles and he kicked them off. When he stood naked in front of her, she had a brief moment to appreciate just how ruggedly built the man was.

He wouldn't look out of place on a professional hockey team with his thickly muscled thighs, defined abs, and broad chest.

Greg obviously took care of himself, and she was about to reap the benefit of his diligence.

Behind her, Tyler shifted until she could no longer feel his body against hers though she knew he hadn't gone far.

"My turn to watch."

Tyler's voice had dropped even more, until it sounded like a gruff rasp that rubbed against her skin, a rough caress on the most sensitive areas of her body.

As if he'd shoved his hands between her legs and stroked her clit.

Her thighs clenched tighter, attempting to ease the ache, but she didn't have time because Greg knelt on the cushion next to her, put one hand behind her head and drew her up for a kiss.

She hadn't been expecting it and he took her breath away as her hands reached for his shoulders.

Greg's kiss had a hard edge, so different from Tyler's. It almost seemed forbidden, like she should be fighting it instead of allowing herself to be dragged under.

He kissed her like he wanted to devour her, to force her to submit. For several seconds, she let herself be devoured, let herself submit.

Sensing her surrender, he pressed harder, his tongue becoming more demanding, his other hand curving around one breast before pinching the nipple between his fingers.

He pushed her into each sensation, prodding her to fall, to give up control.

But where Tyler pushed with restraint, Greg didn't have any.

He sped forward with barely controlled speed, almost too fast for her to process.

But that was kind of the point, wasn't it? To lose herself in the rush and the speed?

No, not lose herself. Immerse herself.

She kissed him back as her hands slid across his bare shoulders then around to his back. Drawing him closer, she arched her back, pressing her breast more fully into his hand. She wanted him to knead her harder, pinch her nipple tighter.

The hand at her neck flexed, his fingers pulling at her hair. His lips ground into hers until she thought he'd split her lip. Then he pulled back and dragged his teeth down her neck.

She gasped at the strength of the shudder that tore through her, her fingers digging into his shoulders until she thought she'd draw blood.

And when he bit her nipple, she couldn't keep from crying out.

Her eyes flew open when she realized how she sounded. Like a woman lost in passion. With a man who wasn't hers.

She turned to find Tyler staring at her, eyeing her like a hawk. Still naked, he sat in the chair nearest the chaise, his erect cock in hand.

As Greg sucked on her breast, Tyler stroked himself with a hard, twisting movement that looked almost painful. He obviously liked what he saw because his cock stood stiff and ruddy red.

If he'd been closer, she would've reached for him, wrapped her hand around his cock and pushed him over the same edge she was teetering on.

Instead, she watched his hand work his cock, watched his hand twist over the bulging head before sliding back down the shaft.

She could have lost herself watching him, but Greg refused to let her.

After a fierce squeeze, Greg released her breast before shoving his hand between her legs and cupping her.

Her eyes closed as he pressed two fingers inside her slick channel, buried them deep and stroked her on the inside.

Her already sensitive tissue quivered in response, clenching around him, trying to suck him deeper. He rotated his hand until he got his thumb in a position to prod her clit, rubbing her, stroking her. Bringing her to the edge then backing off until he had her begging for release.

She needed it, needed that release. If she didn't get it soon, she might melt down and lose her sanity.

"Tyler, please."

"Tyler isn't the one you need to be asking for release, Kate." Greg's voice felt like an electric shock through her body, making her muscles go rigid. "Ask me for what you want."

Her eyes flew open and she found herself staring into Greg's green eyes. So pale. So different from Tyler's.

His fingers twisted, his knuckles scraping and tormenting.

She gasped, arching toward him.

"Say it, Kate. Come on, I know you want to. You know Tyler wants you to."

And she wanted to give Tyler a show as much as she wanted to get laid right now.

She laced one hand through his too-long hair and yanked. "Fuck me, Greg. Right now."

In the next second, she was moving. Greg shifted until he lay on his back on the chaise, head at the flat end, feet planted on the floor at either side. He lifted her over his lap until she had one knee on either side of his hips and her sex spread over his cock.

With his hands on her hips, he held her suspended over him, all the lovely muscles of his abdomen taut and sharply defined.

She kept waiting for him to lower her onto his cock but when she looked down, she saw he was so hard, he'd need help getting his cock in position.

She had no problem giving him a hand.

Reaching down, she wrapped her hand around his thick erection, watching Greg's eyes narrow until they were almost shut. His cock pulsed as she squeezed, her other hand slipping between his legs to fondle his balls.

Greg let her play with him for only seconds before he growled, "Enough. Condom. Now."

Turning, she found Tyler holding one in his hand, which he reached over to hand her.

Their gazes connected as she took the foil packet and tore it open. She had to tear her eyes away to roll the condom on Greg's cock, watching him as he watched her hands work on the sheath.

Once she had him covered, she rolled her hips forward until she was positioned at the perfect angle.

Again, she looked at Tyler, whose gaze shifted to where her sex teased the tip of Greg's cock.

The sensation was decadent. Wicked. And so insanely hot, she knew she'd only have to think about this later and she'd never be cold again.

Settling one hand on Greg's shoulder, she rolled her hips again, rubbing his cock between her labia, taking him a centimeter deeper with each movement.

The feel of the head lodged there, not quite inside her body but no longer a tease, made her want to force her body down, take him as deep as she could until he filled all the aching places inside her.

That first round of sex with Tyler had only made her hungrier, hotter.

She knew what was coming, what they were building toward, but she didn't want to rush. She wanted to draw it out. Make Tyler crazy with lust. Make Greg beg for her to finish him.

Looking down at Greg, she watched his lips flatten into a straight line as she sank a little deeper, until the head had breached her body and began to stretch her channel.

Relief and greed for more warred as she wriggled down his

shaft. Each slight shimmy lodged him deeper, made his lips draw flat and his cheekbones stand out in stark contrast.

She swore she felt his hands on her hips tremble before he clenched her tighter. He didn't try to force her to go faster, though, simply held his body almost perfectly still, letting her do all the work. Have all the control.

Shooting Tyler a quick glance, she saw he'd released his cock, both hands now clamped on to the arms of the chair, as if holding himself back. His body seemed poised for movement. As if at any moment, he'd launch himself at them.

Just the thought of what would happen then made her shiver.

And slide a little farther down Greg's shaft.

She was so wet, he went easily. She didn't want easy.

She wanted rough. Wanted hard.

Wanted dirty.

She sank down and took the rest of him inside in one smooth motion.

Moaning at the sensation of being filled so completely, she dug her fingers into his pecs, the hard muscles tight. But not as hard as the one impaling her body. He felt like silk-encased iron, thick and hot and burning her from the inside.

Her eyes closed as her body reacted to the intrusion, clenching around him until she couldn't bear to stay still one moment longer.

Using her thigh muscles, she lifted her body until only the tip of him remained. Then she sank, hard and fast. Almost too fast. Too hard.

Not enough.

With her eyes closed, she set a rhythm that would get her what she wanted as fast as possible.

Already, her womb began to contract, sharp ripples of excitement spreading through her lower body.

Greg let her control the pace though his hands stayed glued to her hips, holding her steady. She felt ready to fly apart when suddenly Tyler moved behind her and wrapped his arms around her shoulders.

"Hang on, baby. I don't want you going off yet. I want to make this even better."

That rough whisper in her ear made her shake in his arms. On her hips, Greg's hands held her steady, refusing to let her move though she tried.

Thwarted, she contracted around the cock in her pussy even as she rubbed against the one she felt at her rear.

With her eyes closed, every sensation was heightened. The feel of Greg's hips between her thighs, the feel of his shaft as it seemed to thicken every second. Tyler's body against her back, the brush of his chest hair sensitizing her skin.

His arms tightened as she bucked back against him, trying to get him to do something, anything to relieve some of this pressure building in her groin.

"I want your ass, Kate. Can I take you there while Greg fucks your pussy? I swear you'll enjoy it."

She nodded because she couldn't speak, the excitement had stolen her breath.

She'd never had anal sex, hadn't really even considered it before, but now she was dying for it. Wanted him to bend her over and fulfill his promise to her.

He didn't answer, but he did run his lips down her throat until he opened his mouth over the juncture of her neck and shoulders and bit on the tendon.

Crying out, she felt herself falling forward, felt her breasts crushed against Greg's broad chest, his cock still embedded deep inside.

Tyler's hands began a slow slide down her back, teasing, petting, kneading, until he reached her ass.

Then he caressed, warming her until she was sure her skin had to be bright red.

The difference in the angle of penetration caused her to arch her back and Greg thrust, short and sharp, to keep himself seated as deep as he could.

She wanted to move again, felt like she had to move, but the men holding her between them had taken back the control. They made the rules and she obeyed.

At the feel of cool liquid dribbling between her ass cheeks, she moaned. When Tyler's fingers followed, rubbing the slickness around the smaller, puckered entrance, she held her breath.

"Breathe, Kate." Greg's voice was followed by another thrust that gave him even more depth than she thought possible at this angle. "We don't want you to pass out. Trust me, you'll want to be awake for this."

"Then you better hurry because I'm going to take care of this myself if you don't."

Both men laughed, though neither released more than a breath of air. She felt it to her bones.

"Trust me, sweetheart." Tyler pressed his thumb against the tiny hole. "You don't want us to hurry. You want us to take our time."

When he breached her, the pressure on such sensitive tissues made her gasp. And that was only his thumb. How the hell was she going to take his much thicker cock?

She didn't have a lot of time for rational thought after that because he began to do wicked things with that thumb.

Twisting. Stretching. Making her ready.

She tried to stay still, didn't have a choice, really, because Greg held her so tightly, but the need to move had become a necessity. And the need for release pushed her into a state of fevered awareness.

Greg's cock felt like an iron pole shoved inside her, heating her from the inside. Tyler's thumb felt cool as he pressed further.

At first, he used only the tip, but as she squirmed, he sank to the first knuckle. And still she wanted more.

She bore down and heard both men groan. The sound of their desire fueled the fire consuming her. She became a creature of pure sensation, living only for the next release.

Turning her head, she bit Greg's neck, felt him buck beneath her. Heard him swear, one hand moving from her hips to her neck, where he pressed her closer.

"Fuck, Tyler. Do her. Now."

Greg's words barely penetrated her brain but she knew what he wanted.

"Yes. Do me. Tyler, please, just—"

She moaned as she felt Tyler's thumb retreat only to be replaced by the broad tip of his newly sheathed cock, so much bigger than his thumb. With one hand spread across her lower back, he held her still as he pushed forward.

Oh, God. *Yes.* That's what she needed. That bite of pain. That sense of too much.

And it was too much. In the best way possible. She couldn't speak, couldn't think.

She could only hold on while Tyler began to move. So slowly at first, it was almost excruciating. Every nerve ending in her lower body flared, sending confused signals. Pain. Pleasure.

But not enough of either.

"More."

Greg's breath bathed her neck in moist heat just before he turned her head and took her mouth. She sucked on his tongue, giving into the wildness of his kiss as Tyler continued to press forward, filling her until he had nowhere else to go.

When he stopped and held steady, she felt Greg still as well, pulling away from her mouth.

No, no, no. That's not—

Greg began to retreat and the nerve endings in her pussy began to pop and snap in response. She clamped around Greg, around Tyler, making it harder for Greg to move.

Still he managed enough to shoot her straight to the edge of orgasm as he thrust back in. But then Tyler began to move and her overloaded system lost all hold on her response.

The men began a wicked rhythm, rocking her between them, pumping inside her with smooth strokes. She sensed their control, the way they coordinated each motion to maximize her pleasure.

So much. Almost too much.

She felt as if she had too much energy contained in her body. Too much emotion.

Tears formed, but she wasn't upset. With her face buried in Greg's neck, she reached behind her, searching for a connection to Tyler.

He caught her hand, linking his fingers with hers as she bent her arm across her back. That point of contact anchored her even as she felt the first ripple of orgasm filter through her.

"Jesus, Kate. You feel so fucking amazing. I can't get enough of you."

Tyler's lust-infused voice pushed her past ripples and into a full-blown orgasm that tore a cry from her throat as both channels contracted.

"Ah, fuck." Greg groaned, the sound penetrating through his chest into hers. "Can't—"

She had the sensation of falling even though her body was impaled by and sandwiched between two men. She let her climax implode, sucking both men along with her.

Seventeen

❧

Greg returned to his room when Tyler carried Kate back to his apartment.

He'd wondered if Greg would follow, but he just brushed a kiss against Kate's temple and waved good night before disappearing.

Tyler didn't have enough brain cells left to form a coherent argument for Greg to come with them. And right now, it wasn't a major priority.

There'd be time enough tomorrow to figure out what the hell was going on with his friend.

Kate was mostly asleep as he walked to the bathroom, but he knew she'd sleep better if she had a shower.

"Oh, don't even think about taking me anywhere but to bed." She punctuated her words with a tug on his hair. "I'm tired. Want to sleep."

Smiling, he set her feet on the floor but kept her upright by holding her against his side as he turned the taps in the shower. "You will. But you need a shower."

"Hmm. I guess that'll be okay. But put my hair up. And you're doing all the work."

He laughed, loving the grumpy tone of her voice, the warmth of her body. The way her cheek felt against his chest. "I'm fine with that, considering that's what I've been doing anyway for the past couple of hours."

Her hands clenched against his back and her fingernails dug into his skin. Though he doubted he'd be able to get it up again, at least until tomorrow morning, his brain registered the fact that he really, really wanted to.

"And you do it so well."

She sighed then, the rush of air against his chest sparking a more tender emotion. One he hadn't felt in years. Now wasn't the time to blurt it out like a lovesick teenager who'd just gotten laid for the first time.

He was a grown man who knew enough to realize the first time he told a woman he loved her, it should be special.

At the very least, she should be awake enough to appreciate the words.

The woman in his arms could barely keep her eyes open, even though she held on to him with a tight grip.

Almost as tight as his.

The water warmed while he turned to grab an elastic band from the kit she'd left on his vanity.

With a few twists of her hands, she had her hair gathered into a sexy, messy mass on top of her head. He couldn't wait to let it fall again.

She stiffened when he moved them into the spacious marble stall, moaning a little when the spray hit her, then gave an adorable growl and buried her face in his chest as the water soaked her back.

It didn't take her long to warm up, though.

He held her for several minutes, until she felt like a rag doll in his arms, loose-limbed and pliable.

Then he reached for the scented body gel he'd put in here earlier, just for her.

The name had caught his eye in the gift shop earlier this week. Sweet Seduction. When he'd sniffed it, the spicy scent with a hint of sweetness beneath had reminded him of Kate. He'd had bottles of bath gel and body lotion sent to his apartment.

He poured the gel on a puffy and lathered her back. He didn't linger, because they were both tired, but he did make sure he stroked a few key areas several times.

He stayed away from places he knew would be tender, using his hands to wash her between her legs rather than the puffy. And he didn't linger, even though her hips rocked forward as if she wanted him to.

After he'd maneuvered her around so he could wash her front, he used the same gel on himself. Yeah, he'd smell like a girl, but at least it'd remind him of her when she wasn't around.

"I'm thinking about spending some time up at the spa this week. Can I stay with you?"

She didn't say anything right away and for a second, he thought she might have fallen asleep on her feet.

Then she rubbed the back of her head against his shoulder. "Sure." Twisting around, she looked up at him, her eyes barely open. "I'd like that."

As he bent to kiss her, he felt like he was sealing the deal. Hopefully, she'd sign on the line as well.

* *

"Kate, I'm so glad I caught you before you went to work. I have great news. The producers want to meet you immediately. I know we talked about you coming up to visit the theater this week but I've been talking you up since the woman they'd wanted to hire as my assistant took another show. I know it's short notice, but would you be able to come up to the city tomorrow for an interview?"

Tuesday morning, Kate had a brief moment of panic as she froze, mouth hanging open as she tried to think of the words she needed.

Tyler looked up from across her dining table, eyes narrowed as she finally got her tongue unstuck. "Dinah, hi. Tomorrow?"

Her former professor began to laugh. "Sorry, sorry. I know I sound like a crazy woman but honestly, I'm hoping you'll say you can be on the next train up here. I need you, Kate. Like yesterday."

Well, she couldn't exactly say no to that, could she? She took a deep breath and took the plunge. "Sure. I can be there."

She'd call in sick to work. Tomorrow was Wednesday, never particularly busy. Then again, Joe thought every day was busy.

"Oh, that's wonderful. If you can get here by ten, we can talk a little beforehand. Do you have a pen? Let me give you the address."

A minute later, Dinah rang off and Kate sat staring at the address just off 53rd Street and Seventh Avenue that she'd scrawled onto a piece of paper Tyler had handed her, along with a pen.

Her heart raced as panic tried to overtake her.

She felt Tyler's gaze on her but she couldn't meet it.

This job was everything she'd ever wanted. Everything she'd studied for, dreamed about.

And it meant leaving Tyler.

"Kate? Everything okay?"

No, it wasn't.

She couldn't do it all. She'd learned that lesson from her mother. You had to pick and choose carefully or you'd regret your choices for the rest of your life.

She'd already made a huge mistake with Arnie—

"Kate."

Her gaze refocused on Tyler, who stared at her with concern written all over his face.

"I'm fine." She forced a smile, but Tyler wasn't buying it. He continued to stare until she felt compelled to spill the whole story.

"That was my professor from college. I'd called her a few weeks ago about potential jobs in New York."

"Right after you broke up with your fiancé, I assume."

"Yes. I figured if I was going to make a change, I might as well do it big, right?"

His expression didn't change as he nodded, watching her like a hawk. Waiting for her to continue.

"I really didn't expect anything to come of it."

Why did she feel like she was apologizing? She had nothing to apologize for.

"And tomorrow?" Tyler prompted.

"The producers want to meet me."

"So this is a done deal?"

"No."

"But you want the job?"

She opened her mouth to say yes but the word wouldn't come. "I'd have to think about it."

"Why? Isn't this exactly what your degree is in?"

She sighed. "Well, yes, but it's a huge decision. I'd have to move to New York City and find a place to live that won't bankrupt me. And even though I love the city . . . I'm not sure I want to live there."

Tyler leaned back in his chair, in a position she knew meant he was formulating a response. "But this job, it's a foot in the door."

"It's off-Broadway, but yes, if I'm good enough, I could move up the ranks."

"I don't think there's any doubt you're good enough."

Tears welled at the confidence in his voice. He believed in her.

"You'll need pictures for your portfolio. Do you have one? What about a resume? Is yours current?"

Her head began to spin as Tyler rattled off questions. So much to think about. And why did it feel like he was pushing her at this job? Was that her guilt talking?

"Tyler, wait. I appreciate all the ideas, but I don't have enough time to do more than update my resume. I can't take new photos, there's no time. Although I have two pieces—"

"What about Sabrina? Maybe she could model for you tonight. Or I'm sure Annabelle would be willing."

Her brain hadn't gotten that far yet but she immediately latched on to the idea. "That's brilliant. I'll text her and see if she's free tonight. But . . . Shit. I don't have studio space and I can't—"

"No problem. We'll do it at the spa. We'll find a bare room and I'll get Greg to come up and take them. He's handy with a camera."

Once again she was speechless. An Oscar-winning Hollywood producer was going to take photos for her portfolio so she could show it to a pair of up-and-coming theater producers who might hire her as a costume manager's assistant for an actual off-Broadway show.

And the man she loved was helping her get a job that could potentially break them up.

"I'll call Greg now, see what his plans are. Why don't you contact Sabrina and see if she can make it tonight. If not, call Annabelle."

She had to bite her tongue to keep back the words that wanted to escape.

"Who died and made you boss" probably wouldn't be a good thing to say, because he was right. About everything.

Still, she couldn't help but feel he was pushing her away.

Tyler stood, drawing his phone from his pocket and walking toward the front window. "Hey, Greg. I need a favor for Kate."

She remained at the table, struck dumb by Tyler's efficiency as he steamrolled Greg into driving up to take the photos then making sure they had a room at the spa ready for them.

At one point, he turned to her and raised one eyebrow. She knew what he was thinking. Why the hell wasn't she on the phone getting in touch with Sabrina?

Good thing Sabrina's number was plugged into her phone or she wouldn't have been able to remember it. Her brain was running at full speed, tripping over everything she should be doing to prepare for tomorrow.

None of which should include a last-minute photo shoot by a famous Hollywood producer simply because she wanted to show off two of her new pieces.

But those pieces are awesome.

She had to agree with herself. The steampunk costume she'd made for Sabrina to wear to Philadelphia's Comic Con was worth its weight in gold. She'd found everything at thrift stores and antique shops and combined them into one kick-ass steampunk chick, full of in-your-face gadgets and baubles.

The second piece she'd made for herself. The gown was total fairy princess. Lavender velvet bodice, satin and velvet skirt with a pattern she'd hand stitched. There wasn't one edge that wasn't trimmed out with lace. It had thirty buttons down the front and a boned corset.

She'd made it with the intention of wearing it to the Pennsylvania Renaissance Faire, but it'd never seen the light of day because she and Arnie could never agree on a weekend. Either she had to work or he had to work or they'd had some family obligation to attend, so the dress had hung in her closet.

And now it might net her the job of her dreams.

But did she still want that job?

Yes. Of course you do.

Her gaze settled on Tyler, still on the phone. He looked to be in his element, taking care of things, making plans.

She wasn't going to let a man interfere with her plans. Not even one as perfect for her as Tyler.

She picked up her phone and called Sabrina.

* *

"Sorry, I'm late. Traffic was a bitch on the turnpike. Hey, Kate. Nice to see you again."

Kate smiled at Greg, wondering if she should be embarrassed by the man she'd had sex with last weekend with the blessing of her boyfriend. "Hi, Greg. Thanks for doing this for me. I really appreciate it."

She'd wondered how he'd handle the situation and was relieved when he brushed a kiss against her cheek and squeezed her shoulder. No trace of snark or innuendo to be found.

The load on her shoulders lifted by the tiniest bit, enough to make her realize she'd been stressing over that as well.

The pile of stress had seemed insurmountable only minutes ago. But the stress had seemed abstract. Greg's arrival had made everything that much more real.

He was here to take pictures for her portfolio so she could interview for the job of her dreams tomorrow.

The job that would make it nearly impossible for her to continue her relationship with the man of her dreams.

The man who was practically pushing her onto the bus for New York.

Maybe she wouldn't get hired. There was a good possibility she wouldn't.

Maybe she wouldn't want the job. Did she want the job?

That was the question that'd been rolling around her brain more often than any other all day.

Taking the job meant moving. It meant giving up her home, giving up the client list she'd been building for wedding gowns and burlesque costumes and lingerie.

It meant giving up the boutique.

And for what?

An off-Broadway show that *might* have a shot at moving to Broadway. And what happened when the show closed? Would she be able to return to her life here? Would the clients she'd cultivated so carefully still want to work with her?

God, she just wanted tomorrow to be over.

"Kate," Sabrina called from the next room, which they were using as a dressing room. "I can't get this damn buckle done."

Kate turned to go help but Sabrina walked out, head down as she fiddled with something at her side.

And walked right into Greg.

"Oh, jeez, I'm sorry. I didn't see . . . you."

It would have been funny if Kate had been in a laughing mood. For once, Sabrina had nothing to say. She just stared up at Greg, like he was the most handsome man she'd ever seen. Or he was an alien from another planet.

Greg's smile didn't falter as he patted Sabrina on the shoulder like a child. "No harm, no foul, kid. Nice costume." Then he turned back to Kate. "You make this? Honey, you can come work for me anytime. That's camera ready."

She smiled, but she knew it was strained. "Thanks, but there's no way I'm moving to LA. I'm really not much for big cities."

And you're going to move to New York?

She shoved the thought out of her mind. "Greg, this is Sabrina. Sabrina, Greg."

She didn't add anything to the introduction. If Greg wanted Sabrina to know who he was, he could fill her in. Otherwise, she was going on the assumption he'd prefer to remain just Greg the photographer and not Greg the hot Hollywood producer.

Sabrina took the hand Greg stuck out, finally rousing enough to realize she was staring at the man.

"Hi. Sorry, I just . . . You look really familiar. Have we met before?"

Greg smiled again and took a step back. "Don't think so."

Sabrina tilted her head, studying Greg for another few seconds, as Greg turned to address Kate.

"Are we ready to shoot, Kate?"

"Whenever you are."

"Then come here to me, Sabrina."

As Greg gave Sabrina directions on where to stand and how to pose, Kate stepped back to Tyler's side.

"That's a work of art, Kate." Tyler's voice was pitched low enough that only she could hear. "If they don't hire you for the position, they're fools."

She heard his sincerity and wondered if he was going to let her go without a fight. Maybe he didn't care for her as deeply as she cared for him. Maybe she was reading too much into what had, so far, been a mostly sexual relationship.

How would he respond if she told him she loved him?

"Thank you for the vote of confidence. But . . ."

His gaze narrowed on hers. "What?"

She had no clue what he was thinking at the moment.

"What do *you* think I should do? Should I pack up and leave my dad and my friends and . . . everyone I know to go live in a huge city in an apartment on the top floor of a five-story walkup with no air-conditioning that costs me three times what my apartment does here? What if I hate it?"

"And what if it's everything you've ever wanted and you love it?"

The words sounded forced, as if he didn't want to say them but had to. Still, his expression remained placid. Unmoved.

What was it going to take to rattle that calm? She wanted him to show something, anything, of the emotions he was feeling, give her some clue as to what he was thinking.

But why should he? She hadn't told him how she felt. And now wasn't the time. Not with the others here.

One day at a time. Just take it one day at a time.

She turned back to watch Greg shoot Sabrina, not answering his question because she didn't know how.

Greg had Sabrina standing with her back to the wall, head tilted up as she looked at the camera.

"That's good, babe. Now smolder."

Sabrina burst into one of her unrestrained laughing fits, and even with everything on her mind, Kate had to join her.

"I bet you say that to all the girls." Sabrina's hands went to her hips as she sent Greg a look that definitely didn't smolder. "Smolder, my ass. What the hell does that mean anyway?"

Kate was about to answer when Greg took a few steps forward until he was close enough to Sabrina that, if she took a deep breath, her breasts would brush against his chest.

Sabrina's eyes widened and she looked as if she wanted to take a step back but she was already up against the wall.

"I want you to look at me like I'm the man you want to throw down on the ground and screw his brains out." Greg reached out to take one of Sabrina's curls in his hand and draped it over the curve of her ample breast, enhanced by the leather corset. "Can you do that?"

Now, twenty-two-year-old Sabrina was not a virgin. Kate knew that because Sabrina the motormouth told her everything. But Kate also knew that the girl's few sexual encounters hadn't prepared her for Greg.

Kate opened her mouth to tell Greg to back off, but Sabrina found her footing.

Planting her hands on her hips, she fluttered her lashes and pouted as she stared straight up at Greg. "I think I can manage. Why don't you take a few steps back and let me show you?"

"Let's see what you got then." Greg retreated about five feet then held up the camera. "Do it."

Sabrina stood still for several more seconds as Greg snapped pictures. But finally, she moved.

And damn but the girl could smolder.

It would've made Kate smile if she hadn't had so much on her mind.

The photos would be great. She knew she was qualified for the job.

But would she be losing a more important part of her life if she left?

* *

As Sabrina began to loosen up in front of the camera, Tyler felt every muscle in his body tighten.

New York City. Kate was moving to New York City.

He had no doubt she was fully qualified for the position. The producers would be fools not to hire her, especially after they saw her portfolio.

This could be a career maker for her.

But it meant she'd leave him. She'd be busy creating a new life for herself. Carving out a career, settling into a new city.

Hell, he'd be just as busy if he agreed to take the chairmanship of the hotel board.

"Tyler." Kate had pitched her voice low enough so only he could hear. "Is everything okay?"

He turned to smile at her. "I'm fine. Is something wrong?"

Her eyes narrowed, focused intently on him. Dissecting his response. "No, nothing's wrong. You're . . . awfully quiet."

Go ahead. Tell her you love her. She'll stay.

"I've got a lot on my mind."

Her smile was bittersweet. "I know what you mean. So what's at the top of your pile?"

Damn it. He wanted to tell her how he felt, but he didn't want to sway her decision on this job in any way. He didn't have the right. And he didn't want to mess with her head while she had to make such an important decision.

"Hotel stuff."

She waited for him to say more, to open up. Share.

But he already felt his walls going up.

Damn it, he wanted her to sign the contract Jed had given her for the boutique. Wanted a binding legal document between them so she couldn't leave.

Hell, maybe you should just put a collar on her and make her stay.

Shit. That's the last thing he wanted to do to her.

After what she told him about her parents, she'd hate him for trying to manipulate her life. Which is exactly what he'd be doing.

No, she had to *want* to stay with him or the relationship would be meaningless.

"Hey, Kate. Come look at these. Greg must be a damn good photographer because I actually look good in these."

Sabrina's summons broke their connection and Kate turned toward her and Greg.

"I had no doubt you would look fantastic." Kate gave the girl a bright smile. "I really appreciate you both taking the time to do this for me."

Sabrina's answering grin could light up an entire room. The girl had energy to spare. Then again, she was probably all of twenty years old.

"You know I'll do anything for you, Kate." Then she pulled out a frown that could rival any two-year-old. "I am *so* going to miss you when you leave."

As Sabrina wrapped her arms around Kate's shoulders and gave her a hug, Kate glanced at Tyler with an expression he couldn't decipher.

What the hell should he do? The only time he'd been thrown for a loop like this had been when Mia died.

He'd reached the anger stage and pretty much stayed with that until he hit acceptance. He'd never really gotten to denial or bargaining. A year after they'd buried his former fiancée, he'd decided he was done mourning, and he'd managed to live without emotion since.

No grief. No longing. No love.

He'd stuffed them all away in a deep corner somewhere inside.

Then he'd met Kate, and those emotions had started to creep back into his life.

He didn't want to lose her. But he didn't want her to stay and later regret her decision.

Greg stepped in front of him, drawing him out of his thoughts. One look at his friend's face and Tyler frowned. He looked visibly tense.

"What's wrong?"

Greg shook his head and his expression became the one he usually reserved for dealing with the press.

"Not a thing."

Which was complete bullshit. Tyler knew something was up. What the hell was he missing here?

"Are we still shooting, Kate?" Greg asked.

"I assume so. Greg—"

"Then I think we should get started. I need to head back to Philly. I've got some work I need to finish."

Yeah, right. Greg had told him he had tonight and tomorrow open. What the hell had changed?

The girls were still talking. Well, Sabrina was talking. Kate was nodding and adding words here and there, but he could see the signs of her distraction in her half-hearted smile and the way she kept biting on her bottom lip.

When Tyler nodded and said "Sure," Greg turned to the girls. "Hey, kid. Great job. Nice to meet you. Kate, why don't you get changed so we can wrap this up."

Sabrina's mouth had dropped open the second Greg had called her a kid.

Her hands went to her hips again and she drew herself up to her full five-two height and stared straight at Greg. "I don't think twenty-two is still considered a kid in this country. Then again, maybe it's the generation gap."

The side of Greg's mouth twitched, and Tyler wasn't sure if Greg was ready to laugh or grimace.

He did neither. "When you hit my age, anyone under thirty is still a kid." Then Greg turned and nodded at Kate, completely dismissing Sabrina. "Why don't you go get changed, hon. I'm not gonna have much time to process these before I have to print them out."

Kate nodded and took a scowling Sabrina by the arm. "Give me a few minutes to change."

With one last scowl at Greg, who was studiously changing the lens on his camera, Sabrina let Kate lead her back to the dressing room.

When the girls were gone, Tyler walked over to Greg. "What's going on? Did something happen?"

Greg shook his head but didn't look up. "Nothing's going on. There're a few things I need to take care of. The pictures shouldn't need more than a quick touch-up."

Tyler looked down and saw Greg flashing through the pictures of Sabrina.

"They look great." And he meant it. Greg hadn't lost touch of his artistic side since becoming a producer. He knew how to frame a shot for maximum impact.

Tyler had no idea why Greg no longer directed. Damn shame that he didn't, because the guy had a gift. Especially in the close-up shots. Sabrina looked—

Ah.

Tyler looked up at Greg, who stared straight back, as if daring Tyler to say something.

Tyler knew now wasn't the time. But later . . .

"Thanks for doing this for Kate. I know she appreciates it."

Greg nodded, knowing Tyler had given him a break. "Have you told her how you feel about her yet?"

A break Greg apparently didn't intend to offer Tyler.

"I don't want to influence her decision."

Greg's gaze narrowed. "But you don't want her to go, do you?"

He was saved from answering the question by the girls' return. Sabrina had changed back into her jeans and T-shirt while Kate wore one of the more demure role-playing costumes she'd brought.

But not demure enough for him not to get aroused just by looking at her.

The top of the outfit was made from strings of fake pearls, draping down to cover all the right places but with just enough movement to suggest that if she moved the right way, she'd expose a breast. The bottom was a tiny, purple satin skirt that barely covered her ass and was encrusted with tiny pearls in a wave pattern.

Christ.

"Wow, Kate." Greg gave a short whistle. "That's a stunner, babe."

Kate rolled her eyes at him but smiled at the compliment. "Thanks. The top gave me fits trying to get the pearls to drape right."

Greg's wolfish smile made it perfectly clear he appreciated the look. "Then let's get started. Hey, Sabrina. Nice to meet you."

The last had been thrown over Greg's shoulder as he moved Kate into position against the wall.

Sabrina opened her mouth to say something but must have realized Greg had tuned her out.

Instead, she turned to Tyler and gave him a smile that held half her normal wattage before saying good-bye and practically running for the door.

Amazing, really, how attraction could cut you off at the knees that fast.

At Sabrina's age, she'd brush it off in a few days.

In Tyler's case . . .

Hell. He wouldn't be brushing it off anytime soon. Because his feelings had gone further than simple attraction.

But that still didn't give him the right to interfere in Kate's dreams.

* *

With a groan, Kate unkinked herself from the driver's seat of her car and stretched.

Her eyes felt gritty and she kept yawning, although she didn't feel that tired.

She'd been drained after the photo shoot last night and had fallen asleep only minutes after Greg and Tyler had left. She didn't even have time to pout over the fact that Tyler hadn't stayed. She hadn't woken up this morning until her alarm had gone off at five a.m. Ugh.

Then, of course, traffic had been miserable. There was a reason most people around here took the bus from Reading on weekdays.

The upside to the drive was that she'd had plenty of time to think.

Which was why she hadn't gone directly home.

Looking at the front door to her parents' house, she sighed. She needed to make the right decision and her dad had always been the person to tell her the unvarnished truth, no matter if she wanted to hear it or not.

Later, she'd talk to Annabelle, who always saw the upside of everything.

But first, she needed her dad to lay it on the line for her.

She knocked to announce her presence then opened the door and stepped into her childhood.

The white brick ranch house on the outskirts of town had been built in the '70s and the exterior showed it. Inside, the décor was stuck in the '90s. Her mom had never gotten around to redecorating before her death.

And her dad never changed a thing.

"Hey, Dad," she called out. "It's me. Where are you?"

"In the kitchen. I was expecting you earlier."

Damn, she should've called on her way home. "Sorry. Traffic was heavier than normal."

Walking into the kitchen, she took a deep breath and her stomach growled when the mouthwatering smell of her dad's spaghetti sauce hit her.

Her dad turned away from the stove long enough to give her the once-over. "I understand. Sit. I'll get you a plate."

She did as she was told, watching her dad dish her a huge portion of spaghetti and meatballs. "Daddy, I can't eat all this. I'll explode."

He gave her a stern look that made her feel five years old again. "You're skin and bones. Eat. Then tell me why you look like you have the weight of the world on your shoulders."

Her first-generation Korean American father had guilt trips up his sleeve for every occasion. She'd never doubted his love for her, but Tiger Moms had nothing on her dad.

What he and her mom had ever seen in each other that made them decide to marry was a total mystery.

Teddy Song was stoic, demanding, occasionally judgmental, and set in his ways. He expected a lot from the people around him and even more from himself. His position as the chief financial officer for the state-run geriatric home gave him the chance to combine politics and money and he loved it. Loved the challenge.

He couldn't understand why she was content working for a dry cleaner while her hard-earned degree went to waste. He'd expected her to "make something of herself." And that hadn't included tying herself to Arnie, a man who drove a delivery truck and working for a dry cleaning business.

After he'd poured them each a glass of wine, he sat across from her and waited.

She took a deep breath. "I've had a job offer. For an assistant costume designer."

He nodded, as if those came along every day. "That sounds promising."

"It's in New York City at an off-Broadway theater. They expect the show to do well enough to move to a Broadway venue when a stage opens up. The company's financially stable. It has a good reputation and I actually like the people. I'd be working under one of my professors from college."

"It sounds like a great opportunity. So why are you hesitant to take it?"

Trust her dad to get right to the point. Which is exactly why she came to him.

"I've met a man—"

"The man who's stayed at your house recently? Is he the same man you go to Philadelphia to visit?"

Well, hell. She should have known he'd hear. Her father didn't seek out gossip, but he did stop at Tracy's every morning to get his coffee. Someone down there must have filled him in.

Now she felt like a guilty teenager. But that didn't mean she had to show it.

Looking her dad straight in his eyes, the identical shape and color of hers, she said, "Yes, it's the same man."

"And he treats you well?"

Okay, that wasn't what she'd expected him to ask and it threw her off track. "Yes. He treats me very well."

"Do you love him?"

She blushed, a fiery heat consuming her cheeks. But the answer was easy. "Yes."

Her dad didn't bat an eyelash. "So you're going to throw away this opportunity because you're afraid this man doesn't want you to take the job. Has he told you not to take it?"

She wanted to leap to Tyler's defense, but that would have been an irrational answer to a straightforward question. Her father might read something into her response that wasn't true. "No, not at all. He's encouraging me to take it."

"Then what's wrong?"

What's wrong was that he was encouraging her to take it. Hell, he was practically putting a foot on her ass and shoving her out the door.

Okay, maybe that was a little overdramatic but still . . . Tyler wanted her to take the job.

And she wasn't sure if she didn't want the job because she knew it would take her away from him or because her goals had changed.

Shaking her head, she sighed. "I'm not sure."

"And what is it you're unsure about?"

She almost rolled her eyes but caught herself in time. "If I knew that, Dad, we wouldn't be having this conversation."

Sitting back in his chair, he crossed his arms over his chest. "And why are we having this conversation exactly?"

Suddenly, she knew exactly why she was here. "Why didn't Mom become a photojournalist like she wanted to?"

Her dad nodded as if he'd expected her to ask the question all along. "The simple answer is because she didn't want to leave you behind for long stretches of time. And because she thought I didn't want her to go."

"Did you?"

He shrugged, such an odd movement coming from him. "I wanted her to be happy. I knew she wasn't, although she was a natural teacher."

"Really?" She'd never known that about her mom.

"Oh, yes. And she enjoyed it too. It just wasn't enough for her. When you started high school, she began to apply for jobs at the bigger newspapers. She had several interviews but . . ." He paused, then sighed. "The market fell apart. Newspapers were folding left and right and if they weren't closing, they certainly weren't hiring. Most were cutting staff to save money."

"So she missed her opportunity."

"Yes. And I couldn't do anything to help her."

And here was her opportunity, practically knocking her over.

"I've also had an offer to open a boutique. In the spa retreat they're building only a few miles outside of town."

"I've heard about that. Seems like a risky venture, with the economy the way it is."

"So you don't think I should do that?"

"I think it will require much more of a sacrifice from you. Starting your own business is a huge undertaking. Would you be able to stick it out?"

A sharp retort sprang to her lips but she managed to bite it back and think about what he'd said. He'd asked a legitimate question.

"Yes, I could."

"And do you want to open a boutique?"

With a heavy sigh, she set aside her fork. "It was never really something I gave a lot of thought to. But the more I think about it . . ."

"The more appealing it becomes." Her dad shocked her by nodding, his usually stern mouth curved in an even rarer grin. "Have you thought about what will happen if this boutique fails to take off? Then again, the show could close in a matter of weeks and you'll be out of a job there as well. But opportunities like the one you're being offered now don't come around often."

He hadn't said anything she hadn't already thought of herself but, coming from her dad, it did help her see things more clearly.

"Kate, I love you."

As much as she'd always thought her father expected more from her than she could do, she knew he did. Still, every time he said it, it made her grin.

"And I'll support whatever decision you make," he continued. "I'll only say that controlling your destiny is a heady proposition. But business and pleasure don't always mix. I would hate to see you lose everything, but to not have attempted it might be even worse."

*　*

Tyler glanced at the clock for what had to be the hundredth time in the past five minutes.

She had to be home by now. Why hadn't she called?

Probably because she hadn't wanted to tell him her decision.

She'd be crazy not to take the job in New York. And he'd be crazy to try and influence her decision.

"Are you even listening to me?" Jared's voice broke into his thoughts, splintering his single-minded focus into a hundred different pieces.

"Frankly, no, I wasn't." He sighed and watched his brother raise an eyebrow at him.

"Jesus, Tyler. You need to figure out what you're going to do about the chairman's seat. I can't make the decision for you, but the more I think about it, the more I think you need to do it. The GoldenStar was Granddad's baby."

"I know that. It's what's making this decision so damn hard."

Tyler shook his head. "I don't think we should let it slip through our fingers. The other hotels—

"Are the board's," Jed said. "I don't give a rat's ass about those. But Granddad built the Philadelphia GoldenStar. I think it should stay in the family."

Jared was right. Tyler knew that. But Jared wouldn't be the one with the extra weight on his shoulders. It'd be Tyler, because that's what he did. He took over. He made the major decisions and he dealt with the consequences.

And if he did, he wouldn't be able to give Kate and their relationship the time it required. The only times Mia had complained during their years together had been when he was spending so much time getting Haven off the ground.

Yes, she'd understood that a project that huge demanded every ounce of his concentration. But she'd expected him to at least acknowledge her presence occasionally. To put some effort into their relationship.

But he'd taken her for granted.

"I know this is asking a lot from you right now," Jed continued. "But we can do this together, just like we've done with Haven and the Spa."

Tyler looked at Jed, saw a conviction there that made him smile. Yes, they could do it together. And with both of them working on it, it wouldn't be such a colossal undertaking. It'd still require a shitload of time, but they could do it.

Jed wouldn't let him down.

And Kate . . .

Yes, he knew that sometimes life just sucked and there was nothing you could about it.

You really couldn't have it all. He should know that by now.

* *

Tyler checked his ringing phone and paused before answering it.

"Hello, Kate. How did your interview go?"

"It went well. Really well, actually. Which is kind of why I'm calling. I need to talk to you."

Tyler mentally braced himself. Maybe he wouldn't be the one breaking off their relationship.

"I'm glad to hear the interview went well. What did you want to talk about?"

He couldn't keep the cool tone out of his voice. It matched the icy sensation coating his guts.

Even though he knew this was for the best, he'd still had the slightest hope that things would miraculously work out.

"Tyler, is something wrong?"

Her tentative question solidified his decision. "No, I'm sorry. I've got a lot on my mind."

"Oh. Did something happen?"

"I've decided to accept the chairman's seat on the GoldenStar board. It's going to take up a hell of a lot of time."

She paused. "Then I guess it's a good thing I'm going to accept the job in New York."

Thank God she wasn't here, because he was pretty sure he looked like he'd just gotten kicked in the gut. At least that's how he felt.

There'd still been a part of him that had hoped . . .

"I'm glad it worked out for you."

Another pause. "So you don't have a problem with me taking this job?"

"No." *Yes.* "Should I?"

"No. Of course not."

Did he detect a hint of sarcasm creeping into her tone? Better to ignore it. "When do you have to be in New York?"

"They want me there by the end of the week, but I couldn't leave Joe in the lurch. I'll start the following week. I'll be staying with Dinah until I can find an apartment."

"I'm sure Jed would be happy to help you with that. He's got several friends who live in the city—"

"Tyler, what's going on?"

"I don't know what you mean."

"Yes, you do. Don't play semantics with me."

"You're right. I'm sorry." He took a deep breath. "I'm not trying to be cruel but I think, with everything we both have going on right now, it's better if we make a clean break. Now."

* *

Okay, now Kate was pissed.

She knew exactly what he was doing. The bastard was pushing her away deliberately.

And she knew why. Hell, she even understood to a degree.

But he was taking the easy way out and, damn it, she wanted to call him on it.

Even though she felt like he'd shoved a knife in her gut.

She wanted to scream and rant and rage at him. Wanted to tell him she knew exactly what he was doing and why he was so very wrong.

"Kate? Are you still there?"

Through gritted teeth, she said, "Yes, I'm still here."

"I know this may seem abrupt but—"

"*Abrupt* would be a good word for it. But I can think of another."

He continued as if she hadn't spoken. "I'm not going to have much of a private life in the next few months and I don't believe I'll have the time I'd like to devote to you."

Oh hell, now she felt tears burning at the corners of her eyes. And she absolutely refused to show him how weak she was. "Then I guess you're right. We should end this now."

It was his turn to pause.

Isn't as much fun to be on the receiving end, is it?

"Then we're in agreement." His voice had taken on a cool tone she'd never heard from him before. "We had a great time together, but we both need to focus on our careers at the moment. I'm sure we'll see each other again."

At Jared and Annabelle's wedding, she assumed he meant.

"Have you told Jared you're not going to sign the boutique contract?"

Oh, this man made her furious. "No. I'll speak to Jared tonight. He's with Annabelle. I saw his car parked at the shop when I drove by."

Little did he know exactly what she planned to tell Jared. She had a plan forming. One she'd thought to discuss with Tyler—before he'd dumped her, that was.

"Kate . . ."

"Yes?" She let her sarcasm run free in that one word. When he paused again, she knew he'd heard it.

"I'm sorry this didn't work out. You're a special woman and I've come to care about you. You're going to make a wonderful costume designer."

Damn him. If he didn't stop talking now, she was going to cry.

Gritting her teeth, she forced herself to say, "Thank you. Good-bye, Tyler."

And she hung up before he could say anything more.

She wanted to throw her phone across the room, but that

wouldn't accomplish anything other than a trip to the mall to buy a new phone.

Tears wanted to flow but she blinked them back. She refused to shed tears over this.

She was mad. Furious.

He hadn't wanted to fight. He'd just assumed the worst, cut his losses, and run.

Overbearing, manipulative—

No. Now who was being unfair?

Had she told him she loved him? No, she hadn't.

Had she fought for him? No.

Would it have made a difference? She had to believe, yes, it would.

She picked up the phone and dialed.

"Hey, Annabelle. Can I talk to Jared?"

Eighteen

❧

"Hello, sweetheart, I'm so glad to see you. It's been a while."

Tyler hid a grimace as he walked into his parents' home. "Hey, Mom. I know it's been a while. Sorry. There's been a lot going on."

"Oh, I know that. I wasn't trying to lay a guilt trip." Shutting the door behind her, she wrapped him in a tight hug then waved him through to the sitting room where he saw his father sitting on the couch.

"Dad, I need to talk to you."

His mom stopped in the doorway. "Would you like me to—"

"No, Mom, stay. Please."

His father put down the newspaper. "What's up, Tyler? Have you decided what you're going to do?"

"Yes, I have. I've decided I don't want the chair."

His parents exchanged a look he couldn't decipher before his dad turned back to him. "I understand. I'm—"

"But I want the Philadelphia GoldenStar."

His dad's mouth quirked into a grin as he exchanged another one of those looks with his mom. "And how do you plan to sell that deal to the board?"

"I don't. I've read Granddad's will backward and forward. There's nothing in the will that says once I take the chair, I can't sell the chain."

His dad nodded. "You're absolutely right. There isn't."

"Granddad made sure that if the family wanted to keep the Philly GoldenStar, we could. Vasser will bitch a little but he already has a hotel in Philadelphia. He doesn't need another."

His father's grin started to spread. "That's also true."

"Vasser only wants the European hotels, but he knew the board wouldn't split the assets."

"Yes, that's what I believe too."

"And you knew I'd only really want the Philly hotel."

Smiling outright now, his father nodded again. "Yes, I did."

"Jesus, Dad, then why all the dramatics? Why the hell didn't you just tell me to sell the damn chain and keep the Philly hotel?"

Now his dad lost the smile. "Because it had to be *your* decision, Tyler. Not mine. What if I'd sold the chain and you decided you wanted it? No, this was the only way it could work."

Tyler tried to find the flaw in his dad's logic but couldn't. Which just pissed him off more. Not at his dad but at himself.

"I can't believe I didn't figure this out sooner."

"Would it have made a difference?" his mom asked as she sat next to his dad and took his hand. The outward display of affection was so unusual from his parents it took him back for a few seconds before he thought about his mom's questions.

Would it? Would he have done anything differently?

Would he have pushed Kate away?

"Tyler?" His mom sounded worried. "Did something happen?"

Yeah. He'd fucked up. Royally.

He looked his mom straight in the eyes. "How did he get you to forgive him?"

His mom's eyebrows arched in shock before she began to nod. "There was more than enough blame to go around, in our case. Still, your dad apologized and told me he couldn't live without me. We had to forgive each other so we could move forward."

He thought about that all the way from his parents' house on the Main Line to Haven in center city.

He needed a plan. But first he had to get through the rest of the folders on his desk. Several hundred files that he needed to go through before he met with the GoldenStar board of directors on Monday. He needed to have all of his ducks in a row when he dealt with them.

But the one duck he truly wanted, he'd already shot out of the water.

* *

Friday afternoon, Tyler would have gladly shot his brother after he walked into his private office on the fourth floor.

"You're a coward," Jed said. "I know I've said that before, but this time, you threw away something amazing because you think you're going to lose Kate anyway. Fucked-up logic, if you ask me."

Tyler didn't bother to look up. His eyes burned, his head hurt, and he had an ache in the pit of his stomach that wouldn't go away and that he refused to acknowledge.

Jed dropped into the chair on the opposite side of his desk, forcing himself into Tyler's field of vision. He stopped reading long enough to glare at his brother before transferring his attention back to the file.

"So what's the plan?" Jed continued. "Bury yourself in work for a few years before you decide it's time to find another woman? Or are you just planning to skip to the spinster uncle stage? You do know you're an idiot, too, right?"

Yes, he knew he was an idiot, but he wasn't about to give Jed any more ammunition by admitting it. And he didn't have the time to argue.

"What are you doing here besides bothering me? Where's Annabelle? I'm sure *she'd* be happy to see you."

Jed grinned. "I know she'd be happy to see me. But I have an early meeting tomorrow so I figured I'd stay here for the night. I'm heading back as soon as I can."

"Everything okay at the Spa?"

"Yep."

"Do you need me for anything?"

"Nope."

"Then what the hell are you still doing here?"

"Apparently annoying you."

"Jed, I've got a hell of a lot of files to—"

"And all of that can wait. You should take a break. Get a drink. Chill in the Salon."

Right. That's the absolute last place he wanted to be. Too many memories. Talk about a mindfuck.

"I'm presenting everything to the board Monday. I've got too much to do—"

"I'm sure you do. But I think you're going to want to check out the Salon. Now."

Jed held his gaze, and Tyler realized exactly what his brother was telling him.

Hope made his chest tight, made his heart pound. Lust made his blood burn.

And relief made him almost light-headed. And froze him to the chair.

"Tyler—"

Getting up, he practically ran for the door.

* *

What if he didn't show up?

Kate had been asking herself that question from the moment Jared left her in the Salon to go talk to Tyler.

He has to come.

If he didn't . . . Well, then she'd screwed up her life but good.

She'd stepped way out of her box this time and was hoping like hell that it paid off.

And when he doesn't show? Then what, smart girl?

Wow, she'd never realized how bitchy her inner critic could be. It sucked to be on the other side of it. And how had that happened?

She knew exactly when that had happened. When she'd called Jared and Annabelle to ask for their help.

Which is how she'd ended up practically naked in the Salon, waiting for the man who'd almost broken her heart.

If he didn't show, her heart *would* break. But she'd go on. She wasn't about to let a man ruin her life. Not even the one man she apparently wanted more than her dream job. Which, in reality, had turned out not to be her dream job after all.

That dream had been usurped by another that was just as demanding and creative as the one she'd said no to.

But if he didn't show . . .

She was afraid her heart would be scarred forever.

With a sigh, she started to pace. If Tyler didn't get here soon, or if Jared didn't return, she was going to wear a path in the exquisite Turkish rug beneath her feet.

And she should really stop pacing, because if he walked in, she didn't want him to see her so nervous.

Then again—

Out of the corner of her eye, she saw the wall to her left split apart.

She sucked in a quick gasp before her heart started to pound.

Tyler.

She bit her lips, which wanted to quiver, and forced herself to stand her ground rather than run to him and throw her arms around him.

Just because he was here didn't mean their problems were going to magically disappear.

"Tyler."

Did he look happy to see her? Was that a hint of a smile she saw on his face?

God, I hope so.

"Kate."

Silence descended as they stared at each other across the room.

She knew what she wanted to say, knew what she should say. What she wanted to hear in return.

But all that emerged was, "You coward."

He nodded, a dull flush covering his cheeks, but he didn't look away. "You're not the first person to say that to me today. And you're both right. I am. But do you know why?"

She swallowed, her heart pumping in overdrive. "I have my suspicions, but I'd like to hear it from you."

"Because I was afraid if I let myself love you any more than I already did, and you ever left me, I'd lose myself."

Tears welled at the tone of his voice, at the conviction she heard in it.

"The first time . . . with Mia . . . I thought I'd never get over it. Never be the same person. Never let myself care that deeply for anyone again. I honestly thought I was saving both of us from heartbreak further down the line. I'm sorry. I never meant to hurt you."

"And now?"

He shrugged, his mouth twisting with a grimace. "Now I realize that no matter what happens, if we never see each other again or if we spend the next fifty years together, it will hurt just as much. But I know I don't want to spend the rest of my life without you."

The weight on her chest eased just enough that joy began to filter in.

Still, she wasn't ready to give in just yet. The man had dumped her. And on the phone! That deserved punishment.

And she knew exactly what kind.

"That's a nice sentiment." She put her hand on one hip. "But I'm going to need a lot more convincing."

His eyes narrowed and he finally let his gaze drop.

She'd picked her outfit carefully for this meeting, and when his gaze returned to hers, smoldering with heat, she knew she'd chosen correctly.

The hem of her black skirt hit her at midthigh, conservative at first glance. As was the prim, white, short-sleeved shirt. But the skirt fit like a glove and a slit up the left leg gave tantalizing hints of the electric blue thong she wore beneath. And the wraparound shirt revealed the cleavage formed by her blue lace bra. The bra matched the thong that was getting wetter by the second.

"I figured since we were going to be working together at the spa, business casual would be appropriate for this meeting."

He nearly choked on a laugh. "If that's business casual, I've been doing it wrong for years."

His voice held a distinct roughness that made her want to rub up against him. Naked.

"Then why don't you come over here and I'll give you some tips."

She expected him to try to take over now, assert his dominance. Instead he obeyed immediately. He didn't run, but he didn't take his time either.

When he stopped in front of her, she had to tilt her head back to look into his eyes. Such beautiful eyes. She reached for him with one hand, traced his jaw and his lips with one fingertip.

"What about New York?" he asked. "The job?"

"I decided that wasn't the risk I wanted to take. I enjoy working for myself. I want to make the boutique work. I want to grow my wedding dress design business. I want to make burlesque costumes and role-playing gear, and I want *you*. I'm still angry with you, but I can't imagine my life without you."

He bared his teeth in a grin that made her shiver.

"Good." Now she heard that note of command in her voice and she shivered. "Because I don't want to live without you."

Lifting his hand, he began to undo the bow at her waist holding her shirt together. "I love you, Kate."

The bottom dropped out of her stomach at the matter-of-fact way he said those few words. So very Tyler.

As was the way his fingertips caressed the bared skin of her breasts. Perfectly. And when he bent his head to press his mouth to the curve of one aching mound, she sucked in a sharp breath.

"And I love you."

She nearly groaned when he took a step back before he reached into his pocket and pulled out his grandmother's ring. The one she'd found at the flea market. Taking her hand as tears formed in her eyes, he slid it onto the ring finger of her left hand. "And I can't imagine another woman wearing this. It was meant for you to find. And you were meant for me."

She lifted her hands to cup his jaw. "And you were meant for me. Now take off my clothes and make love to me until I can't see straight."

His smile had sharp edges. And she loved it. "It will be my pleasure, sweetheart."